THE FLYING SAUCER MURDER CASE

A GEORGE TIREBITER MYSTERY

BY DAVID OSSMAN

—MIRRORFOTO

ELECTRONIC STOOL PIGEON BETRAYS BABS

This is a close-up view of the wire recorder that was used to obtain Barbara Graham's voice allegedly fabricating a phony alibi for her whereabouts the night Mrs. Monahan was murdered in Burbank. (See story on Page 3.)

The Flying Saucer Murder Case
A George Tirebiter Mystery
©2018 David Ossman

Published in the USA by:

BearManor Media
P.O. Box 71426
Albany, Georgia 31708
www.BearManorMedia.com

ISBN: 978-1-62933-193-5 (alk. paper)

Design and Layout: Valerie Thompson

TABLE OF CONTENTS

Chapter 1

Slaying Horror Told by Witness at Guarded Trial
He Wanted Money, "But No Killing"

There was a nasty murder trial going on that simmering summer in Los Angeles. John and Suzie Q. Public lined up in the marble lobby of Superior Court and a deputy checked them over for weapons. One prosecution witness's life had been threatened — the gap-toothed lowlife had turned state's evidence. His name was True — John True. True or not, "his enemies" were going to use a "napalm bomb" on him, so the Sheriff said.

Another witness, a dark-haired dream-boat-type guy named Sam Siriani, a "sharp-looker" in his plain clothes, turned out to be an undercover cop. What's more, he came armed with a "Dick Tracy" mini-wire recorder. Super-spy stuff in 1953. On the wire, good-looking bad-girl Barbara Graham, mother of three, accused bludgeoner and garrotter, could be heard to offer Sam 25 Grand to be her "love-nest alibi" for the night of the Widow Monahan's murder. "Babs," (who had let her auburn hair down from its tidy bun, almost as if she knew Susan Hayward would win an Oscar playing her in the movie version), hastily conferred with her lawyers.

All of this I knew, not because I read the *L. A. Mirror*, which landed in the shrubbery or on my bungalow roof about four in the afternoon, but because Mrs. Whitmer, my neighbor (and tenant) in Rose-Bud Court took the bus Downtown to the courthouse every day and stopped by sooner or later to deliver a daily summation through my screen door.

"I could have that recorder in my handbag right now," Mrs. Whitmer said, opening her scuffed leather purse and showing me a bottle of One-a-Days, a couple of Christian Science publications, and a lot of tissues. "Think of it! What will we do without our privacy, Mr. Tirebiter? A priest in his confessional could record everything anyone said to him!"

"You've certainly got something to think about there, Mrs. Whitmer," I said. I hoped my teakettle would start to whistle. I put the kettle on when she came to my door, for an escape clause.

"Well, I'm not going to court tomorrow, anyway. Dr. Kinsey's coming from Bloomington to speak at the Statler. He thinks women are sex fiends, you know."

"He does?"

"They say even the footnotes are steamy."

"Footnotes to . . . ?"

"'Sex Life of an American Female' it's called. They're all talking about it on the radio, but they don't say anything. So that's why I'm going to the hotel for the press conference. Maybe he'll say something."

"I hope he will," I said. My kettle shrieked. "Sorry, Mrs. Whitmer."

"I think you drink too much tea, Mr. Tirebiter. Entirely too much caffeine stimulation for a young man."

"I'm cutting down. Don't forget your package." I handed her the square brown box from a vitamins-by-mail company in Wilmington. The postman left packages with me if the bungalow tenant was out, which they were much of the time. Working people and students, mostly, filled out the Rose-Bud's ten fractional addresses. Mrs. Whitmer lived at 628-1/2, Apt. A, W. 30th Street. My bungalow, Number 627, had started out as a quiet place to write. It had turned into a busy place to live.

She popped the box into her handbag and negotiated the two steps down to the walk. Mrs. Whitmer was just south of seventy, I suspected. Big and fragile-boned under her dark bag dress and blue cloth coat.

I had another package — a 100-proof Relska Vodka carton ("It's Tasteless") sealed with brown gummed tape and tied with twine, addressed by United Parcel to Travis Wispell at 627-1/4. I had inherited Wispell and Mrs. Whitmer when I bought the Court from an Old Hollywood screenwriter named Oliver Tulley almost two years before. Tulley had inherited them from Rose and Bud Levy who had owned the place for ten years or so before they decided to move on to San Juan Capistrano back in 1948.

The Rose-Bud is horseshoe-shaped and my front bungalow, like Mrs. Music's across the way, has a bay window looking South onto a quiet residential block off Figueroa Boulevard.

The low roofline of Wispell's bungalow, third back from the street on my side, was topped by a tall scaffolding decked with short-wave antennae. Wispell worked somewhere Downtown as a dental technician, made gold fillings and porcelain molars by day, and spent his nights scouring the planet for ham radio operators to talk to.

He hardly spoke to me, except to bark an occasional location — "New Zealand, 20 meter band" or "North Pole last night, Tirebiter. 32 kilocycles at 8 megahertz." Numbers to that effect. I carried the Relska box out and left it in front of his door, then got my hose and sprayed water down the central grass strip, which was turning yellow in the August heat-wave.

I thought about Buffalo Bill and his horse, and where I had left them — Bill in the shack filled with dynamite and Soldier Boy trapped in the corral at Pistolwhip Ranch. Top of Chapter 12. Only one cliff-hanger to go. The last movie serial, all mine.

I watered my way to the inner end of the Court, where a pair of two-bedroom bungalows pointed their front porches down the grass strip, toward the Washington palms and the three-story Victorian pile across the street. On the left, Mrs. Whitmer's windows were darkened, as always, with greying blinds, the glass panels on her front door with rectangles of shirt cardboard.

The Perrys lived on the right, 628-1/2, Apt. B. Sally, cute as apple strudel, had Little Joe trapped in a playpen on the shaded cement porch while she vacuumed the living room. I knew tall Will Perry would be bent over a canvas under blue-white lamplight in the back bedroom. I could see one of his paintings through the open bungalow door — a four-by-five foot view of a wheel-shaped Earth Station orbiting high in Space above the rusty sands of Mars. It looked like a Technicolor photograph of the real thing.

Two Court bungalows seemed to stay in the hands of USC students. The current girls, Becky and Wilma in 629-1/4 had decided that a summer in L.A. was better than one at home in Grand Rapids, Michigan. They had moved in the previous fall and majored in something that didn't seem to take up too much time.

Next to them, at 629-1/2, camped the Two Bobs, would-be Seniors, one of whom was soaking up the surf in Hawaii, the other actively pursuing Becky and Wilma in lieu of vacationing cheerleader types from Sorority Row, a block away.

It was still hot. The water on the sidewalk steamed off. Daily watering is an L.A. habit, regardless of its usefulness. The very trickling of sprinklers can induce meditation.

"More dead than not."

Travis Wispell appeared beside me, his jaw jutted, looking like a man who had stared at teeth all day. He stared at mine while I sprayed the grass around his stoop.

"It's part of my routine," I said. I moved the hose to the other side of the steps so he could walk up. He looked at the box I'd set there, shook his head, unlocked his door, opened it, went back, picked up the box.

"Lighter than I thought, from the size," I said.

He opened the screen door and looked back at me. "Man's life work," he said. "Ought ta weigh more'n that." The inside door closed with a solemn thud.

The afternoon sun was far enough along to shine directly onto the fronts of the bungalows on the east flank of the horseshoe. Wilma, the reckless one of the blonde co-eds, had changed into red shorts and a candy-striped vest. She sat in a white Adirondack chair that took up half the porch.

"Last blast of the day," she said. "Cools the clanks." She let out a lungful of Herbert Tareyton. The girls had a little 45rpm record changer plugged into their radio and it was playing a stack of singles — "April in Portugal," "From Here to Eternity," "Return to Paradise."

"Good to the last beam," I said and, brain-break over, stepped to the side of my own bungalow to turn off the hose.

There was a loud sizzling buzz, like a pit full of strangled snakes, and "Paradise" was suddenly lost. A high-pitched scream tore the afternoon apart and died.

"It came from in there!" Wilma was pointing across the Court, at Travis Wispell's door. Becky appeared and said with a frown, "Our lights are out."

Bob-the-Blob emerged wearing bathing trunks and a USC Athletic Department sweatshirt. "Power's off," he offered. "Hey, Wilma."

Sally Perry stood in her living room, holding her useless vacuum cleaner. Little Joe watched it all through the bars of his playpen.

I tried Wispell's door. It was locked. I pounded on it. "Mr. Wispell? Anything I can do?"

Bob-the-Blob wandered up behind me. "Maybe you should break in."

"Go around and look through the side window." I pounded again. Bob sniffed at the door. "You smell something?"

Mrs. Whitmer came out on her porch in feathered pink bedroom slippers and a daisy-printed wrapper and hailed me. "I was using my little diathermy machine, Mr. Tirebiter, and the fuses blew. What in Mercy's name was that noise?"

"I'll see. I'll get the keys." They were on my dresser. When I got back, Bob was still making sure the front door stayed closed.

I unlocked it and pushed it open. The Blob came in after me. "Smells like a weenie roast."

"There's the weeny," I said and pointed at Travis Wispell curled up in a corner of his radio-broadcasting-equipped living room, steam rising from his bald scalp. His power was off for good.

The County sent an ambulance, the City provided a detective, and sure enough a *Mirror* photog was there to catch Sgt. William Cummings of the Homicide Squad, square-jawed and straw-hatted, in the act of gazing wryly down at the late Mr. Wispell. The dials, tubes, and transmitters behind the cop and the corpse looked like a video spaceship, so the next day's *Mirror* captioned the picture:

"SPACE PATROL" DEATH
**Body of denture-maker Travis Whispell, 59,
killed by electrocution. (See story on Page 4.)**

It turned out that Mrs. Whitmer's diathermy machine was a vintage Dr. Pratt's Electrocyser — also sold as "The Tingler." Her regimen, she had told me over time, included mild zaps from Dr. Pratt for her lumbago, quarts of the only yogurt I had then ever heard of anyone eating, and nude sunbaths ("skin-soaks") on her rooftop, shielded from view by beach towels hung over a clothesline. Dr. Pratt's Tingler was not responsible for the murderous power surge.

Sgt. Cummings sealed the doors to the bungalow, pending an examination of the ham rig by radio experts. The ambulance took the body away, and the news photographer, a cheerful, sandy-haired, bow-tied guy named Ken Adair, took pictures for the Page 4 story: **"SAID SHE WAS TERRIFIED!** Wilma Bishop, 19, heard the screaming," and a long shot of the Court captioned **SHOCKED ROSE-BUD TENANTS ASK "WHY?"**

There were four lights — big white globes on fluted green iron posts — set in the grass down the center of the Court. They went on again about an hour after dark, and the City Power electrician finally climbed down from a pole in the alley. Bob-the-Blob and the co-eds had long since gone to Currie's Ice Cream for malts, the Perrys had gone to the 6:45 show at the Figueroa Theatre — "Dream Wife" with Cary Grant and Deborah Kerr — and Mrs. Whitmer had lit candles, which bothered me because her place was full of paper — stacks of *National Geographic, Look* and *Coronet,* the *Christian Science Monitor.*

I sat on my steps and drank a beer, considering the difficulty of writing dialogue for dumb animals.

None of my other tenants had come home, which was like them. Between my bungalow and the late Mr. Wispell's lived Audrey Gage, a perky brunette with bangs and a smile that would peel the paper off your bedroom wall. She'd moved in recently, had a job at the Auto Club over on Adams, and was often out in the evenings.

At the end of the row was Mr. O'Toole — an Irishman and former merchant marine invalided by a scramble in Singapore with a Tahitian boilermaker, "over a tattooed whoor," he told me with a grin. He was on disability, occupied himself at the burlesque houses on Main Street, and kept up with shipmates at Downtown bars.

A young woman, daughter of an earlier tenant, was holding on to the bungalow at the opposite end. Gideon Selz, a studio film composer, had used it for years as a home-away-from-Palm Springs, usually when he was in a production crunch. After his death in February, she had visited occasionally. "Going through Dad's papers," she said. Her name was Abby, a poised blonde with the look of an underfed fashion model. The rent had been paid for the rest of the year. Her lights were on timers, so someone seemed to be home at night.

I finally went inside, turned the desk light and the radio on and put fresh paper in the Underwood. Kat Music was the tenant I was waiting for, and I knew that on a Tuesday night she wouldn't be back until eleven.

Thomas Cassidy had just finished announcing the second half of the Hollywood Bowl concert over KFAC when I spun the last canary-yellow page of "Buffalo Bill's Horse" out of my typewriter and set it down on top of a squared pile of pages at the back of the kitchen table.

The sweet, sharp song of Brahms' violin concerto filled the Bowl and swept through my radio, along with coughs and stirrings of the audience, the occasional drone of an airplane and, once or twice, the strains of a fire-engine siren clearing traffic along Highland or Hollywood Boulevard.

The canary-yellows hunkered like a thin gold brick next to a slightly thicker stack of baby-blues — "It Came From Under The Bed." Next to that, a beat-up wooden In box gathered together a dog-eared assortment of pulpy mimeo sheets and termite-inspection stationary I'd bought for a dime at a tag sale in the Shrine Auditorium parking lot. On them was my novel. I was calling it "Street of Broken Glass" because I wanted it to hurt. It hurt so much I hadn't added any pages to the In box since early June. That hurt most of all.

I rolled in a final yellow sheet and typed:

"BUFFALO BILL'S HORSE"
Episode 13, "Soldier Boy and Wolf Man"
by Ty Pritter
Second Draft, Aug. 18, 1953

Brahms' *Adagio* came in for a soft landing and the Bowl echoed with held-back hacking. Never mind — the big *Allegro* third movement could drown out a flu epidemic. It almost drowned out the knocking on my front screen door.

"George? Are you awake?"

"Am I ever! Come in, Kat."

Mrs. Music came in through the music that filled the living room from my hi-fi speaker. She stood in the kitchen door and filled the kitchen with her own music. I was in love with Kat, but I hadn't told her so since I'd discovered I was, about two weeks after she moved into the opposite front bungalow back in January.

Kat was one of those "petite" sizes and wore her hair short, in the fashion favored by most women, with a chocolate wave dipping over her forehead. She filled out a lamb's wool died-to-match in a soft beige, with a bright Liberty scarf tied around her throat — her business outfit at KTTV, "That good-looking channel eleven!"

"You just getting home, Kat? Coffee? Beer? Coke? Me?" I met her at the doorway and suppressed the desire to kiss her hello.

"You never pick up your paper." She handed it to me.

"Kid likes to stick it in the pyracantha and rip the outside pages off." I'd only gotten it because the carrier boy said he needed five more subscriptions to qualify for a new bike. He must've ridden the Schwinn out-of-State, though. The route had been taken over by a pimply lad with horn-rim glasses, a Rams cap and no pitching skills.

"You finished 'Buffalo Bill,'" Kat said, pointing at my yellow script pages. "Do they kiss at the end?" She stood on tip-toe and slid up onto a bar stool next to the pass-through counter. That brought her golden brown eyes closer to mine.

"You bet they do, Kat. Big smooch out there in the romantic desert, and they gallop together into The End. Just Bill and Soldier Boy. Riding off the silver screen forever. The last of Columbia's To Be Continueds."

"Don't start blaming television for the end of Saturday movie matinees," Kat said. "And you're going to boil the coffee."

Rescuing the coffee and pouring Kat a cup, I said, "I accept the inevitable and — especially if you'll be there — I embrace it."

"Uh-hunh," she said.

"We had a death in the family today, Kat."

"Who? What happened?"

"Mr. Wispell."

"Hmmmm. Well, he wasn't my favorite uncle or anything. But it's too bad. Heart attack?"

"It's actually kind of strange. He was electrocuted by his short-wave rig. Accidental is a good possibility, the sergeant said. They think he had some sort of illegal power booster."

She shivered. "Glad I missed it."

"I wish I had. I found him."

"And you finished the script anyway? Good for you, George."

"Spence Bennett is shooting this thing somewhere out in the desert next week, so my deadline is what? A month ago? I just couldn't think of another way a horse could rescue Bill."

"You said you were stuck last Friday."

"Right. Well, it finally came to me. Wolves. Solder Boy valiantly saves Bill from a pack of wolves. Won't let them get anywhere near him." I gave her a hopeful smile. "Thought I might do the same for you."

She smiled back. The cadenzas of Brahms' concerto soared.

"Both the college boy contestants made passes at me tonight," she said. "Before the show, Pomona told me he'd like to have me on the receiving end of his next panty-raid and Claremont Men's invited me to hang out for Homecoming. Me, who's knocking at Thirty's gate."

"What do they know? Who won?"

"Roger Fingerhult form Claremont. He made exactly the same invitation for Homecoming to the girl — Ann Marie Murphey, seventeen, from Loyola — and presto! another 'Hot Date!'"

"*Amor* Conquers *Omnia*."

"It does Tuesdays at 8:30 on Channel 11." She sipped her coffee. "The producers are talking a new quiz show, George. Something with big big prize money. Like hitting the Irish Sweepstakes. I think they'll let me come in as an Associate, and if they do, I'm putting your name in for M.C."

"You put in my name and you'll get a call from one of those cheap-suit 'Business Consultants' at *Red Channels*."

"He'll say, George Tirebiter, Miss, is an agent of the Red Nemesis."

"You'll say, How do you know?"

"He'll say, Anonymous tip."

"He sure as hell won't say it was Lillie."

"And you told them she lied about you?"

"Sure. I made it real Billy Wilder stuff. Wife, soon to be ex-wife, rats on husband. Confesses he led a double life. Voted for Norman Thomas. Joined the Civil Liberties Union. Put Commie propaganda in the mouths of innocent actors. She lies through her teeth to get her comeback role."

Kat laughed. "Misses Oscar by a mile. Career over."

"Succeeds in blacklisting husband, which he survives by changing his name and writing lines for horses, extras and Things."

"I'm still going to put you in for M.C." She closed her eyes and slipped down from her seat on the stool. "I have to go to bed. Good night, George."

The music was over. The radio thundered with applause, which faded under the reverberant tones of Tom Cassidy as he seamlessly segued listeners back to records at the studio for the rest of Your Gas Company's Evening Concert.

Before she could leave, I asked, "We're still going to the Bowl on Saturday, aren't we?"

"Would I miss a glorious Birthday night of Cole Porter under the stars, George?" She put her hand on my cheek. "How's the novel coming?"

"Um, well, you know. Ty Pritter has all these deadlines. That looping dialogue for "Julius Caesar" is due Thursday and he hasn't started on it, and Darling wants Ty to give him the monster movie before 3-D goes the way of the Zoeopticon, and he's supposed to do a twenty-page synopsis of a new Smartee Boys mystery for an editor at Grosset . . . that's under the name Dixon W. Franklyn, of course."

"At least all of you are working." Kat walked into the living room to the tune of Ravel's "Daphnis and Chloe."

"Good night, George," she called. "Sorry about Mr. Wispell."

"I'll see you in my dreams," I said.

The screen door slammed like an off-stage gunshot.

Chapter 2
Errol Flynn Asks New Tax Hearing
Disagrees with Uncle Sam

I was considered something of a celebrity around the Rose-Bud. Not because I wrote for the movies. Nothing in that. It was because some of them had listened to me on the radio — 7:30 Friday nights over CBS. (The rest had probably been tuned in to "The Lone Ranger" on NBC.)

Network radio was the apex of modern entertainment, a galaxy-wide stage prepared by a handful of creative visionaries so as to release America's national imagination. Also, so as to mold them into faithful consumers of "nationally advertised brands" with a quick commercial right to the jaw. Me, George Tirebiter, I sold soap.

My show, "Hollywood Madhouse," went off the air in May of 1946, after five years of good ratings and good laughs. The soap king from New Jersey was making pretty bubbles with a screenland songbird that year, though, so she got my time-slot. When you're dead, you're dead.

When you're just buried alive, you can claw your way out. Maybe. I got back on the air in 1950, just as radio was coming up for the third and it looked like last time, playing a hard-boiled bozo named "Max Morgan, Crime Cabby." Max lasted a year. Radio — news and noise — is still with us. America's national imagination has moved over to television, however, where it's had another beer and dozed off.

No, people in L.A. didn't much care if their landlord or next-door-neighbor had written or directed, or even starred in a movie or two. Still don't. Common as beans. But being a one-time radio star, that gave me a little more razzle-dazzle room. A lot of people were pleased to find my character voice stuck in their imaginations. That gave me *former*-celebrity status around the Rose-Bud.

Now, about those flying saucers.

It was a hot, smoggy Wednesday morning. For the past couple of weeks, the air above the city had been steadily replaced by greasy amber smudge from half-a-million cement incinerators and tons of leaden exhaust from a traffic jam of pre-war, pre-freeway gas-burners.

I was about to walk the couple of blocks to the B of A at Adams and Figueroa where I could deposit the Rose-Bud rent money. Of my dozen tenants, one or two were always late with their contributions. And the very late Mr. Wispell, for reasons kept best to himself, always mailed me a postal money order. It had arrived in the morning mail.

My eyes were watering from smog, not sentiment, as I ripped open the envelope containing Wispell's final financial testament. So I thought. On a single sheet of mimeo paper he (or someone) had typed:

"On 16 August, 1:18 AM I received following at 405 kc — 450 TE SA AFFA SWAP YOUR R 450 K SWAP T ARE YOU APPEAR TO YOU LATER WHEN AS OR SHIP COMPREHAND DA DA K SE EE WID26 Q QRA WID26.

"I swapped frequencies to 450 kc and received at 1:27 — ZORG N UH ZEL BALA WON'T BE THERE UNTIL 14:20 YOU WILL SEE US IN THE SUN AT HIGH TIME TOMORROW VV THIS KAN BE THE SALVATION OF SOLA IF ALL PLANS GO ACCORDING TO OUR WILL.

"I asked, can you give us a sign tomorrow? Reply came at 2:11 — YES YES ZORG MAYBE BALA DANGER TO US N N YOU LAST CONTACT UNTIL SATURDAY YOU WILL HAV TWO VISITORS FROM OUTSIDE WAS AFFA ZO OR ANS DE DE YOU WILL SEE US Q Q

"Do not send me the documents we discussed, as I don't want them around the place if these visitors come.

"All my tests show this is the real thing. Their hand is stretched out. Come Saturday. We're not too old yet to ride in a Flying Saucer."

I was standing on my porch, wondering where Travis Wispell's money order for thirty-two dollars was, when Homicide's best, Sgt. Cummings, ambled into the Court, as square-jawed as ever.

"'Mornin' Mr. Tirebiter."

"Good morning, Sergeant."

"You told me you entered Travis Wispell's apartment about a minute or so after the lights kicked off?"

"A couple of minutes."

"Nobody inside?"

"Just the body."

"How hard did you look?"

"I didn't look."

"Then you come back here and call the precinct."

"And the fire department for the rescue squad. He looked like a blown fuse, but I'm no doctor."

"No cop either. Let's go inside outta this air, you mind?"

Inside, Sgt. Cummings took off his hat, wiped his forehead with a white cotton handkerchief, then wiped the inside of his hat.

"Coffee?" I asked.

"Sure. That college boy stay with the body?"

"No, I closed the door. The side door was locked, too, and the tenants — everybody who was home — stood around outside. Everybody you talked to yesterday was out there when I got off the phone. Sugar? Milk?"

"Both. Nobody in the bungalow?"

"Nobody I know of. You think somebody electrocuted him?"

"I got a radio guy coming to check the wiring today. Shoulda been here by now."

"It was Aliens. Flying Saucer guys. Here's your java, Sergeant."

"Yeah. Wise guy."

"Sure. They move by atomic molecular recreation. Poof! They're in your bathroom. Poof! Gone!" I handed him Wispell's letter. "This transmission came this morning instead of the rent money."

Sgt. Cummings drank his coffee and read the page.

"Crap," he said. "Excuse my French. Look, the finger-print squad is due here any minute. We're gonna take the place apart. I'm pretty sure the guy was murdered, Tirebiter. This is screwy, but it's evidence." He folded the letter into his notebook, pulled out a pen, squared his jaw at me and said, "Tell me what you know about this guy."

➤✦❧

Sgt. Cummings, being the creative L.A. cop he was, gave the flying saucer crap to the press. The afternoon *Mirror* gave his hard jaw and shiny shoes another spot on Page 4.

ELECTROCUTED BY ALIENS?
Detective Says Dead Man Talked to Saucers

Travis Wispell had a brother in Tucson as well as brother hams around the world. Clarence called me while the death squad was laying waste to the death scene. I said I was sorry about his brother.

"The po-leece said they'd — mm, be investigatin' his — ah, it." Clarence Wispell had a cold, which his Arkansas accent blurred through, making him sound slowed down, like a record played at a lower speed.

"I'm sure they're doing that right now. Up-to-the-minute stuff. No hicks on the force out here," I said.

"Cain you holt onto Trav's belongin's until I get up to Los Angleez next week? I'm a con-ductor on the Santa Fe. Gotta arrange my routing."

"The rent's paid a month in advance, Mr. Wispell."

"Gonna send him home to Ash Flat. Hasn't got nobody but me, anymore, anyways. Spent all his money on that dang radio hobby, so I know he don't have much goods in the house. Keep an eye on it for me, will ya, Mr. Typewriter?"

"Whatever the police leave, I'll keep under lock and key."

"Thank ya kindly."

I rang off and went back to reading "Julius Caesar," making note of any ad libs I might put into the mouths of Assorted Plebeians: "We will be satisfied! Let us be satisfied!" "None, Brutus, none!" "Peace, ho! Let us hear him!"

A handful of actors whose specialty was dubbing the many voices of crowds would be shouting these words, or something like them, at the projected image of Marlon Brando as he proclaimed "Friends, Romans, Countrymen!" Hedda Hopper and the rest of the world agreed: Stanley Kowalski and John Gielgud together in Shakespeare? It'd never work.

My pal John Houseman, one of Hollywood's few quality movie

producers, thought it would, and had slipped me the job. It was only a few pages, but every little thing helped.

"The will! The will! Read Caesar's will!" I proclaimed.

"Didn't find no will." Sgt. Cummings stood, his hat in his hand, looking in through the screen door. "Didn't find no box."

"He took it inside."

"Did you see it when you broke in?"

"I didn't break in. I opened the door with my master key, which I had every right to, being the owner . . . "

"Yeah, sure. Didja see it? The box?"

I thought. It hadn't been in the living room. I shook my head.

"Well, it ain't in there now, and I'm not thinkin' it was there yesterday evenin' when I put my seal on the door. Anybody comes around lookin' for the guy, you let me know. Here."

He banged on the screen. I opened it and took a card from his fingers.

"Call me. Keep yer eyes open and yer nose out, we'll get along fine."

He put on his straw hat, walked out to the grey Ford two-door parked at the curb, folded his long legs to get in and drove off.

"Revenge! About! Seek! Burn! Fire! Kill! Slay! Let not a traitor live!" I called after him.

Will Perry opened his door and yelled, "Hail, Caesar!"

"Doesn't even look like rain," I retorted.

"What these people in California need is some good old Iowa downpours," he said, joining me in a patch of sulfurous sunlight. "Thunder and lightning. Wash the skies clean."

"They don't have weather here, Will. Bad for business."

"And still we come. Say, George, drop in and see a picture!"

Will had become something of an overnight success in the world of science fiction pulp magazines. At 26, with a checkered career of hometown advertising, insurance sales (he'd played the carnival and county fair circuit brokering coverage against polio) and three months in an army infirmary with a slipped disk behind him, he'd decided to teach himself how to paint. He'd sold his first cover to *Galaxy* not long before moving into Rose-Bud with his very pregnant wife. Since then, he'd rendered fantastic and haunting Other Worlds for *If* and *Amazing* and *Fantasy & Science Fiction*.

"I call it 'Io in the Sky-O.' It's in a sci-fi art show this weekend at the Hollywood Hotel."

A melon-sized Saturn hung high in a blue-black starry sky, its rings constructed of tiny rocks with sapphire highlights of ice. Its moon was a rubble of dark cliffs and cracks bathed in amber planet-light. Up one perilous canyon-side a band of Earthmen in white spacesuits and cyclopean helmets climbed. You knew they were Americans from the Stars-and-Stripes on the backs of their packs.

"What's it the cover for, *Galactic Geographic*?"

"Book jacket. 'Tales of Space Conquest.' It'll be printed this big." He framed a paperback rectangle with his long fingers. "Say, a girl called me from Harryhousen's office at Warners a few minutes ago, George. They want to see some pictures. Bradbury put in a plug for me."

Ray Bradbury was a personable young fantasy writer who had made a name for himself with a collection of short stories called "The Martian Chronicles." You either loved Ray for his basically Middle Western view of the universe, or you hated him for the way he didn't bother to put the science in science fiction. Warner Bros. had just released a film based on a story of his about a lonely sea monster who falls in love with a foghorn, invades Manhattan and is finally killed at Coney Island.

"Matte work?" Mattes were paintings that served as movie back-grounds — medieval castles, distant landscapes, space vistas.

"Maybe. Hope so. I guess we stumbled into this sci-fi thing at just the right time, George."

"Mars may be Heaven, but Martians scare the Hell out of people."

"That's only one side of it. We're really going out there, George. You can't stop people from wanting to reach out from the planet. They'll do it, too. Little Joe — he'll be thirty in 1981. I bet he could be living on the Moon by then, if he wanted too."

"He'll probably have to. The Rooskies have the H-Bomb. Listen, Will, the detective told me somebody might have been hiding in the bathroom when I went in to Wispell's."

"That's a scary thought. How did he get out?"

"Bathroom window. We could see everything else from out here. Must've gone through the hedge and into the yard next door."

"Let's have a look."

The shrubbery between the Rose-Bud and the turn-of-the-century house to the west was a typical neighborhood combination of dense and prickly pyracantha, clumps of pencil-thin bamboo, a ragged stand of bottle-brush and some papyrus. Will slipped into the narrow space between the back of Wispell's bungalow and the planting.

"The cops have been all over back here, Will."

"Look."

I could see there was a dog-sized hole through the bushes. Will bent double and put his head and shoulders in.

"Back of a garden shed. I could wiggle through, but it'd help if I were a foot shorter."

"There's a gate to the alley in their backyard fence."

"The game's afoot," said Will, snaking out from behind the hedge.

"A foot-print anyway. An alien footprint."

"Now why would an alien kill old Mr. Wispell?"

"Because he was tuning in on their alien frequencies."

"Is this something you're writing, George?"

"No, it's something Wispell wrote. He was trying to talk to flying saucers, Will. Maybe he was talking to 'em!"

The house next door to the Rose-Bud was owned by Anna and Milt Birnbaum, both psychiatrists. Milt was on the Education faculty at USC. Anna had a modest practice out of an office at the front of the house. Neither had been aware of any disturbance or movement in their backyard Tuesday afternoon — or anytime, until the police crawled under the hedge and started dusting their back gate for fingerprints.

I wondered about the tenants on either side of Wispell. Miss Gage was at work, I guessed. I hadn't heard her come home or leave in the morning, so I decided I'd drop in at the Auto Club and pick up a strip-map for my jaunt to Santa Fe on Sunday. Maybe she had something to add.

As for Mr. O'Toole, he stood in his doorway, wearing a stained undershirt and oily khakis, absently adjusting his crotch as we spoke.

"There's nuttin' to be said, sir. I left me place about two for the Follies. It's little Betty Rowland strippin', sir. They call her the Ball of Fire, and it's not just on acountta her head of good Irish red, sir."

He brushed his hand through his own unkempt Sunkist-orange crop. A cigarette dribbled ashes down his front.

"No strange noises behind the bungalow? Ever see any visitors drop by Wispell's, day or night?

"As for the noises, sir, only the dog from next door, nosin' around in the bushes, as it sometimes does. An' I never seen nobody 'round his place at all.

"You told the police that, I guess."

"Well, sir, I did, but I did see himself in a place that gave me a start when I caught sight of his face. Seemed no reason to mention that to the Sergeant, sir. A man's reputation and all."

"Really?" I said. "But, just a second. The Birnbaums don't have a dog."

"It wuz a mutt, all right, sir. Snufflin'. Whinin'. I heard it at night a couple a times lately. Don't sleep at all well since me injury, ya know, sir."

"Some neighborhood stray, must've been. Where did you see Mr. Wispell?"

"Well, sir, I got a shipmate, Bill Meeghan, who come into a bit a money from an uncle er somebody. He took me to that joint on Western — Strip City they call it. Jennie Lee was playin' — th' Bazoom Girl she is! And Bill says, 'Wait 'til ya get a load of 'em! They's as big and solid as the Bells of St. Patrick's!'"

"Mr. Wispell was there?" It seemed unlikely, but there were a dozen heavily advertised burlesque theaters and clubs around L.A., and even a confirmed molar man might yearn for a front-row seat, if the seat was in front of Tempest Storm or Lili St. Cyr or Georgia Southern.

"He was that, sir. I didn't like to say nothin' to him. He was with another fella. Looked like an A-rab, he did. Dark complected. The A-rab was friends with some a the people workin' there, an', after his act was over, the comic sat right down at the table with 'em. There's a man you oughta put on the wireless, sir — he's got a hunderd voices he can make jokes in. Bruce his name is. Lenny Bruce."

The dank smell of O'Toole's apartment had crept around his body and was wafting past me. Stale beer, sweaty clothes, Barbasol and Camels. A man's room, with hair on it.

"I'll look into it," I said. "And thanks — about the dog. That might be a clue."

"God rest his soul, sir."

Tempest Storm at The Follies.
From Mr. O'Toole's Private Collection.

CHAPTER 3

LA FREEWAY LINKS OPEN FOR MOTORISTS' USE TODAY
SOME RELIEF FOR HEAVY TRAFFIC CONGESTION IN HOLLYWOOD SEEN.

Did I say that I'd kept one precious possession after my divorce? It was housed under wraps in the garage off the back alley — a red Mercedes convertible. It would get me to Santa Fe in a couple of days of heady driving on Route 66, my trip paid for by Howard Pingo, a studio chief for whom I did the occasional odd job. He'd called me a few days before. Wanted to go for a drive. That meant he'd like to have a private talk. Last time it was about his contract problems with a starlet who out-bazoomed the Bazoom Girl. This time we were northbound on the Pacific Coast Highway . . .

"I'm ramblin', Tirebiter. You know I think better this way — ramblin'. Hear me out now, Tirebiter. Think of the exhibition angle alone! We make a picture. *Variety* review says, 'A show-biz sonic boom!' It out-grosses 'From Here to Eternity' and 'House of Wax' put together. *Reporter* says 'H-Bomb B.O.' Could be a deep well. Could be dangerous. I like dangerous, how 'bout you? What do we say to the movie-goin' public? We say, 'Say, folks, this ain't just some ordinary color-spectacular wide-screen deepie! This is Top Secret!'"

"What is it exactly, Howard?"

"Well, they tell me the science boys have developed this thing as a weapon, so what? If you can weaponize it, you can SoNorize it. I can have some flacks design a big, glossy 'Weapons For Peace' program for schools. Posters. Star names. Toys. You know I like your ears, Tirebiter. You listen, okay? You listen, come back and tell me about it. If the test goes off big like they tell me, SoNorization'll make Cinerama look like a stub-party at my subassembly plant in El Segundo!"

AUTOMOBILE CLUB OF SOUTHERN CALIFORNIA.
LOS ANGELES.

Pingo chuckled the way only a millionaire can. I kept driving

Driving was SoCal's royal sport, so naturally the architects of the Southern California Automobile Club had built a home-base on the order of Castles in Spain. High arches, white stucco and lots of wrought iron with baroque cement frosting, planted with stubby palms and an abundance of tile-red bougainvillea. The main door looked like it would keep an army of Don Quixotes at bay. It let me in with a sigh of ice-cold air.

Audrey Gage was one of several girls working behind the map counter in a room big enough so it should have pigeons roosting on the painted beams. She handed the woman in front of me an arm-load of maps that would take her all the way to Vancouver, Canada — not the easiest journey in the days before interstates and by-passes — which the woman stuffed into her Bullock's shopping bag and carried away.

"Why, good afternoon, Mr. Tirebiter. Are you going somewhere?" Audrey dazzled me with her perfect smile.

"Yes, but, actually, Miss Gage, I was wondering if you had heard about your next-door neighbor, Mr. Wispell?"

Mysteriously, she tightened some muscles in her face and the smile faded for a second into a smoky bedroom gaze. Her eyes widened just enough to lose their innocence and gleam like some predatory cat's. In a flash it was gone. She was just another pretty face.

"Why, I don't believe so."

I explained about the death and asked if she'd noticed anything — like a dog behind the bungalows, for instance. She shook her head "no." Her hair re-arranged itself like a basket of cute kittens over the shoulders of her stand-up-collared, plum-colored dress. She glanced behind me and looked worried.

"Mr. Tirebiter, I'm sorry, but unless you'd like a map . . ."

"How do I get to Mecca?" It just popped out.

"Mmmmm," Audrey pursed her Red Delicious lips. "That's near Indio." She reached into a near-by slot, gave me a map of the Coachella Valley and growled. For an instant, her tongue showed between her lips. Then she looked right past me again and said, "Next, please?"

The Wednesday mail brought two different mimeo'd invitations to Ty Pritter. There was the regular Thursday meeting of the Los Angeles Science-Fantasy Society with guest electronics professor Harry Upthegrove from Cal Tech. There was also the weekend UFO convention at the Hollywood Hotel that promised to "lead mankind into a New Age and the vibrations of Aquarius."

There was science-fiction and then there was UFOlogy. Science fiction was, obviously, fiction, however speculatively based in scientific fact. As far as I knew, UFOlogy was a cult of alien abductees, hollow earth believers, and Seekers into the Unknown. The two didn't have a lot to do with each other.

It was Marilyn Monroe who inspired me to break into sci-fi. She had played small, unforgettable roles in half-a-dozen movies by mid-1950. I went on the air again early that year, sponsored by Dreemo Cigars, playing a tough cab driver who picks up the occasional body, or murderer, or scared blond somewhere along the Pacific Coast Highway. I got to bring in one scale-priced talent per week, and when I heard that wispy voice in "Clash by Night" and "All About Eve," I knew there was a script for Marilyn.

She was booked to play a Malibu cocktail waitress rescued by Max Morgan from the pounding midnight surf at Zuma Point. The show's plot revolved around a Mr. Nice Guy who gets in the cab with a "Harvey"-type invisible pal. The role was filled by John Archer, a one-time radio "Shadow," by 1950 a busy movie actor. He told me to be sure and catch the premiere of his new

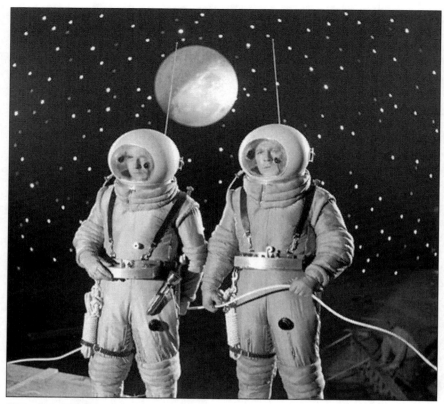

"Destination Moon" (1950)

picture, "Destination Moon." I did. As a matter of fact, I took Marilyn.

She held my hand and whispered with her nose in my ear. Things like, "That's the most gorgeous rocketship," and "Oh, I hope nobody has to stay behind by himself!"

I was a gentleman. Marilyn owed me nothing for the job and the date was purely professional. But our names were linked in the *Mirror*'s movie column and word didn't take long to get back to my wife, Lillie. She'd been living in Santa Barbara for years, the devoted follower of Swami Ram Deva, but chose this public opportunity to sue me for divorce. Naturally the brouhaha kept me from ever seeing Marilyn again.

Except for the weekly broadcast and a couple of rehearsals, "Max Morgan" didn't keep me very busy. My years of making the occasional movie appeared over. Nothing else seemed to be clicking, so, inspired by Marilyn and "Destination Moon," I picked up a handful of sci-fi pulps with busty blonds on the covers, and re-read "The War of the Worlds." The result was a novelette called "Nomads From Neptune," about a warrior race from another galaxy who terrorize a small town when they invade one-by-one disguised as tourists, a truck driver, newly-weds, and various government officials.

"Nomads," got me invited to a meeting of the Los Angeles Science Fantasy Society, where sub-cultures of sci-fi fans mingled — scientists from Cal Tech, be-spectacled high school boys, pulp enthusiasts who lived for nothing more than steady blasts of Space Opera, even the occasional professional writer or artist. I had met Will there, and Bradbury. As Will had said, I stumbled into the sci-fi thing just in time. "Phil Starke" joined "Ty Pritter" at the Underwood, and by the summer of 1953, with two space stories sold to the movies, I was back on my fiscal feet again.

I'd stopped going to LASFS on Thursdays, partly because there was a seething hostility between believers and non-believers in something called Dianetics. A few of the leading writers were behind it — men like A. E. van Vogt and Bob Heinlein. I'd read their books and thought they were pretty military-minded. Benevolent dictatorship, preferably by super-men, was their idea of the World of the Future. If Dianetics was out to convert men into super-men, make mine milk.

A few minutes after five the phone rang.

"Hello," I said.

"We talked on the phone," she said.

"We're talking now," I said.

"I suddenly felt that we had."

"Had what?"

"Talked on the phone."

"This is George Tirebiter," I began.

"I knew it!"

"How did you know it?"

"Your name is right here on this postal money order."

"The one with Travis Wispell's signature?"

"How did you know?"

"I'm psychic," I said.

"My sister's psychic."

"Funny, I knew that too. One thing I don't know is your name, Miss . . . ?"

"Kaawi. That's the language of poetry."

"I could write a sonnet to thank you for sending that money order right on to me. 627 West 30th, L.A."

"I thought we could effect an exchange of energies."

She had a low voice, kind of sweet, but it sounded even more disconnected from her body than the usual phonecall voice. It was as if she were sliding sideways into her next thought.

"Energies," I said. "If you mean trade the contents of my envelope for the contents of yours, that'd be swell, but the police took it from me. Something about evidence in a murder case."

There was another long sideways pause. Then she said, "The Hollywood Hotel."

"It's a dump."

"We're having our convention there this weekend. I'll bring Travis's check."

"Can't you just send it to me?"

"Something tells me not to do that." The way she said it made me think of Xenomorphs with glowing multi-celled eyes.

"The police will have no idea what his messages mean, you know."

"One of them seemed to mean that the late Mr. Wispell was expecting visitors from Outer Space to drop by this coming Saturday."

"Oh, we all are."

"Shriners? Knights of Pythias? Girl Scouts?"

"Flying Saucer International."

"I'll be there."

"They'll be there, too," she said. "Well," she said, her voice slipping sideways, "live in the light."

"Oh, yes. I try to keep on breathing right through the dark parts too."

"That's important," she said.

The line went dead.

>€€

I shook the too-many-words writer's clutter off my mind with an evening walk around the SC campus, as far as the Coliseum and back past the Shrine Auditorium. A mockingbird was performing an extensive repertoire from his perch on a palm in front of the theater. Traffic was busy on Figueroa Street, searchlights playing over Felix Chevrolet. I turned into the quiet of 30th Street and looked up the alley beside the Rose-Bud. The blue-gray flickers of television glared out from under the shade of No. 629 — the almost-always-empty bungalow leased by the late Gideon Selz.

From the co-ed's windows I could hear Gene Norman on KLAC, smoothly introducing "the fastest selling single in history," which turned out to be the familiar strains of the "Dragnet" theme, followed by Stan Freberg's dragon-slaying parody — "The legend you are about to hear is true, only the needle should be changed to protect the record."

Bob-the-Blob, no surprise, had a game on. The Yankees, World Series-bound, were winning.

Kat's place was quiet. "Hot Date!," the show Mrs. Music worked for, aired live on Tuesday night. That made her weekend Wednesday and Thursday. Her mother lived twenty miles east in the foothills of Monrovia, celebrated home of the world's largest date-packing plant. Both Kat's brother Dale and her husband Mike had been listed as missing in Korea. Mike for two years.

For the past week-and-a-half the POWs had been coming home. Every day a small miracle graced the news pages: **"Lost" Dad Returning From Korea. Father Comes Into The Life of a Baby. Blind Vet Sees Joy.** Not to mention **WEDS ANOTHER, FINDS MATE ALIVE IN KOREA.**

I had already noticed that Mrs. Music was going to be darn sure she didn't make that mistake.

Where there is no hope, there is boundless hope. Kat had driven out that morning to be with her mother when the next hundred names of those released were announced. On the other hand, I had a date to take her to the Bowl on Saturday, which was her 29th birthday.

⊰⊱

When the phone rang early Thursday morning, the long-distance voice on the other end seemed to be fluent in a dictionary-free language.

"Tirebiter? O-Man."

"Yes. Who?"

"You're gonna be Mr. Pingo's ears, huh, Tirebiter? Yeah. Uncle Sammy thought he'd be interested. We can trust him with this. It's Micronics."

"It is?"

"Don't ask what Micronics is, that's strictly for tapologists like Hoppenhower and all the rest of those leftist engineers! But they delivered the big one this time!"

"They did?"

"Look, Tirebiter, if we use this stuff on the Reds, which we can do anywhere in the Red World, it'll better than hydrogenize 'em. Poof, right?"

"If you say so."

"I know so. Now, between us, in some commercial version applied to small-scale houses — well, Mr. Pingo deals with me. See ya next Monday."

"I'll be there."

"I figure this'll make Pingo a little taller, me a little fatter. Maybe you too, Tirebiter! Don't miss the Big Bang on the way to the bank, Bozo!"

That made me feel slightly hydrogenated, if not SoNorized, so I sat on my steps with my second cup of coffee at hand, reading the last thing I'd written when Mrs. Music's door opened. She was especially pert this morning.

"Morning, George. Here's your question."

"Fire away."

"Why is an oyster heap like an English poet?"

"Hmmm . . . because it is Shelley?"

"Oh . . ." She walked across the dead grass. "I thought it would be harder than that."

"Depends on who's answering."

"I have to have twelve funny riddles about famous English writers for Johnny by Monday."

"How did it go at your Mother's?"

"Nothing yet, but, you know, we've been waiting a long time. I drove back this morning."

"Ah . . ."

"What are you reading?" She sat on the step beside me, pert as anything.

"An assortment of Roman ad libs. For Housman. I got this one from Antony and Cleopatra — 'the hand of death hath wrought him.' Made me think of Mr. Wispell."

"Sad. What do you know about Mark Twain?"

"Only his obscurer works, the better to steal plots for radio shows."

"We might need an expert on Mark Twain."

"I'm a quick study. What for?"

"That new quiz show with giant money if you can answer all the questions about whatever your specialty is."

"I thought you had me up for M.C."

"That's another show, 'What's My Name?' I'll get you on television yet, George."

"Well, I could bone up on Twain, you could exert your influence as head question writer and get me on the show, I'd answer everything, win the big bonanza, and buy a couple of steamship tickets to Honolulu."

"That's after we got out of jail for fixing the game. Naughty, naughty."

Kat rose and brushed off her skirt. "I've got a busy day, George. New work-frock at May Company, dentist, and a couple of hours at the library. You?"

"I'll run these pages over to Metro. They've got a walla session at 10:30. Drive on to Santa Monica, walk out the Pier, listen to the seagulls. Read 'The Big Sleep' again. It always helps."

"The writer's life." Pertly, Kat walked away to the street and down to the corner to catch the bus. I thought again how crazy it was for me to be crazy about her, but there it was.

Whoever had killed Wispell had de-materialized out his bathroom window with a 12-quart cardboard box full of not more than ten pounds of something. "A man's work," he'd called it. His last words. No, not quite. "Ought to weigh more than that," he'd added. Was it full of the documents he had told someone not to send because of the "visitors" he expected Saturday?

When and if Sgt. Cummings thought to add two and two and end up wanting my rent check as evidence in the bargain, I'd tell him about Flying Saucer International. I had a feeling he wouldn't want to go out there in alien Hollywood crackpot land looking for Wispell's killer, though. He'd be tracking in his own territory — old-fashioned, crooked Downtown L.A.

The radio experts spent a couple of hours dismantling Mr. Wispell's ham rig, which they dutifully carted off to Headquarters. They sealed his front door again. Poor guy, murdered maybe because of that box?

I was the only one who knew about Wispell's visit to Strip City. The *Mirror* offered up an enticing assortment of burlesque ads on the Nitelife page, across from an ad for Clifton's Cafeteria that displayed a seven-course Sunday Dinner for 89 cents, plus tax. Playing Thursday, tonight, were "Girls a' Poppin" at the Toddle House, "Go Girls Go" at the Colony Club, and Miss Switzerland along with Lenny Bruce, Strip City, Western at Pico.

Having wrapped up that high-toned Additional Dialogue for Willie The Shake, I deserved a little low comedy — at least maybe a one-liner about a dead dentist.

Strip City's big red and yellow neon sign blinked on and off above the one-story façade, which was bathed in blue. Next to the door posters proclaimed "Strip-a-thon Every Monday Night!" and "Beauty Contest Discards!"

Inside, the place was like the Stork Club as remodeled by Jean Paul Sartre. The walls were No Exit Black, the upholstery Early Jungleland, the stage the size of a screen star's bed, with big blue neon strippers flashing their red be-tasseled pasties on either side.

The torrid August evening was held at bay by a numbing blast of air-conditioning. An impassive olive-skinned face above a too-tight collar showed me through the chilly darkness to a table. As far as I could see, Thursday night's early show was a full-house less than a sell-out.

LAPD on Pasties Patrol.

On stage a familiar-looking beefy man in a peacock-blue silk suit was acting drunk. It was time for his punchline:

"Aw, hell, I spill more'n that!" The four-piece band segued into a grinding version of "Harbor Lights" and Mr. Beef bowed slightly to acknowledge the deafening cheers of the crowd.

"Thank you, thank you. Well, lovely girls are a dime a dozen around Hollywood, they say. Here's one worth a buck-twenty all by herself, the enticing Rusty Amber!"

Rusty danced onto the stage in a cocktail dress knocked off of a last year's Paris design — blood red, with a wide patent leather belt and shiny stiletto heels. She would have looked at home in a *LIFE* magazine essay on suburban entertaining. In a little while, the dress was on the floor and Rusty was posing suggestively in half a slip. Unfortunately for the pace of her act, the slip caught on her left heel as she tried to step out, and it took a couple of irritated shakes to get it off. She finished up in a red satin g-string and bare breasts. Whether or not a stripper's nipples had to be covered was, in the Greater Los Angeles Area, a matter of politics, pay-offs and expertise in tassel-tossing.

I had a gin-and-tonic and watched the gyrations of Tarana, Strivina and a glacial milk-fed blond who turned out to be Miss

Switzerland. The house was a little fuller by the time she finished bumping her way through "Perdido." Another round of drinks and bring on the laughs.

Lenny Bruce was in his late twenties at this time, five or six years before his big break as a "sick" comic. I had never heard anything like him. He did a routine in several voices based on a news item, the Army's proposed tours of the Alamagordo A-Bomb crater: "Get the schmucks, the PFCs in there and clean up that radiation before Ike gets here!" "But Major, they're glowing in the dark now!" "Good! We can keep the place open all night!"

All too soon he brought on the next act, "The star of my new flick, here she comes, Stacey The Strippin' Steno!"

Stacey the pelvic redhead, began her routine in full secretarial habit, with glasses and a steno book. Bruce sauntered backstage. I wrote a note on my cocktail napkin, passed it to the waitress and took my second drink to the bar. Bruce showed up on the stool next to me a couple of minutes later, a sharp-toothed grin on his face.

"Hiya, Tirebiter!" He gestured at the Steno, now down to her basics. "It ain't no submarine, but it's pretty nice."

"Lenny Bruce, you're a funny guy."

"You too. I heard you on the radio." He stuck out his hand. "Looking for talent?"

"You'd be it, if I was. No, I'm looking for some information. About a neighbor of mine who was killed on Tuesday."

Bruce whistled. "Come on back to what my agent calls a dressing room. 'Course he's a nudist."

The back of the dive was a warren of cramped two-person dressing-rooms. Tarana and Strevina, one almond-eyes, the other a sorority-type girl sat in theirs, painting each other's toe-nails. Bruce shared his six-by-six quarters with Mr. Beef.

"Meet Bob Carney, Tirebiter. M.C. and funny man."

Carney stuck out his paw and grinned like I'd just bought the first brand-new Buick Roadmaster on the lot. "I worked for you once," he said. "Nineteen-forty-seven in a picture with Dixie Cupps. Harry Rose and I did that "Gimme a drink before the fight starts" routine with Dixie for you."

"Sure. I recognized you. That was one funny bit."

"Old as Methuselah's cat." He smoothed the line of his toupee in the mirror. "Lennie wants me to do it for a movie he's writing."

"It's a great routine, Bob." Bruce pantomimed a drunk trying to keep his too-large pants from falling down before the rest of him did. "He's like W. C. Fields when the stuff gets stuck to his shoes in that golf bit."

"You said you were writing a movie."

Bruce preened a little. "I wrote myself two parts. One's an absolutely hip Jew like me," he said, moving like a cool cat under his real gone threads. "The other one's Charlie Chaplin in 'The Great Dictator.'" He duck-walked out the door, tipping his transparent bowler and spinning an invisible cane. He came back and said, in a vile German accent, "Der firing squvad avaits you, Bop!"

Carney slipped back into his iridescent suit jacket. "I just did a bit for Tab Pictures, Tirebiter. Thing called 'A Night in Hollywood' with Tempest Storm. Did the old eight-day cigarette gag. I'm in the book."

Bruce rolled his eyes to the ceiling and wailed like a *yiddishe mama*, "Mine boy! Mine boy! Ven you go, burlesque goes mit choo, Bop!"

There was applause and hooting from the meager house and Stacey the Steno strode back through the curtain wearing pointy pasties and a modest g-string. "No peeking," she said to me and joined Miss Switzerland in their dressing room. Bruce closed the door.

"You're the nightclub world's answer to Cornelia Otis Skinner," I said.

"I heard her on the radio too. She did people from Times Square, right? The immigrant, the actress, a lady down from the Bronx, shopping. Yeah, I dig that. It's a play and I'm doing all the parts. Or sometimes it's me alone out there and all the shit outside is so weird I just want to get to everybody, open 'em up, you know, so they can figure it out by themselves. So, what about a murder?"

I explained. He listened.

"Yeah, Wispell. Big jaw. Like Rondo Hatton. He was with Eddie Haroot. Eddie's got a couple of record labels — Jazzology, Bluetone. Said the guy had a record project for him, might bring in some capital."

"Record project? The guy made gold teeth."

"Aficionado of cool sounds, is what Eddie said. The cat said zero to me, man. Now he's cold as Pops Whitman. You should talk to Eddie, man."

"Thanks, I will."

"The cops don't know about this connection here?"

"I haven't passed it on. Wispell was my neighbor, Lennie. LAPD has a lot of murders to handle, you dig."

"I do dig. And listen, man, I'll letcha know when 'Dream Follies' is in the can."

"You're really going to do Chaplin?"

"Sure. You know, Adenoid Hinkel Meets The Four Boobs."

"Ask me to the premiere. I'll wear soup and fish."

"Where they're gonna premiere this piece a shit, you gotta be sure and keep your raincoat closed."

Chapter 4

Reaction to Kinsey

Sex Survey Stirs Wide Controversy

"We're inclined to believe that Kinsey gets his answers from braggarts, exhibitionists or those who are more or less abnormal."

The paper was full of sex. It sizzled on my porch Friday afternoon. Sex and death. **Kills Wife With Hammer, Drives to Police Station.** That kind of thing. **Dr. Kinsey's Sex Poll of Women Starts Battle in Nation's Press** for example. **Trial Rubout Plot Bared** found Barbara Graham in court, looking at the photographs of slain Mrs. Monahan and remarking, "Gee, how awful" to co-defendant Emmett (The Iceman) Perkins.

I had to turn to page 26 in the *Mirror* to raise a clue of what the book "Sexual Behavior in the Human Female" might have in store for lovers of erotic footnotes. Buried in the last 'graph was "perhaps the biggest bombshell to set off arguments is the finding that women who have experienced sexual climax before marriage are much more likely to succeed early in marriage in achieving sexual satisfaction."

The previous candidate for "biggest bombshell" had been **Have H-Bomb Russ Boast**, headlined on Page One only a week or so earlier. The Civil Defense Administration had quickly advised that anyone living within ten miles of a "probable target area" dig a deep hole and sink in a concrete bomb shelter. **U. S. Tests Air for Russ H-Bomb Proof. Texan Wounds 2 in Crowded L.A. Bus Depot**. It was that kind of summer, August 1953. Sex and death.

Bluetone Records had an office in Crossroads of the World. It turned out to be on the second floor of one of the Hollywood-style half-timbered buildings toward the back. "Haroot Publications" the sign said. Stairs on the outside led up to the office door, which I knocked on and opened.

There was a receptionist's desk, but no one sat there. There was a framed poster on the wall for the Hangover Club, featuring Rosy McHargue and his Ragtimers.

"Hello?"

"Yes?" Suspicious voice from the inner office. "May I help you?"

"Mr. Haroot?"

A stocky man with a prominent nose emerged with his hand outstretched. "I am he."

"My name is George Tirebiter and I'm a neighbor of Mr. Wispell. I believe you met with him the other evening?"

"Would you care to sit in the office?"

I did so, in a room with artists' photos and a couple of LP record covers framed on the wall. Haroot leaned back in his chair and cocked his head.

"Mr. Wispell died, or was killed — electrocuted — on Tuesday afternoon. He lived in my bungalow court and another neighbor told me he saw Wispell with you at Strip City . . ."

"I am not an habitué, Mr. Tirebiter, but I do enjoy the comedian, Lenny Bruce."

"It was Bruce who led me to you. Could you tell me if Mr. Wispell was pitching something? Bruce said he might be an investor?"

Haroot chucked silently and cocked his head again.

"Surely he wasn't a jazz aficionado?"

"Does this have to do with the poor man's death?"

"It might, I suppose. He didn't talk to you about flying saucers, did he?

"Flying saucers, no. Outer Space Music, yes."

"He was a ham radio operator."

"He told me he had recorded music from Jupiter or Mars or Uranus — someplace. Alien music, and did I want to put it out on a new vinyl LP album. I said, well, does it have a beat? He says, it's more like angel's music, like a lullaby. I said, my customers like bebop, daddy-o. Try RCA Victor Red Label you want a nap."

"So, that was it? Gas Music From Jupiter? Why did he think you'd be interested?"

"No idea." He cocked his head to the other side.

"Do you think he really had recordings from Outer Space?"

"He had something. Wanted to play me a tape he said he'd recorded at home, off his shortwave. I don't know, maybe I should've taken him up on it. Novelty release. Speed it up maybe."

"People like canaries whistling Johan Strauss, singing dogs, that woman who does the Bell Song in flats and sharps. You never know. I mean, if he offered to pay for it . . ."

"I do have a professional reputation to keep up, Mr. Tirebiter."

"Of course you do. Well, thanks for your help."

"If I was, I am grateful." He handed me a book of matches from a bowl on the desk. "My place. Armenian cuisine."

He showed me to the door and stood in it while I walked back down the steps. The matches advertised King Leo's, a few blocks away on Ivar, featuring "Food fit for Leo the Magnificent!"

I walked east on Sunset, wondering what happened to Mr. Wispell's tapes. I assumed he had tape-recorded something he'd picked up while cruising the ionosphere. Home recorders had 7-inch plastic reels, even 3-inch ones, easily carried around in a pocket. I put in a call to Sgt. Cummings at a booth in front of the Hollywood Athletic Club.

"I can tell ya this, Tirebiter, person or persons unknown stuck a dynamo in there, wired up the chair and when he flipped the switch it was like lightning hit him. That's all I can tell ya."

"Are you done with his apartment? His brother is coming in on the train to collect the remains and whatever is left of his belongings. I'd like to pack them up, whatever they are."

"Go ahead, go ahead. We got what we need. Go in through the side door, so the front's still got a seal on it, okay?"

"Right, I'll do that, thanks, Sergeant." I hung up and checked the book for "Phonograph Records, Manufacturing," hunted through a few variations and settled on the Downtown office of Record Magic — "Your voice, your memories, forever!" I called and checked, ten to a hundred 10-inch LPs, 24 cents a disk, paper sleeve 3 cents extra. Had they pressed something about Space Music?

"You must be psychic!"

"That's what my sister says."

The woman on the phone sneezed. "Pardon me. It's the Season."

"Sorry. Did you make something for a Mr. Wispell?"

"We pressed fifty copies of a 10-inch blue vinyl "From the

Saucers to You" for him, yes, delivered on . . . Tuesday."

"In a Vodka box?"

"I wouldn't have thought so, sir." She sneezed again. I said good-bye, wiped the phone on my sleeve and took the bus home.

I'd had a reminder from my editor at Grosset about the Smartee Boys book I owed them. The boy's-book stories were all plotted in advance and then handed to writers like me to flesh out. I re-read the synopsis after I got back from Hollywood. The three teens — two brothers and a cousin — would be involved in a pirate radio station, which is where I came in, I suppose.

I made enough excuses about the thing to reassure New York I was ripping right along on schedule. That delayed my checking in on Mr. Wispell's belongings until the smoggy sunset, which seemed to take an hour to slow-fade out.

Mrs. Whitmer came home after dark in a Yellow Cab. I had another drugstore package, so I stopped her as she walked past my door.

"Oh, my gracious! Mr. Tirebiter! I've been to the Greek Theater! There was a crowd!"

"What did you see?"

"No. Who. I saw Dr. Alfred C. Kinsey himself!"

"At the Greek? Wow!"

"It was all about how marriages fall apart because of sex problems. He said we have medieval attitudes."

"Do we?"

"He said that we've only ever guessed about the difference between men and women. Guessed, is what he said."

"Really. Ah, well, Mrs. Whitmer, so . . ."

She leaned closer to me and said, "'Vastly different and typically feminine reactions.' Those were his words. Even after change of life."

. "Good, well, that's what I hear too and this came from Rexall for you. Swell full moon. Good night."

She leaned perilously closer and murmured, "He said they wouldn't take in any more volunteers now the book is published. Goodnight, Mr. Tirebiter."

'REPORT' HEARD ROUND THE WORLD

She toddled away to her bungalow and shut the door. The mockingbird from the Shrine was now running through its songbook from a phone pole in the alley. I had the passkey in my pocket. Wispell's place was dark and a bit on the spooky side. I walked across and knocked on Kat's door.

She was delighted to join me in a visit to the murder house. It would be like Nick & Nora in the Thin Man movies. "George, you live a very exciting life, for a writer," Kat said, as we went around to the side of Wispell's bungalow. "What are we looking for?"

I flipped on the light inside the kitchen door. Whoo boy! It was going to cost more than Wispell's cleaning deposit to mop up this mess.

"I don't know. The cops took the radio gear away. If there was a tape recorder they probably got that. So, if you were going to hide something the size of a waffle in here, where would you go?"

"Waffle?" She opened the cupboard doors. The shelves were very bare. "Dinner plates for two, highballs for three, box of vanilla cake mix for . . ." She shook it. "For hiding tapes in."

"Wow! You must be psychic. Spill it out."

Kat popped the lid flaps and poured the contents onto the counter. There were no tape reels. Instead, a cigar-sized, tissue-wrapped object thumped down into the flour.

"Pretty good for a first-time sleuth, huh?"

"What is it?"

She unwrapped the thing, which proved to be a blue crystal about five inches long.

"Maybe Mr. Wispell was into crystal radios."

"If so, no wonder he was talking to Mars with that beauty. Let's check his closet."

The bedroom was small and close. Police had roughed it up a little. The closet door was closed.

"You open the door, George."

I did, revealing a meager wardrobe. Two shiny suits, several slump-shouldered white shirts. A couple of vests, twill pants, light overcoat for California winters. Nothing interstellar.

"Do you suppose the police checked his pockets?"

"I will anyway." Suit coats, vests, down the line, nothing in the pockets. Two pairs of shoes gathered dust on the floor and a workaday fedora on the single shelf did the same. There was no tape reel under the fedora.

"Is this interesting?" Kat held out a spherical rock about the size of a little roll of recording tape. Its surface was covered with enigmatic speckles.

I looked at it. "It seems to have the Secret of the Universe written in, maybe Martian, all over it. This could be it!"

"First time gum-shoe and I find the Magic Crystal and the Secret to the Universe!"

"Maybe his brother can use it for a paperweight. Anything else in the dresser?"

"The man had a couple of changes of sox and underwear, that's about all."

The living room, where his ham outfit had been, was fitted with heavy shelves where the amplifiers and receivers once sat. There was a world map with red and yellow pins stuck in it, some with extra flags, on the wall next to the desk, where Wispell had perched, microphone in hand, roaming the airwaves. No sign of any left-behind equipment.

"His tape recorder was probably in a small suitcase."

"I know the kind. It couldn't plug into any other machine he used, so he had to hold up a mike in front of the speaker to record."

"Not much left to hand over to his brother, when he comes."

I poked my head into the bathroom. The window was small and above eye-line over the toilet. No vodka carton could have got through it in one piece. There was a copy of *Look* folded on the back of the toilet. I checked. "Flying Saucers Are Real! Sensational exposé in this issue!"

"Something the boys in blue missed?" Kat stood at the door, looking in with a wrinkled nose.

"Magazine article on flying saucers. Could be a clue."

"I bet you say that to everybody."

"I'm going to go to a saucer convention tomorrow, before the Bowl. I'll already be in Hollywood. I'll pick you up at KTLA."

"Unless you get abducted, George."

"That's right, unless I get abducted."

We went back out through the kitchen door, taking the mystery stone and the blue crystal with us.

"For safekeeping. Maybe protective amulets," I said.

"You're really getting into this saucer thing."

"Maybe I'll pick you up in one."

"Goodnight, George."

"Goodnight, Gracie."

Senator Joe McCarthy was in town from Wisconsin, even as Dr. Kinsey was departing back for Indiana. The Senator's attempt at a news "bombshell" bigger than female orgasm was an investigation of Communist infiltration into — get this — the Government Printing Office where "any Communist spy in the printing office could do more damage than the situation discovered in the Hiss case!"

Saturday's *Mirror* announced a scoop by their staff news-hen, Patty O'Duff — **Oops! Girl 'Spy' Scares McCarthy**.

Seems the intrepid reporter knocked on his door at the Ambassador Hotel and the Senator himself opened up "clad only in white shorts." A revealing news-moment! "He has quite a hairy chest and his build isn't bad," Miss O'Duff wrote.

She caught up with McCarthy and his "council," Roy Cohn at breakfast. "The Senator breakfasted on ice tea and a sweet roll. He talks with his mouth full." Yikes!

I quote: "Why are you a bachelor, Senator? I asked. He turned to Cohn and asked him, 'Why are you a bachelor, Cohn?' Cohn considered for a moment and said, 'I'm young enough not to be considered one yet.'"

In retrospect, a fairly bizarre exchange. As she left, Miss O'Duff displayed her red scarf and shoes and asked the Senator "not to get any ideas they represented my political views." She reported that "he laughed."

The old Hollywood Hotel squatted at the corner of Hollywood and Highland. It had been there long before Sid Grauman built his cinema palace in "Chinese" style almost next door. Always slated for demolition, as the papers liked to say, but reprieved for too many years without much refurbishing.

The Flying Saucer International Convention was in and around the Pepper Tree Ballroom, not far from the shabby reception desk. Tables piled with pulp publications lined the corridor, managed by persons with an indefinite sort of otherworldliness about them.

One unhappy-looking traveler with hat and handbag sat behind a sign advertising "My Flight To Venus." Display boards held misty pictures of dodgy objects apparently proving observation, interaction, and a range of effects from conquest and colonization to domestic harmony and world peace.

One table advertised an up-coming Spacecraft Convention at Giant Rock out in the Mojave. Apparently someone had an apartment under the Giant Rock from which flying saucers could be readily observed. Miraculous appearances of Blessed St. Ufo.

From the Ballroom I could hear voices contributing to a panel discussion of "Goodly People of the Avatar." According to one speculator, they were Sirians (seriously, from Sirius) whose purpose was to redeem Our Earth from Communism and the H-Bomb.

I looked around for a woman who might be named "Kaawi." I

McCarthy Opens L.A. Quiz, Says It Tops Hiss Case

BY ANNE STERN
AND FRANK LARO
Mirror Staff Writers

Sen. Joseph McCarthy today opened a public hearing in an investigation he described as having a more important potential than the Hiss case.

It got under way about 10:30 a.m. in Room 330, Federal Building, before television cameras.

An hour before the hearing began, a crowd of about 150 people — twice as many as the room accommodates — milled outside in the corridor.

Although the Wisconsin Republican disclosed the name of only one witness, he indicated testimony would be confined to his current investigation of an asserted infiltration of Communists into the Government Printing Office.

"Any Communist spy in the printing office could do more damage even and be more dangerous than the situation uncovered in the Hiss case," he declared.

Meanwhile, two women who appeared at sessions yesterday were identified today as Florence Fowler Lyons and Mrs. Mary Mitchell, who have opposed UNESCO instruction in public schools. Miss Lyons said she and Mrs. Mitchell conferred privately with aides of McCarthy. The Senator, however, said that he himself talked to the two women.

Alger Hiss was convicted in 1950 of perjury before a Federal grand jury.

Slated as first witness today was William C. Taylor, 43, self-admitted member of the Communist Party and a onetime functionary in its Washington council.

THE FACE OF SEN. McCARTHY
"His build isn't bad. Chest is hairy."

Girl 'Spy' Catches Senator Off Guard

half-hoped to see her in semi-translucent space-robes, maybe a skin-hugging silver coverall. What there were instead were very ordinary, mostly matronly-looking ladies wearing pyramid hats, a guy with a plaid shirt and hand-painted tie with a saucer and "Dawn of the New Age" emblazoned on it manning the Center of Infinity Library table, and a teenager in capris and cat's-eye dark glasses, drinking a Dr Pepper and guarding the Portals of Light.

Even the Hollywood Book Store had a table, stacked with best-sellers like "Behind The Flying Saucers" by Frank Scully, with its garishly beautiful cover featuring three terrified women in revealing nightwear and "The Flying Saucers Are Real" by Major Donald Keyhoe, featuring a trio of elegant saucer-vehicles menacingly bound for Earth. Keyhoe's brand-new book, previewed in the issue of *Look* I'd found in Wispell's bathroom, showed those blazing vehicles descending through the ionosphere. "Flying Saucers From Outer Space."

There was an information table with "Official Publications" and badges for members of the FSI. A woman in her fifties, not too stylish, a user of air-wick to stop kitchen and hotel ballroom odors, wearing a Volunteer badge smiled hopefully at me.

"Afternoon, sir. Would you like to join?"

"I'm just here to look around. Look for someone, really."

"Well, if they're a Member, I'm sure they're here. The abduction is supposed to happen this afternoon, when the Sun is conjuncting."

"Maybe you know her. She told me her name was Kaawi. She may be interested in radio communications with aliens."

"Interstellar Communication by Radiotelegraphy." That's Mr. Bailey. He has an exhibit room across the way. She could be the young woman inside. Dark dress, dark hair."

There was no young woman inside. There were some chairs and a movie screen. There were copies of "The Saucers Speak" for sale. I riffled through one. Maybe I was on to something here. The gobbledy seemed gookish enough for saucer-speak:

"This is Zo again. I am 5 feet 7 inches tall, and I weigh 148 pounds. I have auburn hair. I am what you would call 25 years old. We all wondered what our brothers from other planets looked like. You were lucky you heard us on the radio the other night. You wonder how long our space flights take us. No, we do not fly as you think, but drift on magnetic lines of force. A landing can be arranged. Our superiors must decide. Fate of all creation here depends on it."

It was a lot clearer transmission than Mr. Wispell's teeth-chattering capital letters, at least. The sales table showed the range of obsessions pursued by saucerians — the Wisdom of Ancient Egypt, the Old Testament and Christian Mysticism crossbred into the coming Golden Age. I had the August copy of the Interplanetary News-Digest in my hand when she caught me.

"The latest news of Space Visitors and their message. You can subscribe — five issues for two dollars. "The Saucers Speak" is also two dollars."

It was Kaawi's voice, low, sweet and forever sliding sideways. I turned and said, "Kaawi? I'm George Tirebiter."

She did have dark hair and a dark blue dress. She was also less than four feet tall.

"I knew you'd come. I have your check," she said, walking behind the book table. "What do you think of the Convention?"

"Are you still planning for a saucer landing on Hollywood Boulevard this afternoon?"

"So they say, Mr. T. Mr. Wispell thought so."

"The note that should have come to you instead of the rent check advised you, or somebody, not to send some documents that you, or somebody, had discussed."

"And?"

"Well, Mr. Wispell got a box from United Parcel the afternoon he died and the box disappeared and I'm trying to trace what might have been in it."

Kaawi looked blank and sat down — up, really, on a wooden stool. She shook her head. "Bailey's got a network of hams tuned in to various frequencies." She hummed in Morse Code. "They get something, they send it in and Bailey sort of translates it. Pumps it out, sells to the mailing list. Goes out to Giant Rock and has a beer with van Tassel."

"I gather you're not a true believer."

"You gave me the same impression."

"You go first."

She laughed. "There's the para-normal for real and there's some things so many people have seen they must be real and there's things we can't explain for real or not. Unlike some other Searchers out there in the hall, I don't think Martians established a base inside the hollow Earth five-hundred years ago and have recently put the Government under mind-control."

"Do Aliens like Ike?"

"He may already have met with them, you never know. I have your missing rent."

The money order was in her bag, under the table. She handed it across.

"Thank you, Kaawi. Sorry I don't have the other half of the energy exchange, but the police . . . say, this is just an unofficial question, but would anybody want to kill anybody over saucer messages?"

"Why would they? It's all made up."

"And you don't know anything about documents sent to Mr. Wispell?"

"'Fraid not."

I put the check in my wallet and checked my watch.

"Lunch break." She looked at a program. "At one o'clock Bill Cooper talks about working with the aliens. Seems we've got a couple of extra-terrestrials in Los Alamos trying to help us win the Cold War."

"What's on the home screen?"

"Here? It's Mrs. Alice Cooper, who was whisked off in a space-ship and had her gonads inspected. She has pictures. Two o'clock if the saucers don't land."

"It would be hell on commuter traffic if they did. I'll check back."

"Not to be missed," said Kaawi.

A noisy crowd of about sixty people exited the ballroom, glad to be free of Alien Avatars and pressing forward for a sunny lunchtime stroll down Hollywood Boulevard.

There wasn't much to look at in Hollywood in the Fifties. A scattering of movie palaces, exotic ones like the Chinese or the Egyptian, or imperial, like the Warners, had arisen in the Twenties and Thirties, along with a few tallish bank buildings and a department store. Interurban streetcars on the Boulevard were being crowded out by heavy auto traffic, shopping was mostly of the shoe-store-hat-shop-tobacconists-optometrists sort and the celebrated corner of the Boulevard and Vine Street milled with out-of-towners looking up and down, wondering what they were missing.

Lunch food — burgers-and-fries, BLT's, noodle soup — could be had there at the Rexall Drug counter, after taking a touristy glance down Vine to the still-glamorous Brown Derby. On the opposite corner, an eatery called Melody Lane offered plush booths, a curvy bar and lots of yummy menu items. Both joints were crowded with saucer-seekers, weary shoppers and visitors from Kokomo, hoping to run into Clark Gable.

I stuck around the Hotel to gawk at the exhibits. There were a number of mysteries available for investigation around the convention. The Shaver Mystery, proposing a honeycomb of world-wide caverns built by a Titanic race "which fled a poisoned Earth 12,000 years ago" was discussed in a "deluxe illustrated edition." The Bender Mystery, in which a Bridgeport Connecticut man was visited by "three men in black" who transported him to a saucer base under Antarctica, was discussed in several pulpy paperbacks. Cookbooks (terrestrial food only) were on offer, beside "Lemurian Philosophy," fiberglass aliens with almond eyes, handwriting analyzed by an attractive dark-skinned woman in a snood, discounted telescopes, and my favorite, "One Hundred Proofs That The Earth is Not a Globe." The last was on sale by a gent with really silly facial hair and a khaki outfit with short pants.

"Hiya," he said. "I'm Charlie Vanpool. Ya don't remember me."

"No, sorry. Where do I know you . . . ?

"Assistant sound-effects man on that show right before yours, 'Million Dollar Man.' Mr. Million handed out the bucks to some patsy and they hadda figure out how to spend it. I mainly handled the shoes. Lotsa walkin' on that show."

"I remember. I never liked it, to be honest. You still in radio?"

"Movies. 'Terror from the Sky,' this one's called. I'm a sound-guy. Funny thing is, I got out of the draft because I'm deaf in my left ear, man!"

"You didn't write this book?"

"Not my line a work. I'm more a radio hobbyist. Tune in on the universe late at night."

"Really? You know Travis Wispell?"

"I met him, sure. He's a radio searcher for Mr. Bailey."

"He was murdered on Tuesday, where he lived in my bungalow court."

Vanpool looked up and down the hallway and ventured, sotto voce, "You want to know what I know? I'm not surprised."

"Really! Have the police spoken to you?"

"Shit no! I hardly knew him. We said hello sometimes in the middle of the night."

"But you know something, you said. Who might have wanted to kill him?"

"Who wants to know?"

"I'm a writer, movies. There might be a screen story in it. Science fiction is hot right now, you know that. Maybe you've got the plot."

"Look, there's big rivalry goin' on and it's goin' on right here today. There are a group of people, the de-bunkers, who are denying anybody ever got abducted in a space ship. They say it's hypnosis, self or otherwise. Now, there are some other people that are getting a lot of time on television and radio telling how they were paralyzed and levitated and stimulated and they're sellin' books and getting paid for speakin'."

"Wispell was a de-bunker?"

"I expected he'd be here today and maybe let on what he had."

"You mean proof that these people are fakes?"

"Maybe one or two."

"Motive?"

"Maybe one or two. But look, man, L. A. cops figure everybody here is certified, they won't care about saucer nuts."

"I came to the same conclusion. That's why I dropped in on the Convention. That and the rent check. Wispell sent me his last alien transmission instead. Go on."

"Well, look, you've got the Coopers. Bill Cooper just finished talkin' about how blond, blue eyed extra-terrestrials mated with apes to come up with humans, and Alice Cooper is going to show pictures of her abductions after lunch. They're an industry."

"Not a cult?"

"Not yet. Then there's this weird Anjello who wrote he met the Saucer Men and ran into Venusians on the street. Who hates him is Reverend Roscoe Curley who says Venusians have green skin so it's tough for them to mingle and besides they're fourteen feet tall and nudists. They had a debate at the Spacecraft Convention at Giant Rock a couple a months ago. Pretty hot!"

"Where do you fit in, Charlie?"

"My brother-in-law." He pointed at the book, "One Hundred Proofs" etcetera. "A flat-Earth guy. Nice but fixated, you know? Besides, I dig life on other worlds. I'm cool to listen in and get a subscription to *Saucer's Speak*. Most of my radio time is 3-D chess with two old guys in Europe. Today's my day off. What the hell?"

"Got it. I'll take a copy."

"Two bucks. Thanks. First I've sold. *Caviat emptor*, man. As they say."

I stood outside the sadly shabby hotel and watched the shiny streetcars go by on Hollywood Boulevard. The interurban Red Cars were doomed by the new freeways, just as radio was doomed by television. Progress.

"Gentlemen Prefer Blonds" was playing next door at the Chinese. Tourists took snapshots in the forecourt, among the footprints. It had a new "Panoramic" screen, which rendered Marilyn and Jane Russell the size of Mt. Rushmore seen close up. Gentlemen obviously preferred Busts.

I opened my purchase. According to flat-Earth guy, the planet was actually a gigantic disk with the Arctic Circle in the middle and a gigantic wall of gigantic ice all the way around. One of the reasons was that the Bible said so, somewhere. There was some contorted astral geometry and a few hand-drawn depictions of the sun going around in circles and an anti-moon which caused an eclipse.

I went around in a few circles myself. According to Vanpool, Mr. Wispell's vanished vodka carton could have held proof of — what? Conspiracy among the crazies? Could he have been blackmailing the Coopers or the Reverend Roscoe? Did he have proof that Alice never went to Venus?

Blackmail. That was grounds for murder, at least according to the movies. Hitchcock liked it. Hell, it was good enough for "The Big Sleep."

Mrs. Alice Cooper wore a nametag on her low-key dress, sported a Toni home-permanent and a shiny necklace. She earnestly wanted to unburden herself of her experience so that You would be Prepared in case it Happened to You.

"I woke up paralyzed," she said, showing a slide of her blank face. Bill Cooper was manning the slide machine and there were about thirty Seekers intently following the story.

"I had this feeling of everything being switched off and that I was levitating and floating. It was like an out-of-body experience, but it wasn't. I never saw myself floating along like that. I was just beamed up, on a beam of electricity and I was inside the saucer. I was sure it was a saucer, from the way it hummed and there were aliens. They had those eyes and they were inside my head."

Mrs. Cooper paused and had a gulp of water. The slide changed to a picture of a fuzzy shape (alien) in front of a bright light (UFO).

"I can see we're all grown-ups here and that's why I can tell you that I woke up in that saucer stark naked!"

Audible gasps and a general shaking of heads from the ladies and gentlemen of the audience.

"And this is what I'm trying to tell you is, the aliens are experimenting on us. They are learning all they can and then what? Invasion? No, it's more frightening than that. They want to breed us and breed with us."

More gasps. An elderly couple got up and left.

"They go right to the sexual parts of the body, men or women, and they take samples and they stimulate the nerves, if you understand what I mean."

Mrs. Cooper looked upward and pursed her lips at the memory of stimulation. Her husband shook his head sadly. Speculation on the extent of stimulation ran through the audience, especially those members who had been keeping up with Dr. Kinsey. The ones who anticipated a slide of the nude Mrs. Cooper would be disappointed.

"They showed me hybrids. Little babies that they make in, I don't know what, petri dishes or test-tubes. There could be hundreds of them, made right out of the bodies of human beings."

The slide changed to a very tricky-looking alien.

"Thank you." There was applause. "My husband and I can answer questions from those of you who want us to sign copies of our books. Thank you and beware."

More applause and a general movement to the book table where the Coopers settled themselves.

"Don't the Grays live in caves?" asked the first in line as she offered the couple a copy of "Flying Saucers Want Us!"

"I'm not sure these were Grays. They told me they had a base on the Moon. There are lots and lots of Aliens here, you know." Alice and Bill signed the book and the line moved on. "Did they smell bad?" asked the next buyer. The whole ufo-ing thing smelled bad to me.

Outside, late afternoon traffic was moving east as the Sun was moving west. No saucer had landed on Hollywood Boulevard while the Coopers were performing. I could sense the disappointment as the Conventioneers broke for supper. They'd be back before the Mystery Ship Hoedown at eight-thirty. Me, I had a date.

I'd gotten tickets for one of the "picnic boxes" at the Bowl, in front of the luminous arches of the shell, and picked up an order of Caesar salad, spaghetti and meatballs. Kat loved meatballs, lamb chops and strawberry pie and I'd tried to master the menu the one dinner I'd made for her. The chops were good and she put her hand on mine and said, "Thank you." I just sat at the table, mentally gaping, tumbling into love.

The concert started at 8:30. Nobody very famous, just hummable, singable, danceable Cole Porter tunes about, yes, love, ending around eleven with "So In Love" and "Night and Day." Whew!

Kat ate, hummed and sang along. After intermission she sort of held my hand during "Don't Fence Me In" and then put hers back in her lap for "Just One Of Those Things." We both Fred and Gingered a bit, exiting the Bowl, and laughed.

I parked in the alley, locked the garage door and we walked past the bungalows to the street. Again, TV-glow showed in the Selz girl's window. She rarely visited, let alone stayed for a couple of nights. The Bobs and the Co-eds were silent. Kat said, "That was the best birthday, George. You're the top. Goodnight," and unlocked her door, smiled heart-breakingly, and went inside.

I sighed. Sighed again in front of my door looking across the Court. Sighed a last sigh as I opened the screen door. Jumped a foot when I saw my bungalow door was half-open.

"Hello?"

The lights went on when I clicked the switch. No one there. Of course, there had been "no one there" when I entered Wispell's living room either. I poked my arm into the bedroom and turned on the overhead fixture. No one there.

What was different? Something was different. My various projects, lined up on the desk, came up one shy. The blue pages, my screenplay notes and dialogue for "It Came From Under the Bed," were gone.

I locked the front door again and checked the back. Still locked. I looked under the bed. No bottomless pit direct to creatures with slavering lips and pointy teeth. Dust balls and my old schoolboy suitcase.

It seemed safe to call it a night. Of course, I had couple of carbons of the screenplay filed away, so the stolen original was only good for a few penciled-in corrections. The question remained, who knew about it? Also, who cared? It was B-movie stuff. Unless, of course, I had inadvertently discovered some saucerian secret. Maybe they — whoever they were — did come from under the bed and got out the same way. Funny business at the Rose-Bud. Up to me to figure it out, since I owned the joint.

Chapter 5

Southland GI's Freed by Reds
Only One Week of POW Exchange Remains
2278 of 3313 Prisoners Released
*144 More Americans Scheduled
for Freedom*

It was a couple of days drive to Santa Fe. Once across Arizona, an in-between state slashed by the Colorado River and Grand Canyon, the territory changed. Time shrank into the past, into pueblos unchanged for centuries, into invisible lines of power stretched across the landscape, connecting sacred sites with mountain peaks and the stars.

Driving, I'd been imagining a scene at KTLA between Kat and her boss Johnny Bennett. She would say: "George Tirebiter! George Leroy Tirebiter! His name will be on everybody's lips again, Johnny. It's true he hasn't had a hit for a few years, but, ah — he's an expert on Mark Twain." And he would say, "I donno, Kat. Maybe we could introduce him on 'Swallow Your Pride.' It's only a hundred-dollar jackpot, but, if the viewers like him . . ." And she would say, "They'll love him!"

I loved her for saying that, even in my imagination.

"George can act like a real person, Johnny."

"No, no. I want to go with housewives, military men, maybe a steelworker or a college professor. Look, Kat — what about a guest spot for George on 'People Are Ignorant?' Linkletter can drop him in Jello for the big laugh at the end of the show."

"How about George for M.C. on 'The Big Bonanza'?"

"I've got either Jack Paar or Hal March sewed up. I could test him though for that summer replacement, 'What's My Name?' All he's got to do is wear a blindfold and look baffled."

"He'd love it."

And this is where my road-fantasy took off.

"What's your interest in Tirebiter anyway, Kat?"

"He's my landlord. The last landlord I had moved houses for a living. One day I came home to Glendale and my apartment building was twenty miles away, in Gardena. Besides, George is . . . well, I like him, Johnny."

That thought took me the rest of the way to Santa Fe.

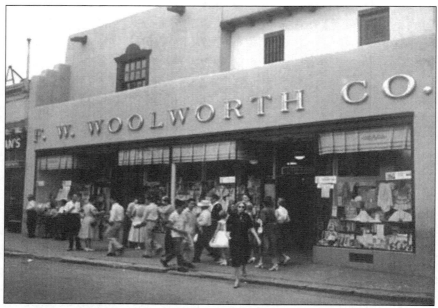

The place to get a fresh Frito Pie in colorful Santa Fe

Santa Fe's Plaza gathered a lot of history around it, including the ancient Palace of the Governors, an indispensible Woolworth's, and the La Fonda Hotel, which occupied all of the eastern side. I'd read about it first, in "Ride the Pink Horse" by Dorothy B. Hughes. She too had been there at Fiesta time. "Cool, dark and rich, more like a Spanish hacienda," she wrote, putting Chicago cops and robbers into Cowboy Country.

I checked in and went into the dining room for *huevos rancheros* and as luck would have it ran into the hard-boiled paperback writer, Mickey Speedway. I'd known him since Chicago when I was a kid. He wrote for the *Trib* and did a feature on me when I was playing Young Tom Edison at the World's Fair. He was young then too. Now a famous writer, his famous writer's hacienda was a few miles out of town.

"What is it now, Mick? Three best-sellers, two movie sales, book-a-year contract? Not bad."

"Sure, yeah. Gettin' up to around a million copies all told, George. Only two bits a copy, but jeeze, with those great cover pitchers, the ante adds up. Men buy the blonds in the tight red dresses, women buy the gun-totin' dicks in tight fedora hats. These people, tourists in the hotel? They buy 'em at the cigar stand and they read 'em. They have a drink, lie awake in their ten-dollar beds and they read 'em. Someday, when even your two-bit hotels got a TV in the room, maybe they won't read Mickey Speedway then — but now? I bet there's a copy of 'My Quick, Hot Gun' in the waitress's purse back in her locker right now."

"So the Windy City's loss is . . . "

"Adobe's gain, George. I'm livin' way down on the Ol' Pecos Trail where nobody bothers the rich gringo novelist in his mystery rancho. *Confidential* sent a photog' out to shoot me in the buff or somethin', but there ain't no numbers on nothin' out here, George. You can't ever find these haciendas — you get 'took' there and forget the way back!"

I'd forgot a helpful fact about local food and I suddenly thought I might never use my taste-buds again.

"Which is ha-hotter, haaa . . . haaa . . . red or haaa. . . green?"

"You want hot, I'll give ya hot. Don't turn around, but Mickey Spritzer just walked across the lobby inta the barbershop."

"L.A.'s favorite mobster?" I fanned my burning lips. "I thought he never left the shoe store."

"Only to see what the boys in the squad-room will have."

"In small bills."

"I hear he gets a cut on every patent leather brogan the city coppers use. And they gotta use plenty."

"And a cut of every racket on the Strip."

"Jeeze, if we don't look out this little burg is gonna enter the 20th century. Gangsters yet! I may havta move to Alaska — Cuba, maybe."

"You want gangsters . . ."

"Been ta Vegas lately?" we said in unison.

Hearty laughter. Gangsters, murderers, headlines, the movies were full of them, newsstands loaded with them, even the romantic, colorful, bustling dining room seemed scented with death for a moment.

"So, George! It's great ta see yer smilin' beezer, but what brings ya? What's the play?"

"Top secret stuff, Mick. It could be just another show-biz gimmick or it could make the movies better than ever. Big test out in Pecos. I'm here for Pingo."

"Bingo you can play at the pueblos."

"Howard Pingo — owns Paranoid Pictures along with Pan-Pacific Airlines. Some buildings around town."

"He owns you too?"

"I meet him once every couple of weeks in the back of a donut delivery van in Culver City and we drive up the PCH to Santa Barbara and back. He's got a few more scars from the last crackup in his rocket car. Doesn't like people to see 'em. He likes to talk, I don't mind listening, sometimes I do a little research for him."

"Hollywood is for addicts, George. Get out while you have a chance." Mick got up, picked up the check, gestured I should let him and said, "Hey, there's a pre-Fiesta dance at the Line Camp tonight, Tex-Mex band, lotsa fun. Friend I'd like ya ta meet! Have a happy count-down! Don't forget ta wear yer dark glasses!"

The test was in a facility off in the piñon hills, buried back in a heavily-guarded Federal arroyo. I had a map and it was a nice morning drive. The local radio station played Perry Como and Patti Page, Eddie Fisher and Tony Bennett.

After a couple of days on the road, musing on what I was calling the Mystery of My Bungalow Court, I had a short list of clues that I'd follow up on when I got back home on Friday.

The idea of Mr. Wispell being a blackmailer seemed remote, but maybe he'd found a way out of a life of false teeth. The disappearing of the vodka box and its lightweight contents wasn't done by an Alien, either. Somebody Earthly had got in Wispell's place and probably the same person or persons had purloined my script pages as well. But why did poor Mr. W get the electrified chair? Where were the Space Music records supposedly delivered to his door? And what did the Munchkin woman, Kaawi, know that she hadn't told me?

⇒✦⇐

I can tell the next part of this story best if I use some of my old radio-writing technique. It works for movies too, easy. It's just — fade out-fade in — bring in the right music underscore, cue the sound-effects — take us to another reality.

In this case, fade out Tony Bennett singing "Rags to Riches" in my car. Fade up the clipping of scissors, the hum of a shaver, the slap-slap of a shoeshine rag. Close-up on Mickey Spritzer, B-movie mobster from nowheresville Cleveland. He's getting spritzed up in the La Fonda Hotel's *barbaría*. The spritzing won't help a man whose nose looks like one of his custom-made ostrich-leather shoes. Mickey's on the phone, long-distance.

"Tirebiter, yeah. He's Pingo's stooge. Pingo thinks he's gonna make a deal on this Secret Weapon without cuttin' Mickey Spritzer in, he's got another think comin'. . . . Well, sure, I'm cuttin' you fellas in . . . No problem! Does Spritzer skim on the family back home? That's why I'm in this stinkin' desert, keepin' an eye on Tirebiter . . . Yeah, well, trust me . . . Yeah? Well, we'll talk about it in Vegas . . . I'll bring Tirebiter with me . . . OK . . . so long . . . give my love to Lake Erie . . ."

He hangs up the phone and gives the shoeshine lad the eye. "Say, uh, canya use light blue on the ostrich? Great." He looks over at the Indian woman waiting to give a manicure and says, sotto, to the lad, "Tell Sweet Georgia Brown over there I need a nail buff, OK? Know what I mean?"

Fade out on the gangster, cross fade to the pulp writer. Pop classical in the background, a Haydn Quartet on the phonograph in an art gallery half-way up Canyon Road. Mickey Speedway is drinking a Schlitz.

"I just had breakfast with him."

The Countess Eldorado, formerly Madge Flotow from Ironytown, Pennsylvania, has a fragile glass of white wine.

"Tell me his name again?"

"George Tirebiter. He might be really good for a sale. Jeezus, Madge, the town's fulla celebrities. Mickey Spritzer, the Mob's man in Los Ang-lis, he's stayin' at the Old Viejo. There's a platoon of Army brass stayin' there too — got a big test out in Pecos today. Top secret shit. George is out there."

"I'd like to meet him. I used to listen to that radio program of his — 'Hollywood Madhouse?' — when I lived in New York, before the War. Before Hugo. Fifteen years ago."

"More like fifty years ago. Radio's dead, Countess. The cigar company that sponsored 'Max Morgan' pulled out on accounta the blacklist. World's gonna pass him by. Doesn't have a TV set, he said, but he's workin' for Howard Pingo and jobbin' at Metro and Columbia and writin' a novel, so . . ."

"So he's Top Secret. Be a darling, Mickey, bring him up to my place tonight from the Line Camp. Maybe I can sell him a desert landscape, or some pueblo pottery."

"I don't think he's a pot kinda guy."

"I can arrange a deal on a Georgia O'Keefe. Something sexy. We can talk secrets. It's worth a martini or two."

"He said he might be writing a Western, maybe you could off-load some of that cowboy junk."

"Perfect! I have 'Shy Dogies,' 'Rodeo Hi-Jinks' and "The Lonely Buffalo' in the back gallery."

"You sell him the store, I get ten percent, like with Heston."

"What about the gangster?"

"He's more the lizard-boot and concho-nugget belt-buckle type. Squat, you know? You sell him that Navajo monster, he'll look like Humpty Dumpty!"

"I'll put something in the window he won't be able to resist. Something murderously overwrought. And Tirebiter, bring him back after a few tequilas for a nightcap. Perhaps he is the answer to a maiden's prayer."

While, unknown to me, these plans were being laid exactly where I was going to intersect with them, I navigated a narrow canyon road toward where my map said I would find the Test Site Area. I suspected it was the low, circular building a few hundred yards beyond the traditional military fences, HALT signs and armed MPs. One of them directed me where to park and another admitted me inside the structure, where I found myself in a sort of ante-room with a hi-fi speaker and a count-down clock. "F-X minus 40" it read.

The O-Man, round as his name and rank, hustled in as fast as he could waddle.

"Hiya, Tirebiter! You're right, I'm the O-Man. Inside Manager at the Bureau of Deals, Military-Industrial Section. Here's some popcorn and a Coke."

"You know," I said, my hands now full, "I can never figure out how to eat the popcorn with a Coke in the other hand."

"Logistics," said the O-Man. "Not my department."

"And your department is . . .?"

"Bureau of Deals. It's where it all happens. OK, listen up. The Army's gonna want to stockpile these, let's call 'em S-Bombs, and keep the technology a secret. What we do is, we leak the info to the technocrats who can use this stuff to keep our country great. What'd we do if the Commies ever got there first? They'd use Tchai-cowsky to take over the Free World!"

"'Swan Lake' is dangerously popular already."

"You ain't heard nothin' yet! If this works, we're gonna wire Radio City for sound."

"It is wired for sound."

"We're gonna SoNorize it!"

What Mr. Pingo wants, Mr. Pingo ends up with. Whatever this thing was, the deal depended on my ears, which the O-Man provided with plugs. Heavy plastic dark glasses were on offer "because there's some chance you could get a flash-burn when they amp it up."

The clock ticked on to blastoff. Meanwhile, crossfade to Canyon Drive, where a plot was unfurling. The bait was in the gallery window when Mickey Spritzer strolled by.

Fade in Haydn. Same unobtrusive Quartet. A doorbell jangles as a door opens.

"Anybody?" says the short fat gangster.

The Countess appears above, at the top of the stairs to the gallery's second floor.

"Of course, darling. Please look around." She preens as she descends the staircase. "If you see something beautiful, just ask."

"Yeah, well, yer not bad, beautiful." Spritzer closes the door. "But it's that belt-buckle in the window — with the nuggets? That thing fit on an ordinary belt?"

"No indeed, nor on an ordinary man. It's a Pueblo Chief's buckle, you know.

"Yeah, well, sure, yeah. I'm whatcha might call a Chief. That's the guy all the braves work for, right?"

"In a manner of speaking. A Chief's belt would be made from the skin of a beautiful but poisonous lizard. Perhaps boots also . . ."

"Mine're ostrich. The designs here, see? On the side? I gotta diamond, club, spade, whatever that other one is, see? They're put on with crocodile. My own design. Got some wet-backs do this stuff for me. I'm in the shoe business, come to Encino, look me up in the book — Spritzer's For Gents."

"Welcome to Santa Fe, Mr. Spritzer. I am the Countess of Eldorado."

"Wow! A real Countess?"

"My late husband, Count Hugo, grew up in a palace before the War. Let me show you the Chief's buckle."

"Yeah, OK, now yer talkin'!"

At fifteen minutes before blast-off, the anteroom had about a dozen people, most of them in uniform, all with eye-shades and ear-muffs. Suddenly, the doors opened, like a theater's, and we walked in and occupied a circle of seats facing a dark blue theatrical curtain. The O-Man introduced me to a thin man in a loose-fitting suit.

"Tirebiter! Like ya ta meet Hoppy Hoppenhower. He'll kinda give ya a ringside blow-by-blow."

"Dr. Hoppenhower, sir, what a pleasure . . ."

"Call me Hoppy, Tirebiter. Glad to meet you. I seldom have time to go to the movies, but the President showed one of your films at the White House when I was a guest in '43. 'Get our minds off the damn wo-ah,' he said."

"Dog Fights Over Broadway."

"That's the one. Mickey Rooney. FDR loved Mickey, you know. Loved to watch him, you know, do him, with the cigarette holder.

'My-ah friends' . . ." Hoppy imitated Mickey Rooney imitating George M. Cohan imitating the President.

"This thing we're about to witness — the S-Bomb? It's yours? I mean, you invented it?"

"Look, I've been told you're Mr. Pingo's special representative. Just between you and me . . ." He lowered his voice and looked away from the gaggle of Generals a few chairs away. "I hope you'll be able to figure a way to get this thing out of the hands of the Generals, away from the military entirely, and give it to the people. For a profit, naturally."

"I thought this was finally the ultimate secret weapon."

"A weapon that can only be used against *people*, sir. I never wanted this. My interest in sonic reinforcement was strictly theoretical. A question of research. I always liked sound — sound and arithmetic. If I showed you a diagram for that thing out there, you wouldn't have the faintest idea what it was. Ninety percent arithmetic and ten percent Cee-o-Two." He smiled, then frowned. "General Bully — that's him there, three stars — he found out we were working on this thing and convinced us that without it we'd lose the Cold War."

"Think so?"

"It was the urge to find out if arithmetic could be made to have a material form — to walk like a man, if you see what I mean. I regret to say it was too great a temptation for us."

"Well, I'm only here to listen."

"It's the end of this world."

A warning horn ah-ooga'd and the group stopped talking for a second. The blue curtain didn't move.

In Los Angeles, I knew the rehearsal for "Hot Date!" was underway. Mrs. Music was pre-interviewing the boys from Thousand Oaks and the girls from Cal Poly. She was pitching me to KTLA, if not because she liked me a lot, then because, well, she thought "people" would like me on the small screen.

I thought about making one of those TV entrances — the music, the applause, the teleprompter — "Welcome to the Super Jackpot Game! The only rule? Don't lose! I'm George Tirebiter! Hello to our first contestant, come on out, Mrs. Eleanor Presky!" Not a lot of work to it, really.

Another ah-ooga! The Generals sat down and faced the curtain. Behind it was what?

"What's behind the curtain?" I asked Hoppy.

"You'll see a wall of black cones, that's about all. But back of that is a new way of thinking. Not an atom in the Universe will be the same after this!" He laughed and wiped his face with a large white handkerchief. "Sorry. Hyperbole."

The lights in the room went down. Ahhh-ooogahhh! Three-star General Arnold Bully got up from his colleagues and found a microphone, which he tapped, to see if it was working. It wasn't. He tapped again and was rewarded with piercing feedback. Hoppy held his head in his hands. "Bad start," he muttered. "Bad start."

General Bully unfolded a page of notes and consulted them, looking for his name. He found it and said, "This is General Arnold Bully, Commanding Officer of Project F-X, speaking. All personnel should now take your assigned places. Visitors and observers outside this room must stay back of the double-paned windows in order to minimize risk of sound-absorption." He glared out at the one-way glazing over our heads. "Remember, if your damn ears fall off, the United States Army assumes no risk in pursuit and exercise of National Defense!"

A murmur ran across the room. Bully squinted out at his audience. "Now, you all know what I think. We need this weapon. The enemy is prepared to send every last man, woman and child into battle against our Fundamental Way of Life. Science has given us a way to split the eardrum and extract the damn Music of the Spears!" He examined his notes. "Ah — Spheres — or Spears, either way, I don't care if you don't like it, just remember, if it works, use it!"

A murmur of agreement and light hand-claps. The room darkened, the curtain pulled back and pale floods lit the Wall of Sound. I stuck my earplugs in and closed my eyes.

A CRACKK! on the naked skin of a snare breaks the silence into an arresting echo of the Big Bang itself. A shockwave from the powerful strike bursts out and knocks us listeners back into our seats, hard. A worried, almost skeptical, silence follows.

SSSSSSHHHHH! SSSSSSHHHHH! Steady brushing, like clusters of comets in 3-D Surround. BOOM BA-DOH BA-DOO pelts the walls on either side of us with clusters of alien harmonies. Overhead and underfoot, tintinnabulating ALANG ALANG ALANG meets a dreamy SSSSHHHHBOOOM.

Only the beginning. Motorcycles ride into the hall, surround us with wild rebellion and vanish, leaving nothing but a hound dog, crying like a fat, red, burnished high-class electric guitar. Piercing red guitar jets twang, bend and go crazy, come toward us and begin to rattle the walls.

The saxophonic cries of the hound that can't catch a scared rabbit shake the room and finally roll away, skid violently at the end, disperse into atoms and explode into flames and screams.

The whole show lasts about three minutes and twenty seconds. Ain't that a shame?

Hoppy Hoppenhower looks at me, bends over and shouts in my ear. "We call that one the Big Mama! Next one's the Little Richard!"

The, let's call it, B-side of the Demo, is a neutron burst of disco-ball flash and something very much like sex after Midnight. Another three minutes of ultra-high-frequency violence. The sound fades away.

Hoppy covers his mouth and says, sotto, "I told you — it's the end of the world. Give this creation fifteen years after it's released into the atmosphere. 1968 will finally bring Peace and Love. Or give it a chance, at least. Hand all this over-amplification to the military and it'll be directed across the borders, its horrific use threatened. Annihilation! Tell Mr. Pingo if he brings it to the people, they'll carry the power along with them, they'll be plugged in to the Vibrations, they'll be free!"

"What do I tell Mr. Pingo it is?"

"We're paying a radio disc-jockey in Cleveland to call it 'rock-and-roll.'"

Howard Pingo stops the donut truck on a corner in Reseda, looks around, pulls down his fedora, gets out, moves smoothly into a phonebooth, drops a dime, dials. The phone rings in Culver City, gets picked up . . .

"Shifty? Pingo. I'm callin' from a pay phone. I've been drivin' around the Valley for a couple a hours, thinkin', you know, and I want you to get back to that guy in D.C. . . . Not that guy, the other one, he's a Senator . . . Yeah, well, look, tell him I'll back Nixon in '60 if that's all he has . . .

"Democrats have got spit in the pipeline after egg-head Stevenson . . . Humphrey's a puff-ball . . . Jug-ear Johnson? Voters find out he bought all those elections in Texas, he hasn't got a chance . . . Shit, man, he's Catholic! You want the Pope in the White House? Look, Shifty — here's what I've been thinkin' — we get ourselves a Charlie McSnerd, you know what I mean? Feed him his lines startin' next year, work him upward through the system and fifteen-twenty years down the line, we've got a do-it-ourselves President! . . . Right! I could get half-a-dozen people from Palm Springs to breed him and back him like a Derby contender. . . .

"Sure, could be a star. Not a major star, though. More a Second Feature type, good voice, respectable, reads TV cue cards . . . Right, the Perfect Host . . . Sure, I've got some names. You come up with some and we'll parlay . . . Oh, Wendell Corey maybe, Ronnie Reagan, George Tirebiter. We can do it, Shifty. We'll talk. So long, yeah . . ."

Mr. Pingo looks around, tugs at his hat brim, gets back in the truck, pulls a U-turn and goes home to his office where he expects Kim Novak will be waiting.

Pre-Fiesta parties had La Fonda lit up, the late afternoon was warm, mariachis played in the Plaza. Before I could escape upstairs to my room, Mick Speedway hailed me from a chair next to one of pueblo-style fireplaces.

"George! Hey, Georgie! Viva La Fiesta! Have a *cerveza*, fella! You've got the dazed look of the already smashed! This is Fiesta, buddy, not the Day of the Dead!"

"If you're dead, probably the best thing you can do about it is have a party."

"Good one, George."

"Do you hear churchbells?"

"What churchbells?"

"They keep ringing them."

"Say, Georgie — I bet it was the big test, right?"

"I'm still hearing it. It was like — like a cry from the bottom of Dante's Inferno. As if all the noise in the universe was liberated at the same instant."

"The Ultimate Weapon. Jeeze!"

"That's if they use it, Mick, which would be to terrible to contemplate. After the second test went off, Hoppenhower turned to me and quoted something about a 'million points of light' from the Tibetan Book of the Dead. General Bully quoted Walt Whitman. No one really heard them, though, 'cause our ears were still ringing. The O-Man promised me they knew how to scale it down for home use. He said you'd eventually be able to wear the weapon, take it around with you!"

"I know a nice, quiet place with a phone, George. Come on, I'll introduce you to a friend of mine. Very influential art dealer in town here. Specializes in cowboy stuff — you know, statues. She's related to European royalty. Quite a woman."

"If she wouldn't mind me making a long-distance call."

"No problem. She's got a sweet little place over the gallery — chilis hangin' from the rafters, buffalo skulls, old baskets — adobe as hell — right up the Canyon."

Canyon Drive was a short walk over a bridge across the Santa Fe River, bordered by tall cottonwoods. One of the cottonwood trees looked exactly like a snake dancer as it moved in the breeze. The leaves rattled. I had to get out of town.

Fade up George Feyer at the long-playing piano. "Cheek to Cheek" segues to "Cocktails for Two." That Old Devil Haydn had folded his Quartet and andante-ed away. The Countess and the Gangster are drinking margaritas. It's the Gangster's third.

"So, Countess! Another jolt of this mag-yarita stuff and you can sell me the Indian that makes the belts. I'll fly him back to L.A. and put him to work in the back of the store. Shit, I'll put him to work in the window! What a draw! Searchlights!"

"I think that the old man who made your belt would not want to go to the City, Mr. Selzer."

"It's Spritzer, honey. Spritzer. Everybody knows me."

"Of course. Perhaps you would want to take the margarita back to Hollywood instead?"

"Ha! I ain't run rum in nearly thirty years, Countess. Yeah, I'll have another splash."

"It's tequila, not rum. A cultured taste, isn't it?"

"Sure. Say, what's a dame with cultured taste like you doin' in the art racket?"

"Making a very good living, Mr. Spritzer. And I also meet many interesting personalities, like yourself."

"Yeah? Well, say, what about you and me having some steak or somethin'? We go back to the hotel where there's somebody I'm supposed to catch up with, you know, keep an eye on. I'll catch up, we'll nuzzle into some dinner, then . . ."

The doorbell rings, the Countess gets up and goes to answer it. The door opens with that jingle bell.

"Mickey! What a surprise!"

Mick Speedway strode up the stairs to the door of the faux-adobe gallery and rang the bell. I followed.

"You'll love the Countess," he said

The door opened with a jingle bell and the Countess smiled at Mick with some relief. "Mickey! What a surprise!"

"Hey, Countess, this is George Tirebiter, that movie writer I told you about?"

"How do you do?" Her hand was chilly and damp. I could see it was from the margarita glass on the end table. Across from her chair hulked Mickey Spritzer, wearing a meteor-sized turquoise buckle on a tooled belt that split him in half as he rose.

"Please come in both of you. This is Mr. Spritzer."

"I heard yer name, Tirebiter."

"Yes, I've heard yours too." I made a dog-smile. "All good things!"

"This is the crime novelist, Mickey Speedway."

"Swell, yeah, hi."

"Yeah, good ta meetcha, Mickey. You're the suede shoe man, right? Say, if we had the Mouse here we'd have a quorum, right?"

"Sure, yeah. I don't get it."

"Say! That's a classy belt-buckle you've got there. Giant chunka turquoise. Musta cost a bucket." He winked at the Countess.

The Gangster was nervous. Obviously, he would have preferred to meet me alone.

"Listen, Countess, maybe I should get goin'." He eyed me. "I got some unfinished business I gotta take care of tonight."

"Please! Gentlemen! It's not often that a woman has three such famous, attractive men at her disposal at at once. It gives me a strange and wonderful feeling of danger. Tonight, I think there is a scent in the air of things that are slightly over-ripe. Make yourself at home, Mr. Selzer."

Spritzer sat reluctantly down.

"Can I pour you a margarita, Mr. Tirebiter?"

"Thank you, sure, but — a what? Here's the thing, I really have to make a phone call if you don't mind, and after that I suppose a drink might clear my head."

"Go down the inside stairs to my gallery. You will find yourself in a room filled with the most beautiful, sexy bronze cowboys. The telephone is there, it's private. You are my guest."

"Perfect. Excuse me, Countess, gentlemen." The stairway was across the room. I smiled back, ever cheerful, at the Mickeys, nodded enigmatically, and walked purposefully away and down. I thought there might be a back door I could let myself out of after I made a quick call to Mr. Pingo's answering service, then I'd send a telegram when I got to Gallup.

I clicked on the Gallery lights and was greeted by a last roundup of bronzed cowpokes, wounded buffalo, noble savages and tired cattle.

"Rope that doggie," I said. "Tote that steer! Very moody, gentlemen. And livestock." I checked the price tag on the wounded buffalo. "Very moody, very expensive, very solid."

There was a back door alright, and a niche near it for the phone. It looked like the Countess had imported her telephone from Waltztime in Gay Vienna. I dialed, it rattled back throatily. Shifty answered.

"Hello, Shifty. This is GLT for Mr. P . . . I need to talk with the man. It's Operation F-X. He'll know. Santa Fe, yes, now, but I'm leaving as fast as I can . . . No, the only Indians I've seen are right beside me here and they're not moving . . . Exactly — like they've been made out of bronze. Look, tell Mr. P I'll meet him in the parking lot. Day after tomorrow. And, Shifty, about the demo here? You can tell him this . . ."

That's as far as I got before an Indian Chief kicked me in the head. In radio, there'd be a big, fat metallic thung-g-g-g, then the antique phone would clatter down ring-a-ding and a weighty body bag would drop to the floor with a thud-badomp.

Mickey Spritzer picked up the phone and said, "Shifty? You can tell Pingo he should never forget who owns him!" Then he dropped the phone and picked me up by the coat-collar. Humpty Dumpty was stronger than he looked.

"Alley-oop, Georgie. It was gettin' too crowded upstairs after you left — time for Mickey the Spritz to splitzville. Sorry about the little tap — this Indian shit is heavier than it looks. OK, now. Let's you and me go for a little ride . . ."

Sgt. William Cummings of The Homicide Squad in his famous "Mask of Death" pose

CHAPTER 6

BABS ALIBI LURE GIRL
SET FREE BY JUDGE
OCOOPERATED WITH BURBANK DETECTIVE TO
HELP UNDERCOVER COP TRAP MRS. GRAHAM

It was Sinatra's very good year. "From Here to Eternity," lifted him from musicals to melodrama and he was opening at the Copa Room, owned by the same gangsters that owned Mickey Spritzer. The Sands was only a year old then, still a two-hundred-room motel with slots and craps tables, before the ultra-Sixties tower went up on top.

I was in a fairly sleezy suite on the second floor. Spritzer had flown me out of Santa Fe in a "company plane" and a couple of bouncer types had driven me to the Sands in a Lincoln Town Car. I had aspirin for a headache and a room-service breakfast, heavy on the hot sauce. The telephone was strangely out of service. I knew what this was about. My ears.

They were ringing. No, the phone was ringing. It was Shifty, calling on behalf Mr. Pingo.

"He's knows about it, Tirebiter. You're safe. There's a deal goin' on, you know? There's gonna be a couple of lawyers, maybe a guy from William Morris, gonna ask what ya heard and it's OK if you tell 'em. This rock-and-roll shit is the H-Bomb as far as ASCAP is concerned. Jukebox mob is scared. Stay cool."

The entertainment lawyers and the agents came and went. I told them I'd heard a tide, a tornado, a cannonade of sound. It was loud, man, loud. Patti Page, Percy Faith, Eddie Fisher, they're going to get drowned in the blues, I said. Mickey Spritzer and his fellow crooks got to divvy up the clubs, dives and venues. That was enough for a while. Mr. Pingo invested heavily in teen-agers and ticket sales rose for rock-n-roll movies only teens could make sense of. The military knew when they were beat, er — beaten, and turned successfully to less entertaining forms of warfare.

I hopped from Vegas to Burbank late on Wednesday afternoon and took a cab home. The Court was quiet. It appeared no one was home on my side. The porch lights were out at Mrs. Whitmer's and the Perry's. Curiously, I could see the television flickering inside the Selz bungalow. I thought I'd give it a check, since I'd seen it on all the way back to Saturday.

I couldn't hear TV or anything else inside. I knocked. Paused. Knocked again. "Miss Selz?" I said. She could be asleep, I supposed. I knocked again. "Hmmm."

Around the side of the bungalow was the kitchen door and a bedroom window. The porch light was off, the window was dark. The kitchen door was open enough for a thin line of bluish light to fall through.

"OK," I said to myself and pushed the door in. Beyond the kitchen the television lit up the living room. "Hello, there! Miss Selz?"

It was wrestling on TV, from Olympic Auditorium. Gorgeous George, with a blonde mane and a silent hammerlock on some guy with a Rooski beard.

Facing the TV, sitting on a low table, was a Relska Vodka carton, sealed, or rather, unsealed, with brown tape ripped back. Since I was expecting a dead blonde, I jumped a foot when I saw it.

Well, I owned the place, so what was the harm of turning on a few lights? The living room was easy, chandelier went on from a switch by the door. Behind the coffee table was a leather couch, well-used, with a couple of afghans folded on it and over it a painting of Orpheus, strumming his lute to a Peaceful Kingdom of lions and tigers and nudie-cuties, oh boy!

The TV was part of a hi-fi system built into a wall of shelves, loaded with LPs, books, manuscripts, more-or-less tidily sorted. There had been a piano, but the Selz girl sold it and it had been carried out the front door shortly after she inherited the bungalow.

Everything was as I would have expected except for the vodka box. I wasn't going to look into it yet.

The bathroom was scrubbed clean as only an obsessive person likely, according to most women, to be a woman, could make it.

Expecting nothing but fresh linen, I popped the bedroom light on and smiled at the prospect. Smiling back at me from atop the bed was Charlie Vanpool, khaki shorts, silly facial hair and all.

I'd seen the movies. I knew he was dead.

In a half-hour the Rose-Bud was lit up like a Hollywood premiere. The nearest patrol car rolled up first with the siren on, followed by two more precinct cars, an ambulance and Sgt. Cummings, looking none-too-fresh.

"What the hell, Tirebiter? You got the corpse motel here? How's your coffee?"

"Not bad — you get used to it."

"I'll have some. Let's do this inside."

"Swell. Good idea."

The bungalows swarmed with uniforms, flashlights and body-baggers. I could hear Little Joe bawling after a burly cop banged on the Perry's door.

"You know who the stiff is?"

"Sure. I said that when I called in. Charlie Vanpool. I just met him Saturday at a flying saucer convention."

"Did ya. What was he doin' there?"

"Selling a book about how the Earth is flat."

"Boy, you know some nut-bars."

"Here's the thing, Sgt. Cummings. Vanpool knew Wispell. They were both ham operators, listening for voices from outer space."

"Now we're gettin' somewhere. Two nut-bars! This Vanpool didn't live here, right? Not in that apartment?"

"I never saw him before Saturday. Wherever he lived, it wasn't here. Look for a place with a big antenna."

I could hear somebody passing between the back of my bungalow and the untidy hedge. Hearing dogs in the back, Mr. O'Toole had said. Something like this scrambling, snapping noise, I thought.

"So how did nut-bar get inta that apartment, and especially, how did he get dead in that apartment? Any ideas, Tirebiter?"

"Glad you asked. Look, somebody has a master key for all ten bungalows. Last Saturday night I came home from the Bowl and my door was open. Nothing gone but my work on a movie script. It was on my desk, there, right where there isn't a stack of paper."

"Why didn't ya call it in?"

"I thought it was weird enough, but you would have called me a nut-bar."

"Maybe you are. Keep talkin'."

"It was for a science-fiction movie about monsters and aliens called 'It Came From Under The Bed.'"

Cummings shook his head. He muttered through gritted teeth. He got up and sat down. He tilted his hat back.

"Look. You tryin' to spook me? 'Cause I don't spook. Somebody wired up Wispell, somebody knocked over the nut-bar in safari shorts, maybe the same somebody, with the same key, came in here and burgled your movie. My advice is get all your locks changed tomorrow. Awright. Who rents the death apartment?"

"The Selz bungalow, you mean. It's been rented by the same family for years. They live in Palm Springs, this is their L.A. *pied-a-terre.*"

"I'll ignore that. Got a number, address, something?"

"Well, a P.O. Box in Palm Springs is all."

"You give that to the cop who's gonna take yer statement. I'm gonna leave somebody around here the rest a the night. Tell everybody ta go back ta bed. We got the body out, the death bunga-whatever-it-is is sealed up. Fingerprint guy'll be here early. I'll be here later and we'll go over the saucer stuff. OK?"

"I'll look after things until then, Sergeant."

"Right. You do that."

Cummings rose and arched his back. His bones cracked. At the door he turned and said, "Where you been, the last few days?"

"New Mexico."

"Quick trip."

"Business."

"Flying saucers?"

"Weapons."

"You get around, don'tcha, Tirebiter?"

He went out and I followed behind so the screen door wouldn't slam. Habit. Outside, I could see that the lights were out everywhere but next door and across the Court. Kat was home. I thought I'd check to make sure she was alright, and besides, I missed her.

I only had to knock once. Kat had her hand on the knob inside, turned it, and was there suddenly, brightly summery in a yellow frock, smiling at me.

"Oh, boy! I'm so happy you came over, George! I was just going to knock on your door. Come in."

Hers was a sweet apartment, furnished with a bent bamboo couch, chair and coffee table. An over-stuffed armchair, afghan covered, sat comfortably under a good reading light.

"What's going on? I just got back from Mother's when an ambulance rolled up and a cop said Stay Put Inside! Who's dead? He said it was a murder investigation."

"They've gone now. The dead man was somebody I met at the Saucer Convention on Saturday."

"God, George! Sit down, please. I've got some good Scotch for special occasions and nervous collapse. How about over ice?"

Kat, in the little kitchen, cracked a tray open and spilled a few cubes into two glasses. I looked around. Photos of her Mother, her husband Mike, a couple of family groups, a pair of framed *Vogue* magazine covers with Erté drawings.

"Sit in the comfortable chair. Tell me everything."

I took the Scotch, clinked my glass with hers and had a sip. "Very nice. Here's to the future."

Kat had a long sigh over that thought.

"Any news?" I asked.

"You mean about the POWs? No. Mother is more broken-hearted every week. There wasn't much of a chance before, but . . ."

The bent bamboo couch was upholstered in jungle plants. Kat perched nervously on the edge.

"Tell me everything."

"About the murder? He was a guy named Vanpool and he turned up in the Selz bungalow, or his dead body did."

"You found it?"

"I think I was lead to it. He told me he was a ham-radio guy and he knew Wispell. Interesting, though, he told me he thought Wispell had something possibly blackmail-worthy on a vacant-eyed couple who claim to have been abducted by the Aliens."

"Wow." Kat took a gulp of Scotch and settled back against the tropical foliage like a buttery orchid. "How was your weekend in Arizona? Tell me everything."

"It was New Mexico and I can't tell you everything. It's Classified." I tapped my heart. "However, it was a thrilling couple of days involving a gangster, a novelist, a phony Countess and a whole lot of noise. Actually, the novelist and the Countess were trying to palm off some big bronze buffalos on me for even bigger bucks, which I don't have. The gangster banged me with a bison and I woke up in Las Vegas."

"Are you making all this up?"

"It's about the Army's Big Test. I was there for Mr. Pingo, then I had to tell a passle of lawyers and a couple of big-time agents, what I'd heard. Which was something like orchestras of electric guitars and untrained saxophones overloading in an abandoned warehouse."

"Wow! Organized crime, defense secrets, show business, and you, George, tied up in the middle! How will it end?"

"Like these arrangements always do, Kat. Pingo and some others will take the American noise-bomb and make it small enough to sell a billion. That means everything is going to get louder. Much, much louder. Have you ever heard of 'rock and roll'?"

"I don't think so."

"You will. Power comes from the mouths of loudspeakers, Kat. That's what the Marxists say, I believe. I shudder to think what will happen when everybody in the world is plugged in."

"For a writer, you sure have fun." Kat took a last sip and rattled the ice around in her glass. "How did the dead man get here?"

"Somehow, our Rose-Bud seems to be in the mix with these characters. Sgt. Cummings calls 'em nut-bars. And, I'm sorry to have to tell you, the locks are compromised. I'm having new ones put in, but be sure you use the inside latches too."

"Now you're scaring me."

"There's a cop out there tonight, so don't worry. Thanks for the drink. I'm just across the way. Scream if you need me." I got up from Kat's comfortable chair. "Really. Any time."

She looked up at me. "Right. Wait a second. I have to tell you something."

I waited.

"I got you an audition, George."

"My God. You did? What for?"

"'What's My Name?' it's called. It's a silly afternoon guessing game, but you'd be host. It's steady work if they like you, and they will like you."

"When's the audition?"

"Next week. Monday on our set before rehearsal. OK?"

"You're a pal."

We rose and walked to her door. I opened it, pushed open the screen. "Thanks, Kat," I said.

"You're a pal, too, George. Good night." She palmed a little kiss at me, standing in the perfect key light, smiled, and closed the door behind her.

Across the way the porch light of the Gage bungalow was on and there was light seeping around the curtains. Music, too. "Night Train," real heavy on the tenor sax, but not too loud. I wondered. Took a deep breath of the much cooler night air and watched as a car pulled up in front, made a U-turn in the alley and parked across the street.

It was a skinny, sandy-haired guy with a bow-tie. Ken Adair, the camera-jockey from the *Mirror*. He came into the Court and I said, "Evening, Ken. Can I help you out with something?"

"Oh, sure . . . oh! Hi, Mr. Tirbiter! More big doings, huh?"

"You're not going to take pictures tonight?"

"Well, no. Not the murder. I'm gonna come with two reporters in the a.m. Front page shot. Court of Death!"

"Thanks a lot."

"Freedom of the Press."

"So . . .?"

"I'm in the Camera Club."

"And . . .?"

"It's Audrey Gage. She's our model tonight. I think that's her bungalow there — 627 and a half, right?"

"That's right. She knows you're coming?"

"There's four of us for 9:30 to 11:00. Maybe Sid or Marybelle could already be here. It's a regular thing, really. She's a model."

"OK. I thought she worked at the Auto Club."

"Extra income. Comes in handy. Look, I'll be back here on business tomorrow and I don't want to lose my time with Audrey tonight, so . . ."

"Goodnight, Ken. Happy flashbulbs!"

"Right. Poppity-pop!"

He walked over to the bungalow, knocked on the door, which opened with a honkin' blast from the sax. Ken went right in. Audrey stepped a step from the doorway and looked curiously at me. She was wearing black stockings, a black corset and five-inch heels. She smiled, flicked a little riding-crop my way and re-entered with a backward flip of her foot.

Chapter 7

The Lonely, Shadowy Years
Easy Prey for Woo-for-Cash Romeos
Three Deadly Mistakes Every Widow Should Avoid

Early Thursday morning I collected the newspapers that littered the hedge. Nothing but sadness. Poor Rose-Bud. We'd be on Page One in the afternoon, but things were still quiet at 7 a.m. I thought it might be a wise thing to be elsewhere for the day, avoiding all the police traffic. Maybe Mrs. Music, on her day off, would be up for a little investigative drive.

Ooops! My beautiful car was still in Santa Fe, unless it had flown home. And what did I want to investigate anyway?

Albert Bailey of "The Saucers Speak" seemed to be the connection between Wispell and Vanpool. According to the flyer I'd picked up when I got my rent check, New Age Publishing had an address on Glendale Blvd. and also offered Bailey's "Voyage to Serpo" and Mrs. Alice Cooper's "I Was a Venusian Bride," among other testaments to nut-bar-ism.

The first of the Death Squad drove up and parked in the alley. A second followed. It had been dumb of me not to have looked into the Relska box, but I forgot all about it until after the bungalow was sealed off. Nothing else had seemed out of place. The plainclothes guys and I nodded at one another. Audrey Gage appeared in her doorway, wearing a modest little dress and low heels, gave me a girlish wave and tock-tocked down the walk and out. Where was the under-the-counter honey in the black silk corset this morning?

My phone rang. It was Shifty. "Tirebiter! Howz yer head? Ha ha! Listen, check out your garage, know what I mean? Surprise!"

I didn't know what he meant, so I checked. The Mercedes was locked in my garage, hood still a little warm. Under the windshield wiper was a menu for the Oasis Café, in the desert near the Salton

Sea. In Mecca, as a matter of fact. I pulled it out and opened it. Scrawled broadly across the "Sand-rich Fare" side of the menu was, "You're in danger. UFO landing site, Thursday night." On the other "Date Malts & More" side was "Kaawi, the Space Angel." I was in luck. I had a map to Mecca, thanks to the Triple A and this year's model, Audrey Gage. I'd start there. Maybe Kat would enjoy a nice drive into the desert. Especially if I might be in danger. It was time to call my pal the locksmith to work on the doors. There would be cops around all day. As I came back into the Court Kat opened her door.

"Saw you," she said. "Saw you striding around the corner. What's up?"

"I got my car back. Like to take a little ride?"

"Sure. Thanks. Looks like it's going to be crazy around here today."

"Let's go before the Sergeant gets here and traps us into making statements."

"Ready in a minute. Can I bring my coffee?"

"Bring a hat. It's going to be hot."

"Where're we going?"

"It's a Nick and Nora sort of thing. UFO landing site in the desert."

"Of course. UFO landing site. Where's our vicious guard-dog Falla?"

"Nick and Nora's dog is called Asta. Falla was FDR's dog. He hated war. Maybe we should borrow a dog from somebody."

"You don't allow pets."

"Not at the Rose-Bud. Someone in the neighborhood's got a dog that gets out at night and prowls in the bushes."

"Not much help."

"Not so far, but I'm thinking about it. Dog — or something — in the bushes.

"It wasn't a dog that got ahold of your master key and started a killing spree."

"Don't say that."

"I can see the headline."

"There's more. A death threat."

"Whose?"

"Me. Mine, I'm afraid."

"Oh, God, George! I'll meet you in back by the garage in five minutes. Where are we going?"

"Mecca."

Kat raised her eyebrows, nodded and went back inside.

I had a couple of things on my mind. One was New Age Publishers. We could stop by the office before heading into the desert. Another was Eddie Haroot and Bluetone Records. Why would he meet Wispell in a burlesque joint to talk about Music from Outer Space? Which reminded me, the records that apparently were sent to Wispell couldn't have got here, or I would have received them. Stolen en route, perhaps by the Rose-Bud Murderer. "From the Saucers to You" they were called. Maybe they were the same place as "They Came From Under the Bed." And the contents of the Relska box, assuming it was empty when it reappeard.

Will Perry came out of his bungalow, looking spiffy, with a large portfolio in hand.

"I'm making the rounds today, George. Warners, Columbia, Fox. Say, what did you think of the art show at that saucer thing?"

"Oh, gee. Sorry, Will. I totally forgot it was happening. I'm sure there was nothing to compete with 'Io In The Sky-O.'"

"It was crazy. Lotsa really bad stuff — drawings of aliens, drawings by aliens, a whole series of fuzzy color photographs of a saucer landing. Behind a hill, of course! You never see them land, because the scale would be off. Sci-fi fans steal every good idea, you know, and then execute them badly."

"Fans will be fans."

"Best thing was a mock-up of a cabin in an interstellar spaceship. Good carpentry. Looked real."

"Who made it?"

"Ah — funny name. Research Group. Lemurian Research Collective, I think. Hey, see ya. Gotta catch the bus!"

The office of New Age Publishing was an angular one-story structure near the corner of Glendale and Alvarado in the Edendale district.

The same building housed the office of Interplanetary News-Digest Inc., Bailey Ent., and Mixville Pictures. Kat and I had fabricated a cover-story. KTLA was researching for a new program on the "para-normal" called "Beyond!" Would Mr. Bailey or any of the other fine folks here like to be on TV?

There were no fine folks in the three offices used by Mr. Bailey's conglomerate. All were dark, shades pulled down over the glass doors. Mixville Pictures (there was a card, hand-lettered on the door) presented to our knock two men in their late twenties, dressed in Levis and T-shirts. Their eyes went straight to Mrs. Music who said, "Hello. I'm Mrs. Music," then their cheeks went red.

"Hi, guys," I said. "I'm George Tirebiter. Can I ask if you know anything about the other offices here?"

"No, actually this was an empty office and we sort of rented it. I'm Dave, this is Phil."

"We're making a horror movie up Alvarado Street in the old Keystone Studio," said Phil. "'The Keystone Horror'."

"Spooky old soundstage. Ghosts of the Kops chasin' around."

"Chaplin started there," I said.

"Right!" Phil and Dave said together.

"Actually," said Phil, "we have seen a lot of our neighbors. Mr. Bailey is usually around. Grizzled."

Dave added, "Sort of Old Prospector look to him."

"Nobody seems to be around today," said Kat. "Are you the writers of the movie?"

"Oh, yeah!" said Phil. "No sense waiting for somebody in Hollywood to see you got chops. We're writing it, we'll film it up the street, our girl-friends are in it. They *are* it, as a matter of fact."

"The stars, Phil means. Look, I think the whole gang here is off to a meeting someplace. They packed into the old school bus they use and drove off yesterday."

"Didn't say where they were going?"

"Not to us."

"Who's the 'whole gang'?" said Kat.

"Let's see. Mr. Bailey's wife Chloe, she's the editor of the saucer journal, and there's a couple of people who work for the publishing part."

"They publish some weird effin' books, too," added Phil. "Imaginative stuff. They even have a record out. LP."

"You're kidding."

"Nope. 'From Saucers to You.' There musta been a hundred copies around."

"All gone now," said Dave.

"Except mine." Phil grinned.

"You copped one? Crazy!"

"That's great!" I said. "Have you listened to it?"

"No, no record player here. I liked the cover."

"It might be a clue in a murder case," I said.

"Double murder case," offered Kat.

"Wow!"

The LP cover art, printed on cheap cardboard inside a glossy cellophane wrapper, must have been featured in the sci-fi show at the Hollywood Hotel. Two almond-eyed Aliens recline in an extra-terrestrial oasis. One Alien plays a lute-thing, the other drapes her (?) tentacle into a silver pond. High in the dark sky are two Alien moons.

On the back, some helpful information:

"Extra-Ordinary Music! Sounds from Outer Space!
The Saucers Have Landed!
UFOs — Threat or Welcome Visitors?
Listen and Make Up Your Mind!"
Recordings by Travis Wispell.
© New Age Publications 1953.
P.O. Box 566, Mecca, California

Next door to the Oasis Café I had no doubt. The little nowhere town was south of Palm Springs, at the edge of the Salton Sea, a lake left over from an irrigation error that flooded a below-sea-level desert. It wasn't Death Valley, but it was hot and bleached-bone dry. "I thought," said Dave, "that if it was crazy and weird enough we could just use it in 'The Keystone Horror' as background music. But we haven't heard it yet."

"Thanks for the information. I'm sure we'll be able to pick up a copy."

"Good luck on the movie," said Kat.

"There's two other people on the bus, a couple, kinda, I don't know, blank-looking, both have white-blond hair."

"It's a school bus? I bet it's on its way to the Salton Sea to watch
the saucers land!"

"Us, too, George?"

"Us too, Kat."

The Mojave Desert is a vast and empty waste that spreads away
east and north from the coastal mountains of Southern California
as far as the Colorado River and beyond to Las Vegas and Phoenix
and deep into Mexico. The Mojave is interrupted by scabrous hills
and barren ranges, but continues on, rocky and baking, colonized
only where someone has found or brought water.

The Coachella Valley is a finger of the Mojave poking south
toward the Gulf of Mexico between snowy slopes to the west and
crumbling gray ones to the east. In it lies the Salton Sea, an eye-
filling sky-blue lake left over from a breach in the irrigation canal
from the Colorado that feeds the agriculture hard-won from this
desert floor.

The August heat had dropped a few degrees and I put the top
down while it was still morning. We drove out Route 66 and
dipped south to Riverside where we stopped for lunch at the bizarre
old Mission Inn. I'd always thought it was a sort of romantic place.

Kat hadn't said much on the way, stared out at the orange groves mostly.

We had sandwiches in the Inn's Spanish Patio, elaborately tiled, like the La Fonda in Santa Fe, seated at a smallish table, also brightly tiled. I looked at Kat's golden-brown eyes as much as down at my plate. After the lunch was done, I started to say something.

"Don't say anything, George. I can tell you're all full of something to say besides you loved the food. Shhhh. I'm having a great time. As a matter of fact, I'm having an adventure. We're pals. We're Nick and Nora! Let's go beard the saucers in their lair!"

We laughed about the silly programming planned for KTTV, we speculated on Mrs. Whitmer's sex life, and finally we left the main route and turned onto Highway 111, the featureless two-laner that would take us to Palm Springs and then all the way to date shakes and UFOs. It was hot and too bright now and I stopped briefly to put the top up. The desert was alive with silence. The road itself seemed threatened by unhappy spirits, hovering, just out of sight. Cahuilla Indians fastened their beliefs deep into the canyons above the wealthy Village, where the shadows of the mountains cast the shadows of gods back on the sand. The Cahuilla and all the rest were checker-boarded out of their lands when the Southern Pacific rails came through, thanks to the gift of every other square section along its desolate route.

We rolled down the gentrified main drag, lined, since the glamorous Thirties, with specialty shops catering to a certain kind of golfer's wife, genteel nightclubs with big stars close-up, deluxe hotels with brilliant blue pools. Away from Palm Drive, the poverty was a century deep.

I filled the tank at a Richfield station while Kat checked the phone book. Gideon Selz was listed with an address in Araby Canyon. We went south out of town, nipped up a winding road and found the place — flat roof, all glass, gorgeous plants, all under a hot afternoon sun, with high clouds just forming.

"Quite the view," said Kat. "This man lived at the Rose-Bud?"

"A sleep-over place, paid for the year-round. Nice man, student of Stravinsky, he told me. Somebody's at home, obviously." Since the place was literally see-though, we could see a woman sitting, reading.

I knocked respectfully at the glass door that led to the living room. The reader looked up, curiously. It was Abby Selz. Good, I could explain the situation quickly and continue on to Mecca.

She pushed back the door and said, "Yes?"

"Miss Selz? Abby? Your landlord, George Tirebiter? This is Mrs. Music."

"Can I help you?"

"Well. it's only about the bungalow in L.A., nothing serious. We were just passing through . . ."

"I haven't the faintest idea what you're talking about. If you're looking for Bob Hope, he's one canyon over."

"I'm confused. You're Gideon Selz' daughter, right?"

"How do you know my father?"

"His place in L.A. — I rent it to him, or I did, before he passed away."

"What are you talking about? Daddy's in the pool. Look."

Abby waved out the opposite glass wall. In the pool a man who looked like Gideon Selz all right bobbed up and waved back.

"That is almost as big a mystery as the one I'm here to tell you about." I felt tipped off balance. "Could we step out of the heat for a few minutes?"

"Certainly. I'll ask Daddy to come in." She walked out more glass doors and said something to her father. Mr. Selz burst out of the pool, put on a terrycloth robe and scooped a gin-and-tonic off the table.

Kat tugged at my arm. "This is coo-coo, George. What's going on?"

"I just hope this is really Selz and we're not being totally Gaslighted!"

"Especially by people who live in glass houses."

In from the diamond-blue pool came Mr. Selz. It looked like him, but I hadn't seen him since around last Thanksgiving.

"George! What brings you by? Haven't seen you since I was stuck on those 'Gents Prefer Blonds' orchestrations. Hello, Miss."

"Mrs. I'm Kat Music."

"Lovely. A beautiful woman named Music! Very pleased."

"Folks!" I said. "Let's all sit down a second, because I'm confused." I sat down. Everyone else did, making a sociable foursome. "Gideon, you are supposed to be dead."

"Clearly, I'm not. What gave you that idea?"

"She did."

"No, Daddy. I get it now. Abby did it."

"Who are you?" I smelled a rat.

"Gail. We're twin sisters. She told you Daddy was dead?"

"Yep. Came one day in February with the news, moved in for a week, sold the piano and started to pack things up. She hadn't been back for a while, yesterday the TV was on, nobody answered when I knocked. Long story short, there was a dead body in the bedroom and the bungalow's been sealed up by the Murder Squad for investigation."

"She'll do anything," murmured Gail.

"The Baldwin was worth maybe five hundred dollars. Anything else gone?"

"I really don't know. I hardly got a look around before I found the late Charlie Vanpool."

"Who's that?" asked Gail, increasingly annoyed.

"I know Charlie," said Selz. "A sound man on that saucer quickie I played the Theremin for. Only engineer in the studio when I recorded it. He's dead?"

Gail got up, pursed her lips and looked out at the liquid blue of the pool. "What are we going to do about Abby? You didn't re-rent the bungalow, did you, Mr. Tirebiter?"

"No, no. But how do I know which one of you sisters is authorized to be there? How do I know which one of you is you?"

"Abby's nuts. She believes the Earth is flat and the Martians have landed. She's in some cult by Mt. Shasta and never comes home, which is fine with me!"

"She must have had my bungalow key copied," said Selz. "But you say we can't access the place anyway?"

"I'd give it a couple of weeks. Maybe the two of you would come in together, so I can tell who's who. New locks on all the doors. Vanpool's the second dead body at the Rose-Bud in the last two weeks. Mr. Wispell was electrocuted, not by accident. That's two murders. The cops are all over the place. We — Mrs. Music and I — she lives in the front bungalow, opposite mine — anyway, we thought we could follow a lead maybe the detectives would miss or wouldn't care about."

"Listen, Tirebiter, Charlie Vanpool — funny beard, right? Always dressed like he was going to climb Mt. Kilimanjaro?"

"Same guy."

"He sent me a record album recently. Thought I might like it because of my Theremin music, which is spooky and outer-spacey."

"Stop!" I said. "Is it called 'From the Saucers to You'?"

"That's the one."

"Have you heard it?"

Selz snorted. "Saucer Music by Marconi, maybe. All bings and pings and sine-waves. A lotta static."

"It was recorded by Mr. Wispell."

"You don't say? Well, that's a coincidence, isn't it? Do the police have any suspects?"

"Not that I know of. Sgt. Cummings doesn't necessarily confide in me." I got up. The house was quiet, pale white and uncomfortable. "Well, I'm glad to find you alive, Gideon. Nice to meet you, Gail. Kat and I are off to have a date shake in Mecca."

"Nice afternoon for a drive, George. Sorry about Abby." Selz shook his head. "We'll clear it all up."

"She must've needed the money and figured Daddy left something of value she could hock or sell."

They walked us to the door. A wind had whipped up, and the palms were swaying. At four o'clock the sun was working its way toward the peak of Mt. San Jacinto. Down 111 were Indio and Thermal and finally Mecca and the salty Sea. The scrub-covered desert floor alternated with thick stands of date palms, grown down here for fifty years or so.

We'd only just got back to the foot of the canyon when Kat said, "You know, George, I don't believe a word either of them uttered. It was like a scene from a play and they had their dialogue all written out."

"What he said about coincidence. There's no such thing. The record connects everybody, doesn't it? Something about it connects everybody."

Top down again, a bestiary of clouds traveled along with us. "See yonder cloud that's almost the shape of a camel?"

Kat pursed her lips and looked, "No, methinks it is a weasel."

"'Tis very like a whale."

The Southern Pacific tracks paralleled the highway, now bearing the unlikely name Grapefruit Boulevard, and a long freight steamed by, on its way to L.A.

"And, look, there's a flock of bats, or maybe a school of rabbits. It's really beautiful in its way, George. Is there a plan?"

"Somewhere along here is the Oasis Café. We're just tourists stopping in to have date shakes. If Kaawi's there, she'll tell us what's going on."

"You guess."

"I hope. If not, we can check out Mecca and go on down to the North Shore. I bet we find a school bus filled with nut-bars somewhere in the vicinity."

The car was suddenly full of the fluttering sound of a flute and a stony burst of rattle. It arose out of the floor between Kat's feet.

"What's that?"

"Oh, George!" She was staring at the sound. With that, the car choked once and the motor went still. I coasted it into an empty spot that might have been the beginning of a trail into the mountains.

Kat picked up her purse and opened it. The rattle and the flute filled the surrounding sagebrush with echoes. "It's these things! The Talismans!"

She displayed the crystal and the stone that we'd found in Wispell's bungalow. The tall blue crystal was lit from inside and sent out a warm, musical tone. The flat, round stone made a rhythmic, crackling series of taps.

I picked it up out of her purse and held it for a brief moment in the palm of my hand. At my touch, the stone shot away from me and into the sky above the car where it vanished.

"I thought we were in the desert to see flying saucers, George, not flying rocks!"

"I think that rock was on its way home, somewhere out there, up in a canyon where the palm trees grow."

"What happened to the car? You didn't run out of gas?"

"Just died." I turned the key, pumped the pedal. Nothing.

"It's obvious, but I'll say it anyway. It's on its way to getting dark and we're way out of town. This is making me very nervous."

"It's an adventure, remember? We're going to get picked up any minute."

"By a flying saucer?"

"Could be." I got out of the car and lifted the hood.

"George!"

"No, really. There'll be some traffic on this road before the sun goes down. We'll flag it. I'll be Gable and you'll be Colbert." The engine looked normal, all the wires and belts in place, battery connected.

"I was already worried about the Walls of Jericho thing, to be honest," Kat said. "What shall I do about this?"

The crystal was still glowing inside her purse, though the tone had faded away.

"I suppose we can use it to flag down . . ."

"A spaceship?"

"A taxi, maybe? A date rancher? The sheriff? Look, Kat, I didn't think this through. About a motel or anything. I'm really sorry. It's been a swell day so far, hasn't it? Well, so far is just about as far as I thought ahead. Date shake, two straws."

"And a murderer or three. Is that a car?"

Headlights grew brighter behind us. Kat got out and we posed by the side of the road, waving. It was a Ford pickup and it slowed down until it rested beside us. The blonde inside was either Abby or Gail Selz. She looked at us, lifted a middle finger, snorted and, before I could say anything, tore off, on down the highway.

"We're neither of us popular with the Selz girls," I said.

"Understatement."

I slammed the hood down. The engine turned over and caught. "All right!"

"What did you do?"

"I hate to say it, but it's magic. Get in. Let's go."

"The crystal is dark again, George."

Behind us, another pair of headlights was approaching. As it pulled near we could see it was an old yellow school bus, which slowed down and stopped beside us. The door hushed open. The driver was The Old Prospector.

"Hello. You OK?"

"A little car trouble, we're fine now."

"That's good. You don't want to be out on this part of the road in the dark of night. It's a cursed place. Heathen Indians cursed it on their way to Mexico when the U.S. Army came after 'em. Well, so long's you're all right, then. Have a nice evenin'!"

The door hushed closed, the old gears clashed and The Old Prospector guided the bus off toward Mecca.

"What are you waiting for, George? Follow that bus!"

Somewhere between Thermal and Mecca, the still-bright sky over the highway created Tricksters dancing among the black shadows inside the date gardens. Two-story-tall palms swayed, squatty ones like spiky mushrooms rattled. Just before it got to be a scary Disney cartoon, lights spilled from the Oasis Café, set off the road, a parking lot in front.

"Date shakes," I said.

We pulled in and parked along side a couple of trucks, neither one a beat-up Ford, and went in like tourists. Red vinyl stools faced a long counter and colorfully decorated back wall advertising date-flavored food and drink from bread to chocolate. Tables for two lined the opposite wall, looking out at the quickly disappearing twilight. Only one of them was occupied — a teen-age couple holding hands. A big guy in overalls sat at the counter stool nearest the cash register, drinking coffee.

"This is so sweet, George!"

We sat at one of the tables and our waitress, a large Mexican woman in her fifties, toddled over. "You know what you want?"

As I wondered what to say, Kat spoke up. "I'd like the Mecca Burger without the onions. George, you probably want onions, right? And we'll share a date shake. Two straws."

The other waitress mixed up our shake and smiled over at us as the shake-making machine shook. The big guy slid off his stool and tossed some change on the counter.

"See you tomorrow, Walter," the waitress said.

"Yup," he replied. "Don't stay up too late tonight, Effie, hear?"

"No chance," Effie said. "We close at eight."

The burgers came and went, fries too. I discovered where the teen-age romance about "two straws in the shake" comes in — you are really hopelessly eye-to-eye with the other slurper. It's a funny situation, but so is puppy love.

No one resembling Kaawi came or went. We dawdled a bit, but it was nearing eight o'clock and the bill came.

"*Gracias, señores*, good night. Don' get lost."

She went back into the kitchen and a faucet went on. Effie hung up her apron and left by the front door.

"What did she mean by that?"

"Damned if I know. Wait! It's on the bill. Look."

"'Rancho Tres Palmas Date Farm. Follow me.' Who's me?"

"I think the other waitress. She's out front in a truck."

I paid up with a generous tip, like a good tourist, and we slipped quickly out and into the chilly night air. The waitress, Effie, flipped on the truck lights and waved to us, "follow me." The truck had "Tres Palmas" lettered on the doors.

"Now we're having an adventure!" Kat announced. "You know, for a writer you sure know how to have a good time!"

As we pulled away, a burst of wind cycloned among the palms, rattling the fronds and tossing the bagged branches of fruit around like big cocoons. Splashes of desert sand hit the car. A large Moon finally rose above the Eastern range and the salty desert shone dully in its light. The truck drove ahead, around the east side of the lake at country-road speed.

"So, George, when we get to the date farm, what's the cover story? We've done TV reporters and tourists so far."

"These people know who I am, maybe they know who everybody is at Rose-Bud. So, be just like you were back at the Selz' — Mrs. Music — and if it helps to be from KTTV, that's good too. Keep it in reserve. I think these people want us for something, some way we can help them, maybe, I hope."

"I'm keeping all my options open. And, in case of anything extraterrestrial, I've got the magic blue crystal that stops convertibles in their tracks!"

A cluster of loose brush blew across the road in a gust of sandy wind. I lost sight of the truck then, for a moment, and when we cleared the little sandstorm, its taillights had vanished. I slowed, looking for a side road off to the left where the truck must have turned.

"The crystal's glowing again! Slow down, it must be along here."

There was an open gate a few yards ahead and the truck idled inside.

"Tres Palmas. Private Road."

I turned in and the truck headed uphill toward the Moonrise.

"This is not turning out to be a swell bed-and-breakfast surprise for Mrs. Music, I hope."

"Don't even think that."

"I'm joking."

We didn't say anything after that until the road flattened out and snaked around a ridge of the mountains to present the pretty picture of a ranch-house, date-palm grove and horsey outbuildings, stark in the moonlight. Two more well-used trucks and three cityfied sedans were parked in front of the house. Curtains were pulled across the picture window.

Effie parked next to the other trucks, I pulled in wide, not liking to risk the Mercedes to more gravel than necessary. We parked and Effie came toward us, hand out.

"Hi," she said. "I'm Effie Hydell, Kaawi's sister. She's inside. Glad you came."

In spite of the cars out front, there were only two people in the living room. One was a tidy, brush-cut man about forty, the other was Kaawi.

"Kaawi you already know, this is my husband, Major Hydell," Effie said.

Kat, who hadn't met the miniature Space Angel, said, "Hi, there! Kaawi as in . . .?"

"It's Indonesian. A kind of yam, I think. You're . . . ?"

The introductions went around. We shook hands and nodded and accepted gin-and-tonics and bowls of different kinds of dates. We were directed to the Mission-style sofa. I could think of nothing but my first question.

"You're going to ask why we summoned you here," said Kaawi.

"No, actually I was wondering why you said I was in danger."

"Your bungalow court is being taken over as a base for forces who wish to create fear and suspicion and make money doing it." That from Major Hydell.

"Sounds like politics as usual to me. Wait a second, don't you think 629-and-three-quarters 30th Street, L.A. is a little small for a revolutionary cadre — only one bedroom, 600 square feet or so. True, there's a nice tile bathroom . . ."

I was clearly being snarky, so Kat cut in. "Who is this mysterious force?"

"They're Aliens," said Major Hydell.

"Don't you have to have aliens to pick the dates?" I snarked. "Wetbacks?" Kat glared at me.

"You don't get it, Mr. Tirebiter. Aliens." The Major got up. He was all muscle. He too was short, Kat's height. "We are in league with them at this time, we are testing Alien weaponry, their anti-gravity drive, all behind closed doors, and much of it just across these mountains, in Arizona!"

Kat looked at me and smiled a warm smile.

Smiling back, I said, "I don't have any aliens of any kind living in the Rose-Bud, except Mr. O'Toole, and he's Irish."

"These Aliens aren't from Mexico and they're not from Mars. The ones that work for the Air Force I'm not supposed to know about, but I'm not stupid. That's not where the threat is." The Major was being patient with me, but he was serious in an oblique way.

Kaawi said, "Mr. Wispell sent me information in code. He could see what was going on, that the Church was moving in, and I passed it on, but it looked like they were ready to do something pretty soon, so . . . "

"That's why they killed him," said the Major. "Vanpool too. Getting too close to the truth."

"The truth? That I've got Aliens infesting my Court?" I didn't want to laugh, but . . . "Quick, Henry, the Flit!"

The Major snorted. "DDT? Very funny, Mr. Tirebiter."

Kat moved away from me on the couch. "George, if your life is in danger, shut up and take this seriously!"

"Earlier this year the Selz bungalow was taken over by a trick. It's been in use since then as a base."

"Both bungalows are cordoned off now and sealed. Nobody can get in or out. They'd be useless."

"That's what you think, Mr. Tirebiter."

"What's happening," said Kaawi, "is they're going to announce the Church of Science Fiction, only they're really starting a cult that owes allegiance to the Aliens."

"Who is doing this?"

"The Coopers," said Effie.

"The Coopers and the Baileys, they've got the Alien transmissions from the saucer people and Selz, rich guy, believes in them, finances them. His daughter moved in on you, right? They've got Rev. Rosco in it too. They want us to believe the answer to World Peace is . . ."

The Major stopped in mid-sentence. "What's that?"

It was the blue crystal in Kat's bag. A steady minor tone. It was getting louder.

"That's my flying saucer alert signal. I always bring it along when I'm in saucer country," said Kat innocently, opening her bag to show a bright blue light glowing from it.

Effie moved to join the Major and held on to his arm. Kaawi sat up very straight. "Where did you get that?"

"It's a prop from a TV show!" Kat shut her bag and laughed.

The Major glared at her. "TV? How did you know such signals existed?"

"Uh, let's see, good imagination?"

Now seemed like a good time either to run like hell or execute a casual exit and then run like hell. I picked casual.

"So, everybody, what can I do to help?"

"Get proof!" said Ellie, still clinging to the Major.

"We need proof that one of them killed what they thought were spies!" Kaawi relaxed back in her chair. "That will kill their awful Church!"

"Proof!" I said, taking Kat's hand and moving toward the front door. "Sure. That's what I've been looking for. Thanks for your help and good luck." Smooth, I hoped.

The Major unlatched the door and laid his hand on the knob. "You may find things at home are very different when you return. Changes mean the Powers are working. We're depending on you."

He opened the door and shook hands with me. I let Kat go out ahead and expected to say to her, after the door closed, "Let's get out of here." There was no one on the porch. "Kat?"

Windy silence and the rattle of the palms. The parking area was empty except for my convertible. "Kat?"

I took two steps toward the car. What little I could see in the moonlight vanished. I don't think I took another step.

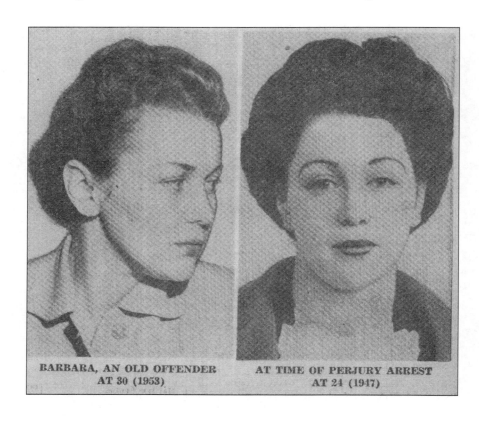

BARBARA, AN OLD OFFENDER
AT 30 (1953)

AT TIME OF PERJURY ARREST
AT 24 (1947)

Chapter 8

Barbara Graham Fights for Life
Her Primrose Path of Crime
Frantic Effort to Escape
the Gas Chamber

I was confined. I didn't seem to be bound, just unable to move. A blank weight pressed against my eyes. The air smelled metallic. The taste of it hung in the back of my throat. I couldn't cough it out. I couldn't cough at all.

I tried to say "Help!" or "Kat!" or "Let me up!" When I tried to say "up" I knew I was on my back and that I couldn't say anything out-loud. The words spun around inside themselves like a frantic tornado through the tall palms. A little panic-fear began in the middle of my body. I heard my name being said. I could only hear.

This is a bath of voices I'm in, I thought. "Illusion," said a splash of words. "You really don't exist," eddied through my ears. "Learn this first. Don't be afraid of it."

"Try not to be afraid as this happens."

"You don't exist . . . you are a vibratory reflection."

"Your soul only used your three-dimensions for transit."

"You cannot visualize your body anymore."

"It is useless to you."

I floated in the bath of words but now without a body. I tried to find a way to be frightened, to be full of terror, so confined and bodiless, but fear was far away, un-grab-able, hopeless.

"You can be anywhere you want to be," said a wave of voices dying into pebbles on the shore.

Since I was nowhere, that rattle of words made no sense. Anywhere? Where was reality?

Down along the lakeshore bonfires are dying back to marshmallow-toasting size. A dozen or more caravans are pulled up in campsites.

A schoolbus occupies Space #1 and from it sounds pour, words slowed, run fast, mixed into the hot crackle of the fires until it becomes a kind of music. I am there, not physically, because that isn't me anymore, but hearing the music.

Mrs. Alice Cooper, a less-than-Venusian vision in pale yellow arises from the depths of the Salton Sea and into the firelight and music. Her voice comes from a trance and puts the listener into one.

"Greetings in the Oneness of the Cosmos, Workers in the Light! Soon you will see the space vehicle that will take those of us willing to embark on such a journey away to a locus in Space that is the center of all thought and all knowledge. The energies are here, have been here for centuries, creating this moment. Join me on the way to Infinity!"

I see and hear her, but it's hard to keep my place in a state of non-existing and I try to lock onto a dog, but the animal immediately snarls and twists away.

There must be fifty people here, waiting for something big to happen. A gaunt man with a rough beard steps into the light from the schoolbus and shouts "Any minute!"

I feel the silence and fear and it triggers my own fear, desperation now that this state I'm in has no ending but endless not-ending.

"You can be anywhere you want to be."

I grabbed on to "you want to be." That's what I want, to be, that would be enough for the instant, but that word "you" hangs like smoke and blows away.

The people on the shore are pointing and gasping. From over the mountain tops a spinning light emerges and falls toward the lake.

I feel as if I have vanished.

I'm wondering where George is. He was right behind me at the door and then he vanished and now I don't seem to be able to see a thing anywhere. His nice car is out here and if I could walk better I could find it, but I can only float inside the dark now and not think about it.

The Aliens are landing. They're horrible like crabs and spiders and lobsters only they look cute to humans so we'll fall in love with them.

They have a hundred sexes and they'll use them all. If that's what's happening, I can't wait. I'm wondering about George. Sometimes he seems like Orson Welles and sometimes he's Andy Hardy. He has a crush on me but I've been captured by the saucer people. I'd yell for him but I can't yell or move my body, yet my body seems to be made of charms and the one down there shines like the Moon and I'm in a place between longing and desire that's full of aches and scars. Longing is real and desire is fantasy. Maybe the other way around. Plundered. I'm being plundered.

The blue crystal says, "You are a welcome volunteer, earth-person. We have only a short time to give you your duties. You must choose your course now. You are one of the communicators. You will listen and prepare the world for our arrival. Learn who is with us and listen."

I have no defense against this. I slip from my skin.

I understand that this is an interplanetary ship and that many of the people waiting on the beach have volunteered to go aboard. We will be stopping at the Moon Base and then on to Io, one of Jupiter's satellites. Training and integration will take place there. We will be returning to Earth to save mankind from its pain. The worst thing is I can't breathe. Suddenly my body appears to me and it can't breathe. Under water. A body under water that can no longer breathe. I forget.

If he'd touch my hand we'd travel together. I feel wanted. I'm all pressure points and tingles. Where are you, George? I think if you touch my hand I'll feel it all over. They need me.

When do you know that you're no longer alive? Goodbye. So little got done. They come from under the bed. I've already forgotten and I remember nothing. Sleep. Be frightened to sleep. Fear awake.

It was something like song-and-dance-man Dick Powell coming to painfully, but perfectly hard-boiled in "Murder, My Sweet." When he emerges to consciousness after being heavily drugged, his sanitarium room appears to be filled with smoke. It's a great moment for a song-and-dance, but none of that for Powell's Philip Marlowe — or me. Kat and I both moaned some instead. I felt she was moaning for me.

Touch my hair. Cup my breasts. Feed me dates. Kiss my lips. Make love to me.

"I would, but I think I'm dead," I moaned back from a bed in a room filled with smoke.

"You're not dead, George!" Kat was done moaning. "Tell me you're not dead."

"I wish I could," I moaned.

"You're not! Open your eyes!"

"Kat? Where are we?"

"I haven't figured that out yet. I think it's a motel room."

I opened my eyes. Heaven or Hell or Motel 6, they all look the same when you've been abducted by Aliens. If I was in a smoke-filled room, the room was pitch-dark and I couldn't tell. It certainly smelled like it.

Kat was sitting up on the opposite side of the bed I realized I was lying in. She turned on the pale light on the night table and turned to look at me.

"Motel room, right?"

"What happened to us?"

"I don't think I want to talk about it, not at this point in our neighborly relationship."

"I thought I was dead. Really. How did we get here? Wait a second."

I got up and went to the window opposite the bed and pushed back the curtain. A giant neon sign proclaimed "Westward Ho." A smaller one blinked "No Vacancy." The Mercedes was parked in front of the room.

"Were we abducted by aliens, Kat? Were you?"

"I walked out of that ranch house and that's the last real thing I remember, except I missed you. What time is it?"

"Four thirty. In the morning, I guess, 'cause it's still dark. I think we're in Palm Springs."

"If we drive back to L.A. right now I'll only be a couple of hours late for work, and I'm supposed to be doing library research anyway."

"You are certainly calm about this."

"Remember the murders, George? Remember what we innocently came to Mecca for? Who done it?"

Kat found her jacket and purse on a chair. She opened the purse and swore. "Gone. I knew it! The crystal's gone! Whatever happened to us — we were drugged or something — whatever, those people we were with? What did you call them? Nut-bars? Coo-coo as loons!"

"Let's go home. If the nut-bars are killers, we'll need a little more proof. By the way, are you aware a flying saucer landed by the Sea-shore and took everybody for a trip to the Moon?"

"On gossamer wings? Are you OK? I'll nap for awhile then take over driving, if you want. Please? Let's get out of here."

The Moon had sunk into the West and we followed it back to the big city, joining the morning work-bound traffic. Students were on the move between early classes when we got back to the Court. Kat had drifted into sleep on the way out of the Village and I left her that way, sweet-faced, peaceful, quite sexy, though I'd pretty much given up on that.

We said goodbye at the entrance to the Court. Kat smiled her warmest smile at me. "Thanks for the date, George. You sure know how to give a girl an out-of-body experience!"

I found my bed and slept until a knocking on my door reminded me that I was no longer dead. I got a robe and pulled it on and opened up.

Sgt. Cummings said, "What is this, Tirebiter? Every time you have a murder here you go outta town? Didn't I say we needed ta have a talk? Where the hell were ya yesterday? Let's go inside. Too late for coffee?"

"Never too late for coffee, Sergeant."

Cummings came in, took off his straw hat and said, "Ya seen the front page?"

"What, **MURDER BUNGALOW — WHAT'S NEXT?**"

"Nah, that wasn't much of a pitcher. Ran it on page four. Got me on page one, yesterday's edition. **MASK OF DEATH** they called it. Got my name right. Sgt. William A. Cummings of Homicide Squad. Ya probably didn't see it because you skipped town!"

I made the coffee. Mrs. Whitmer walked by my open door on her way out, glanced in and shook her head.

"What do you know I don't know?" said Cummings, after he had his hands on the coffee.

"Let's trade some information, Sergeant. I'll give you some ideas you won't probably like if you'll tell me about Vanpool's death and what your boys have found out."

"Vanpool was DOA of shock or heart-attack, somethin' that left no marks. He was brought into your apartment there after he was dead and laid out. Surprised nobody noticed a corpse bein' carried into the back place in front of all yer tenants, but we talked to everybody except Mrs. Katherine Music across the way. Two of you took a drive yesterday, I hear. None a my business."

"I was following a rumor and Mrs. Music was happy to go along for the ride. The rumor is this, and you can do with it whatever you want. I hear there are two camps in the world of flying saucers . . ."

Cummings snorted into his coffee cup. "The nut-bars?"

"Two camps, Sergeant. They're both crazy, but they seem to hate each other anyway. We ran into both groups down in the desert. One warned me that the other one is creating a Science Fiction Church and they tell me they've decided to headquarter it right here at the Rose-Bud. One group or maybe the other abducted Mrs. Music and me . . ."

"And you joined the cult?"

"Whatever they did, we were mesmerized or hypnotized and I experienced my own death."

"Unh-huh."

"Here's what I'm trying to say, Sergeant. The saucers and Aliens that people claim to see and talk to seem to be hypnotic illusions. Maybe there's some exotic drug involved. Both Vanpool and Wispell knew, or at least had a hint about who was behind it. Whoever that is had them both killed. Personally, I think maybe Wispell was blackmailing him, or them."

"Got some names?"

"Start with Gideon Selz."

"You go to see him in Palm Springs?"

"We did, yes. One of his twin daughters was there, Gail."

"I thought you said he was dead, so I checked and he's not dead, so what's the game?"

"One of the twins got into the bungalow, told me her father had died and sold his piano. That would be Abby and she's a flat-earth cultist. Obviously, Gideon's alive and well. But — something about the whole thing — the scene — seemed too — pat, I guess."

"Not surprised. Those twins, Gail and Abby? I checked. Not so hard to check if you're a cop and not a dumb nut-bar tryin' to be Sam Spade. Only one daughter, named Abigail — Abi-gale — that's all. It sure seems easy to put one over on ya!"

"Is the Selz bungalow still sealed?"

"You bet. For one thing, a lot of the place got spit-shined, so the boys are lookin' for fingerprints and not findin' many. And for another, I'm lookin' inta Wispell's dental business. He handled a lot of gold, had a lot a customers Downtown. The ham radio thing? Cover for somethin'."

"What about I put his bungalow back up for rent? You're done with it, aren't you?"

"I guess. His brother gonna pick up what's left? Tell'm we got a crate of radio parts in the evidence room. Gotta keep 'em. You got somebody in mind to do the rentin'?"

"No, but I'll be careful. No nut-bars. A nice retired couple with a son that checks in on 'em regularly. College kids. No Aliens. All Earthlings welcome!"

"Right. So, you think Selz is behind the killings?"

"They lied to us. And why would she want me to believe she was twins? Olivia de Havilland played that game a few years back in "Dark Mirror." You were played by Thomas Mitchell in that movie, by the way."

"Hoo-ray for Hollywood!" Cummings unfolded as he rose, put his cup down, took a couple of steps to the door, turned in that thoughtful, off-hand way cops always do in the movies and said, ""Expect a visit from the FBI. Stay on their good side, no problem.""

"Too late for that."

"So I heard. You get another body here and nobody knows a thing about it?"

"What do I do then?"

The Sergeant pulled his hat down and grunted. "Check yesterday's paper. 'Mask of Death.' I'm glad I was wearin' the light-weight gabardine. Had a fresh shave, too. Call me!"

The screen door slammed.

I had another cup of coffee and pulled on some clothes. The heat spell had died out and the morning was overcast and chilly. I sat on my front steps and thought about redecorating. Every bungalow porch deserved a big red geranium in a nice Mexican pot. The center grassy strip was probably better off dead. Oops! Sorry I even thought that.

Mrs. Whitmer hurried back into the Court, carrying two grocery sacks.

"Can I help?" I took the bags and she sighed.

"I'm indebted to you, Mr. Tirebiter. I have been running to Ralphs for twenty years or more and it's finally got the better of me. I eat less, it costs more and the store gets farther away every time I make the trip. Mercy!"

She took a shiny new key from her bag. "Your locksmith came yesterday. Nice young man. I do feel safer, but I had him install a sliding bar on the inside anyway. Thank you, I'll take my groceries back. Just some yogurt and beef liver for my condition. Bananas and tomatoes were both ten cents a pound but tomatoes are a poison, you know, but bananas have potassium."

"I've always heard that."

"They summed up in the Barbara Graham case, you know. I was there, Mr. Tirebiter. The police stoolie that recorded her, oh, she was angry at him. Turned red like a cardinal and cursed like a stevedore when he came in. And they let that other woman go and she was up for a sentence but they said jail was too dangerous, because she'd be at risk for her skin, the attorney said."

"Sounds like it's all over."

"She's getting the gas chamber for killing that woman who wasn't any older than I am. Choked her to death! Deserves what's coming.

And Barbara's little boy was waiting outside all the time to see her! Well, thanks again."

Miss Gage was leaving her bungalow, dressed for the Auto Club. She waved and said, "Mr. Tirebiter? Are you interested at all in photography?" She asked that with the sweetest, most innocent smile.

"As a hobby? Not much. I have a Nikon I never use."

"Well, I really have to explain that if you'd ever be interested in photographing with a model, I'm very good. The West Side Camera Club comes on Tuesdays. I hope you don't mind. I mean, it's not like I'm using my apartment as a business, exactly — well, not exactly at all! It's an artist's studio the way I think of it."

"So long as you know what you're doing. It's really not my job to police the Rose-Bud, but with what's been going on we all have to be careful. Oh, I met one of the Clubbers — Ken Adair? You pose in costumes?"

"It's all with what the Clubbers want. I have a pretty big wardrobe!" The girlish smile smoldered and she lifted her left eyebrow. "Of very small things!" She laughed like Marilyn. "Or nothing at all. It's whatever you want. Have a good day, Mr. Tirebiter!" She put on her work face and left the Court for her short walk to the Auto Club.

Nude model! I thought. I wonder if randy old Mr. O'Toole knows he's living next to the real thing, so to speak.

Randy Mr. O'Toole and his seabag nearly cattterwhomped me, as my old Irish Mum used to say back in the Emerald City.

"Ooops, so sorry, Mr. Tirebiter, sir. I was just thinkin' if I didn't hurry I'd miss the bus and, sure, I can hear it pullin' away and off she goes. Well then. One'll come again in a cat's tail. Got a minute to spare, have ya, sir?"

"What's up?"

"I heard the dog again, sir, behind the buildin', scruffling about last night. But more'n that, sir, that cottage across the way, locked up by the police it was, but last night me lumbago was actin' up and I saw out me winda that there was a light on in there two a.m.-ish and I don't mind sayin' it was ghostly. It was a ghostly thing, sir."

"No one's supposed to be in there, Mr. O'Toole. Thanks for the tip. I'll pass it along to Sgt. Cummings for you. About the dog?"

"Sounded like it was snufflin' for somethin' like a lost bone er toy. Lookin' around, like."

"That's probably just what it is. I wouldn't worry."

"Just thought I'd say, sir. I'm off now. Greyhound station Downtown."

"Quick trip?"

"Well sir, I got a call from me sister, came in at the Seaman's Hall and I got it a bit late, anyway she's gettin' elderly and wants a bit a help movin' to a nice home up there in Oakland. So . . ."

"Lock your place up tight, OK? I'll keep an eye out."

Off he lumbered. I hoped the burlesque scene was as lively in Oakland as it was in L.A.

Almost nine a.m. The overcast was thinning. The Rose-Bud, so full and lively a few days ago, was also thinning, petal by petal. I walked over to the Selz bungalow and checked the police locks. I looked through the kitchen window, under the shade. Still as the tomb. There were curtains across the front window, thin enough so the shine from a flashlight would easily show through, if it had been a flashlight O'Toole saw.

The Bobs' bungalow had an envelope tacked to the front door. "Mr. Tirebitter," it said. Inside, a sheet of folded schoolbook paper. Unfolded, it read in smudgy ballpoint: "Mr. T. Hold on to things, I'll be back to clean out in a few days. Transferred to San Diego State. Keep my deposit. Bob says he's staying at U of Hawaii, how about that. Thanks, Bob."

Another couple of petals just dropped from the Rose-Bud. As I stood in the entry, two cars pulled up and parked in the alley and another swooped into the empty space across the street. Two men got out of each and all of them looked like B-movie G-Men. One came up to me and flashed a badge.

"Max Shearer. FBI. Inside, sir, please."

"I'm not a danger to myself or others, Agent Shearer. What can I do for you?"

"You can get the fuck inside sir, please. You're in the middle of an operation!"

For Harry Sweet,
I've long tried to
be—
Betty Rourke
11-8-54

John E. Reed
·HOLLYWOOD·

CHAPTER 9

PLUMBER'S WIFE A PIP UNZIPPED!
MRS. SUNBEAM, 37-26-36
TOPS NUDIE CUTIES
MEASUREMENTS BEST OF FINALISTS THAT
JIGGLED BY JUDGES

A tabloid for tired businessmen, that's what the *Mirror* amounted to, with a skinny couple of pages for the little woman tucked inside, next to the sober TV listings and the salacious display of stimulating entertainment at a reasonable price — all the cocktails you could drink plus prime rib dinner slabbed on a plate and a no-name band you and your little honey could dance to for a measly five bucks plus tip, for instance, and on the Sunset Strip, no less.

I had time to leaf through yesterday's *Mirror* while I was under house arrest. Not exactly arrest. Agent Shearer escorted me to my door.

"This matter does not concern you, sir. I apologize for my outspokenness but there are armed Federal personnel on these premises and your life could be endangered. Please remain inside until our operation is complete."

It was over pretty quickly. My neighbors, the Birnbaums, were led away in handcuffs. The rest of the G-force climbed in their cars and melted back into the metropolis. Before he vanished, Agent Shearer knocked on my door and thanked me for my cooperation and said there was no further peril, foreign or domestic. Words to that effect.

Since I was on the FBI's fellow-traveler list I was relieved not to be hauled in alongside the Birnbaums. Left-wingers they were, for sure, but enemies of the state? You never knew these days.

Will Perry knocked on my door. "Damndest thing! Be sure and check your paper tomorrow. I'll be in it! Total surprise! Dick Williams at the *Mirror saw my* paintings at the saucer show and called me up!"

"That's great news!"

"And how about tech advisor on a space movie called 'Destruction Orbit?' It's at United, but I think it really may happen."

"Will, I think it's you that really may happen!"

"Here's the thing, George, the Grandma's been wanting some time with Little Joe, so we're going up to spend a few weeks in Portland. Sally'll be glad for the help and I can do the sketches for the movie out in Grandma's barn. I know it's been crazy for you the last few days, but I guess there's not much of anything I could do to help anyway, so . . ."

And there wasn't, so I waved goodbye as the family drove off in their old Studebaker. The Court looked desolate afterword, like a leftover movie set with the cold wind blowing through its empty backs.

Mrs. Whitmer, the co-eds, Audrey Gage. Kat and me. The last petals on the Bud.

A bike wheeled into the Courtyard and the kid kicked down the stand, got off. He picked a paper out of the saddlebag and handed it to me. "Two dollars a month, sir," he said.

"Worth every bit of it." I gave him a dollar bill and enough change.

"Anybody else in the Court like to subscribe?"

"Don't think so, but I'll ask."

"Thanks." He looked around admiringly. "Maybe I'll live here someday."

"Maybe you will."

The kid rode off and I went back inside. There was a possible clue I'd overlooked that needed looking over. Why had my movie scenario been taken? The carbons were in the orange crate in the closet that I used as a filing system. There were about 20 pages and the answer seemed to be at the very top of the pile.

IT CAME FROM UNDER THE BED
Screen Story by Phil Starke
8/1/53

This is a horror story that takes place in a Los Angeles bungalow and in the underground world that opens beneath it.

Our Hero is Jeff Chandler. He's a family man with a wife Nancy and two children. Both Cindy and Donna, 8 and 11, sleep in the same bedroom.

Chandler came by this house when his Uncle Wilbur passed away and left it to him. Wilbur was an undertaker.

We meet the family at breakfast where Donna begins to spout gibberish about Demons.

Cindy knows the secret — that from a hidden opening underneath Donna's bed Demons do go in and out of the room during the night. She explains and her parents accuse her of inventing a story.

Jeff decides he'll lay in wait for a Demon to appear that night. Nancy begs him not to put himself in danger — "They could be right!" — but he refuses and leaves for his job, which is Boy's Vice Principal at Manual Arts High School.

Jeff is gone and the girls take the school bus, leaving Nancy very, very alone. She hesitantly goes into the girl's bedroom, armed with a broom. (Music sting cue here, lots of terror under).

Like a good, heroic Mom, Nancy gets down on all fours to look under the bed belonging to Donna — the one with all the fancy horses on the coverlet. There is nothing under there but a big dustball. She pokes at it with the broom and the ball rolls away from it. That happens a couple of times.

Annoyed, Nancy crawls halfway under the bed. A bloody, horrible pit opens beneath her and she falls, screaming into it. The pit closes again, becoming the wooden floor and the dustball rolls back to sit guard on top of it.

Maybe there are tunnels under the bungalows and the Aliens use them to get around, delivering bodies and stealing United Parcel deliveries. Comfortable beds here, especially if you're sleeping the Long Farewell. No, SoCal Edison and Your Gas Company and Bell Telephone must have been underground on and off since the Twenties when the Court was built.

What other kind of access to the bungalows could there be? No such thing as a basement in L.A. Maybe, now everyone was gone, I should go around with a broom and poke under the tenants' beds.

The phone rang. It was Shifty. "Hey, Mr. T, this in from Mr. P. You know anything about a door being open and shut at the same time? Great idea, sez Mr. P. Possible road to another dimension if you walk through it. Might have entertainment value he sez. Wants ya ta check it out. The inventor is a guy named Mar-Cel. In the Big Apple. Can do?"

"That's a long way to go right now, Shifty. I can't make it to New York, not this week. I've got empty bungalows and a couple of things hanging and there were the murders, you know, and the police want me to stick around and keep the grass trimmed, if you know what I mean."

"You bet. Keep the grass trimmed, yeah, love it! I'll tell The Man. How long're you out of commission?"

"I'll call. Tell Mr. Pingo I do know something about the door that's always both open and closed already and I'll follow up on it a.s.a.p. Right now, I'm going to sweep out from under the beds."

"And under the carpets, ha ha!"

"I'll check under the carpets too. I'll call in later. Thank Mr. Pingo for the opportunity."

While I had the phone in my hand I thought I'd check in on how things were going at the Flying Saucer Journal or whatever it was. New Age Publishing was in the book.

"Good morning. Welcome to New Age. I'm Andromeda, how can I help?"

"Yes, good morning. May I speak with Mr. Bailey? My name is George Tirebiter."

"I'll ring through to his chakra."

A fairly long pause. Mrs. Whitmer knocked at my screen. "Just a second. On the phone." I gestured at her, "Wait."

"May I have Mr. Bailey return your call?"

I gave Andromeda my number. Mrs. Whitmer called through the screen. "Mr. Tirebiter! I have the nicest surprise! My niece Lorraine has invited me to stay with her over the weekend in Pasadena. She has tickets to 'Queen For A Day' on television. I only hear it on radio, so I'm so thrilled! It's in Hollywood, you know. At Sunset and Vine, Lorraine said!"

"Well, have a wonderful time! She's picking you up?"

"Oh, yes and we're having supper out at Clifton's Cafeteria and Lorraine says they play Hawaiian music there and I've never heard a note of that. Here she is! Aloha, Mr. Tirebiter!"

I watched as she got in her niece's two-door Plymouth. Both waved goodbye at me. The phone rang.

"This is Andromeda at New Age, Mr. Tirebiter. Mr. Bailey will speak to you now."

"Fine. . . Hello?"

"Ah! George Tirebiter. I know something about you, good sir." There was something in Bailey's voice that reminded me of Bob Carney — a Second Banana with an act that went out with the old tentshows. It was the voice I thought I heard when I was bodyless over the Salton Sea, welcoming the Alien Saucer. The Old Prospector.

"And what's that?" I said.

"You write movies."

"Well, movie stories anyway. How do you know?"

"I'm in possession of a scenario called 'It Came From Under the Bed' by one Phil Starke, which is an obvious alias. A shall-we-say-contributor of mine presented it to me as his own. What do you think of that?"

"It was stolen."

"I was afraid it was. If you'd like to drop by the office I'll be happy to hand it back to you." He paused. "Or, I can just as easily put it in the U.S. Post."

"Does this so-called-contributor of yours have a name? Because the Murder Squad would like to have a word with him. Maybe more than a word."

"He goes by Sydney Carton, which, well, we do believe that there is a far, far better world coming in the New Age."

"Clever. By the way, how did the UFO convention go? Was there a sighting at Mecca since Hollywood Boulevard turned out to be too busy?"

"The convention was a sincere attempt to demonstrate to the world at large that we must admit to the presence of Aliens in our midst, that the U. S. Military must confess about their experiments, and that there is much to fear the way the country and the world is going. About the Salton Sea, sir, if you were there you know what took place. We are forbidden to speak."

"I'll come by and pick up 'Under the Bed.' Any way I can contact this Sydney Carton? He might know how somebody had a key to my bungalow, came in, and only stole a crummy movie yarn when he could have taken some classy Shakespearian ad libs?"

"He comes and goes. I have no idea how it was you might have been burglarized. I just print books and magazines here, Mr. Tirebiter. And I don't believe everything I read."

"Do you know anything about a Church of Science Fiction, Mr. Bailey?"

"In the New Age, sir, we shall each be a Church unto ourselves. I'll leave your manuscript with Andromeda. Good day, sir and High Vibrations."

High poppycock! Sgt. Cummings had it right — nut-bars, all of 'em! Except, at least I had an alias to go on and no reason not to assume that "Sydney" had access to the murder bungalows and was maybe the murderer himself.

Gideon Selz had said the Coopers were behind the Church. Or maybe it was the Aliens behind the Coopers behind the Church? The flyer from the Convention had a contact number, of course. Bill & Alice Cooper were represented by the Palmer Agency, 600 South Main.

I got off the streetcar at Pershing Square and walked down Fifth Street to Broadway. Downtown L.A.'s shopping district. Orbach's here, a block away The Broadway, May Company, drugstores, hotels, drab office buildings and a cluster of palatial movie theaters. The Palmer Agency was on Main St. in the Santa Fe Building, up two floors from Thrifty Drug. The Santa Fe Building was next door to the New Follies Burlesque — 14 Big Acts! Betty Rowland was headlining, as Mr. O'Toole had promised. Fifth and Main was the edge of Skid Row, the Greyhound Bus Terminal waited wanly at the corner for the tired, lost and defeated and welcomed the temporarily hopeful into the dispiriting vista of another heartless city.

I checked the occupants on the board in the lobby. The second floor offered a credit dentist, a watchmaker, a CPA and the Palmer Agency. The fourth floor had a surprise: Wispell Denture Mfg. His office was here? I'll check into that later. The Palmer Agency was behind a half-pebbled-glass door with Come In Please lettered across the glass.

"Hi!" I said to the motherly secretary. "I'm interested in the Coopers. The saucer couple?"

"Oh, we like them so much! They've both been abducted, you know."

"I certainly do. How can I get in touch?"

"Would you like to book them for an appearance? They love to talk to Eagles and VFW's and practically anywhere. County Fairs are very good to us."

"They don't appear at Church events, do they? You know, to speak on the Other World, the Worlds Beyond, that angle?"

"They have an appearance fee, of course, but I'm sure your congregation would benefit from the experience. Name and number, I can get back to you early next week. They're in Santa Barbara, you see, speaking to the Society for Paranormal Research."

"Good for them! It's George — Riefenbissen." I spelled it, gave her my phone number and looked around the walls. Eight-by-ten glossies of dog-acts, ventriloquists, burlesque dancers, a woman who stood on one finger on a man who stood on one finger on a bowling pin. What an act!

"Thanks so much. I'll expect to hear from you, then," I said. I walked up to the fourth floor and down the hall past Ace Aquarium Supply, Emmitt Secretarial Services and Yarn, Unltd. Wispell Denture Mfg. was at the end of the hall. It said Private, but there was a light on inside, so I knocked once and opened the door.

"Well, well! What a surprise!"

Sgt. Cummings, straw hat pushed back, sat with his feet up on a table covered with teeth.

"If it ain't Sam the nut-bar Spade! How did you figure this place out? Look it up in the Yellow Pages?"

"Totally by accident, Sergeant. I was visiting another office downstairs. This is where Wispell came every day? Not the best part of town."

"Didn't matter much. All that glitters ain't gold, especially where Wispell was concerned. Just between us, Tirebiter, the guy was skimmin' off the top. Nothin' to do with flyin' saucers. What's new?"

"I got an offer to return my stolen movie story. Seems a regular contributor to the Saucer Journal offered it up as his own. Said my nom de plume was his and his name is a fake anyway — Sydney Carton."

"He stole it?"

"Something about it caught Sydney's eye. I think he had a master key and was prowling all the bungalows. Scary thought."

"A professional wired up that chair, Tirebiter. Somebody big wanted Wispell out of the way. That's the way we're goin'. You have a good day now."

He lifted his long legs from the table and down to the floor. He sagged when he stood up.

"I'm workin' here, even if it don't look like it. Think-time, you know?"

"Think-time is my best friend, Sergeant. Anything else you'd like to share?"

"Not with you. Go home, keep yer nose clean."

"Anything on poor Charlie Vanpool?"

"One murder at a time. Go home."

I left Sgt. Cummings sagging under his burden of thought. On the second floor I glanced down the hall toward the Palmer Agency. An extremely tall person in a long robe and hood was ducking his upper body to go through the doorway. Say, maybe Palmer represents those 14-foot-tall blue-skinned Venusian nudists that Vanpool told me about!

The Follies next door occupied an old Downtown theatre, once a famous playhouse. The Red-Headed Ball of Fire was headlining between a pawnshop and a shoe store. Why not, I thought?

The show was going on — and on-going 11 a.m. to Midnight. The audience was all male and all the males were wearing hats. Even if you were a bum, you wore a hat.

Piano, drums and a couple of saxes in the pit, with a runway around them where strutted the chorines. There were a lot of chorines and they did a routine dressed in abbreviated cowgirl togs and another in hula skirts in front of a piece of scenery so surreal I thought it might be left over from a Mélies silent film fantasy set on the Moon.

The comedy act was pants-droppingly un-funny. The boys out-drank each other while ogling a succession of those same chorines, whose top measurements hovered in the low to mid 40s. Only the Ball of Fire stood out from rest, most of them bus-station dropouts with a high school musical or two behind them. Polite applause as

they walked off, still over-dressed for a take-it-off show. Rowland had been working the Follies stage for a dozen years and she was quick to strip to the legal minimum and strut her stuff with wild whips of her stop-light hair and a serene stroll along the runway in front of the sweaty men gazing up at her while she ignored them.

That's all you get, fellas! Show over. Guys pulled their hats tighter and buttoned their coats.

On the way out, Bob Carney appeared from the Men's Room and waved me down.

"Just one of the low-lifes now, huh, Tirebiter? Ugly habit, strippers."

"I'm a writer, remember, Bob? It's all research."

"Yeah, well, me too. I hadda see Jack and Harry do their good-ta-the-last-drop routine. It's almost spiritual. Hey, I did my bit for Lenny's movie. Funny as hell! And that Stacy the Steno? Burned up the camera! Better than Rowland, younger, and she stripped down from, you know, hat, gloves and handbag, not her nightie. Movie's gonna headline some Main Street joint, down here in the beaver district, haw haw!"

I walked dispiritedly back to the bus stop. Downtown Los Angeles. No place for trees, never had been a place, except for cottonwoods along the marshy shores of the L.A. River, long since gone. It put me in a sour mood. Downtown seemed segregated into the important business and pleasures of men and the frivolous ones of women. Burlesque and shopping. Down-and-outers sleeping on the sidewalk only a block away.

A newsstand across from the minimally green Pershing Square offered sci-fi magazines, two of them with covers by Will Perry and a section of "men's" magazines with titles like *Snap* and *Slick* and *Flirt*. One called Scamp sported a familiar face — Audrey Gage, discreetly topless, smiling like your apartment needed the extra heat. I spent 15 cents and took it with me to read on the streetcar home. After all, there were some provocative articles — "7 Ways To Increase Your Love Life," "Teen Age Sin-Clubs" and "Nudism Explained."

The Rose-Bud looked cold when I got back home. The place had been vacant all day. I walked around each of the bungalows and checked doors and windows. Everything secure. No one at home at the co-ed's. Both Kat and Audrey should be getting back from work soon, so there'll be some lights in a few windows, at least. I put on coffee and left my front door open to see who might be coming in. I made sure the lights were shining on all the bungalow porches.

Maybe Kat would be interested in dinner out. We could drive to the Santa Monica Pier and eat at the Tides where the waves wash in. We could come back, watch television, which Kat deeply understood. She had a set, a $200 Emerson she needed for work. I checked the paper, tonight's Channel 5 Feature Film was "Rocket Ship X-M," and "Mr. and Mrs. North" played before that at 9:30. "Mr. and Mrs. North" was a lift from "The Thin Man," but it had been a huge success on radio and a bright actor named Richard Denning had the lead in both the radio and TV versions.

We could . . . the phone rang. It was Kat.

"Hi, there! I've just been thinking about you."

"Really? That could be dangerous."

"How about dinner on the pier and 'Mr. and Mrs. North' on your Emerson?"

"I'd like to, really, George, but I can't. They want me to learn to floor-direct and the 'Pinky Tomlin Show' is on tonight at 9:00. I just wanted you to know so you wouldn't worry."

"'The Object of My Affection.'"

"Who?"

"Pinky Tomlin. It's his theme song." I hummed it on through "white to rosy red."

"Oh."

"Who did you think?"

"Sorry to miss dinner. I'll be home about 11. If your light is on I'll knock and say goodnight."

"See you then. Stay out of the way of rapidly moving cameras!"

"It's more like don't trip over the g. d. cables. 'Night."

KFAC offered a couple of unambitious programs of pops-concert and dinner music which played in the background as I poured some brandy into my coffee and thought about driving to Santa Barbara and seeing what the Coopers knew about the Church of Science Fiction. A drive-in burger sounded better. As I half-listened, an announcer broke through the line-up of movements from "The Planets" and Strauss Waltzes to advertise King Leo's, Eddie Haroot's Armenian Restaurant, on Ivar in Hollywood. If, as Sgt. Cummings hinted, Wispell was selling gold as well as music from Uranus, maybe he had some sort of deal with Eddie.

I heard footsteps on the walk outside and looked to see. It was

Audrey. I waved to her from my door. She waved back and went in hers. That was when I saw a low light moving behind the curtains in the Selz' bungalow.

Chapter 10

Rocket Shot to Moon Hinted Soon
Mars and Venus Also Potential Targets Projectiles Would Cause Nuclear Blast on Contact

I should have called the cops, but curiosity killed my best instincts. It was just eight o'clock and the radio moved on from pop to the Evening Concert and a Rossini Overture. It made good background music for a sneaky trip as out of sight as possible across the grass strip to Kat's porch and then past the co-eds and the Bobs. There was a steady glow in the bedroom where I'd found Charlie Vanpool.

I could pound on the front door and demand, "Who's there?" Since that might prove to be dangerous, I walked past the front and around to the side and the kitchen door. It was closed. Dark had pretty much settled around the Court. The three center lights on fluted poles came on, deepening the shadows.

I thought a good idea might be to go get my flashlight — the six-battery one that could make a worthy weapon, if needed. Then knock on the front. I moved between shadows down the Court and across to my open door. Rossini had become Mozart. When a car pulled up across the street I realized that however alone I felt, there was life going on all around. It was the *Mirror* photog Ken Adair and a woman I didn't recognize.

"Hey, George, meet Gina Simpson! We've got a session with Audrey tonight, swell, huh?"

Gina held out her hand and said, "I've heard a lot about you." A striking blonde with her figure emphasized by a low-cut silk dress.

I shook her hand and said, "Rumors."

"Hey, Audrey said you had a Nikon you never use. Get it out and get in on a shoot. She's really fun and a super model."

"Not tonight, but you have a good time. Nice to meet you, Gina. You're a photographer too?

"Oh, no. I'm the other model."

"Ah, well, have a swell evening."

Ken and Gina knocked and went into Audrey's bungalow, leaving the court still again. The Mozart symphony had become something with cellos by Villa Lobos that blended in with the traffic on the boulevards two blocks away. The pale light still glowed through the curtains of the Selz bungalow. I got my heavy flashlight and watched and waited.

Nothing happened. There were bursts of happy laughter next door and some flash-bulb flashes. After a while Peggy Lee was singing.

I walked boldly across to the Selz front door and knocked. "Who's in there?"

Silence. I knocked again. Silence. The light stayed on. Maybe something on a timer I don't know about? I unlocked the door and went in. Where the vodka box had been on a coffee table there was a pumpkin-shaped Japanese lantern. It was pretty, but it had no business being there.

"Hello?" In the bedroom, everything had been removed by the Murder Squad. The closet door stood open. I shined my light inside. Pale white stucco on two sides, cedar on the third. Empty.

The mattress was bare and shiny. It had seen some heavy use, I thought, and looked ready for replacement whenever I could rent the place again.

Under the bed? I'd written this scene already, but even so, getting down to shine the flash on the floor gave me a shiver. There was nothing, not even a dust ball. As I got up, I heard a scurrying behind the bungalow on my side of the scraggly fence that leaned against the twin garages on the alley side.

By the time I got around to the back, the scurryer was gone, but I could see where a panel of the fence was missing. Selz' bedroom window was almost directly across from the hole. Gotcha! Or I would have, had I known where to look in the first place. I went back inside, got the Japanese lantern, relocked the front door, and almost went home.

When I'd seen the lantern first I could swear it was moving, then it seemed to be in the bedroom. When I got inside it was in the living room. There was a way in and out that I hadn't found and somebody escaped through it just ahead of me.

Two garages fronted the alley behind the bungalows. The one behind Selz went with the unit. I had assumed it was for storage. The padlock on the door came loose in my hand. There was a car inside, a '50 Ford. The back wall had a few shelves and a large tin Coca-Cola sign mounted like an art-work. Sure! I poked around, found a small latch, poked it, and the sign pivoted away from the wall. Behind the sign, a door, which slid open to reveal the fence. The missing board was directly in front and I could see the bungalow window on the other side.

The secret. I couldn't wait to call Sgt. Cummings and get the fingerprint boys to work this place over. Whoever had been in the garage tonight got out too fast to secure the lock. I figured they wouldn't be back and hurried to get a spare and fasten the door with something I had the key for.

Villa-Lobos had bowed out, only to be replaced by Strauss, one of those heroic German pronouncements. I turned it down. There was a salami in the fridge and I cut some slices and ate them with more coffee-plus-brandy and listened. I was nervous about leaving the Rose-Bud nearly empty and unguarded. The Court stayed quiet for another half-hour, then Ken Adair popped up and knocked on my screen.

"Hey, Tirebiter! You still happening?"

"Sure. How was your evening?"

"Those are two beautiful babes, let me tell you! Say! That's mine!"

Ken burst in and picked up the *Scamp* magazine I'd brought home from Main Street. "I shot this one right next door! How did you know?"

"So your side job is girlie mags?"

"The *Mirror* pays me a few bucks, this crummy magazine pays me a few bucks. Actually, for the cover I got fifty. Not so bad. I put it together. Audrey's going to be a star, Tirebiter. I mean, her picture is going to be on every mag from *Sunshine and Health* to *Chicks and Chuckles*. So long as she's willing to pose, we'll both make money."

"That's show business. She does have an amazing smile."

"See-ductive, that's what. And her friend Gina — spectacular! You really missed something. But, say, this is what I wanted to mention to you. There's talk down at the paper that the Wispell murder has something to do with this other dead guy, Vanpool. Anything in it?"

"I think so. The cops have it that Wispell's about gangsters or money laundering or something. Maybe. I've still got some digging to do about Mr. Vanpool and the rest of the saucer people. Something very bizarre happened the other night down in Palm Springs. Say, here's something you can do for me — check the files for anything about a Church of Science Fiction."

"That's a laugh riot."

"I think it's a tax scam. Check Gideon Selz."

"Oh ho! I'll check 'em out. You get on to something, keep in touch, I'll bring a reporter down. Patty O'Duff. You'd like her. Tough for a news-hen."

"She was the one who bearded McCarthy in his lair, right?"

"That's her. You read the story? The real scoop is the Senator opened his room door in the all-together! Patty is unshockable! See ya!"

Adair left, Audrey's lights went out and the Court was silent except for the wind in the tall palm across the way and the neighborhood mocking bird, working on his encores. Maybe he could learn Ravel's Bolero, now playing. That'd be a sweet little trill to entertain Mrs. Mocker at midnight. I turned the radio up.

Kat was late coming home, which meant her boss would have to give her a lift from Hollywood. Still, it was late. Bolero buddle-de-bump-bump-bumped along until everybody had a piece of the action. It crashed to a close like a door slamming. It was a door slamming. Across the Court I could see Kat's bedroom light shining for a moment. Then it went out and she didn't. "See you in the morning, maybe," I said to myself. I decided I'd go to bed and worry about murder and mayhem and love and sex in the daytime.

※

Over the Sea a spinning light descends and picks us up delicately as a mother bird. I understand about the training to save Mankind. We have helmets and hundreds of contacts wired to our brains to allow the Aliens to do their training. I believe we must take the government into our own hands so the Aliens can give us council. We are free to communicate our Mission. We must leave this Planet Earth. How simple it is. I forget the hours of this voyage as soon as they have passed. I forget where I am and where I am not. I must concentrate on breathing to exist at all.

The blue crystal is back in my dream. Prepare the world for our arrival. Clothe yourself in smoke. Drift. I slip from my skin. The Mission is getting clearer. We will succeed. I am very powerful.

When I return I will fulfill the Plan. I will not remember who I am when I am nonexistent. I am where elephants stand on their heads and remember nothing. I am on the Moon.

Why does he come on to me like that? I shouldn't have to fight him off. I was angry. Cover my head with the pillow.

I wish she'd said good night. Wish I'd eaten dinner. Wish she'd kiss me good night tomorrow.

"One Hundred Proofs that the Earth is Not a Globe" was written by one Howard Bernard, A.B, M.A., Ph.D., printed by an outfit in West Virginia called Interplanetary Press. Maybe he was local. One Howard, three H.'s and one H.R. in the central directory. I called the first one first thing Saturday morning after a lousy night's sleep.

"Bernard residence."

"Hello, I'm calling for Dr. Howard Bernard, is he in?"

"Sorry, he's already left for the office. Shall I take a message?"

"Well, I could call him at the office, if you'd give me the number."

"Dr. Bernard is booked for the day."

"I see. Does he by any chance write books?"

"Dr. Bernard is a widely published authority on *pitirosporum ovale*. It's a fungus. Is it he whom you're looking for, sir?"

"Not unless he believes the Earth is flat."

"I'm sure he does not. Good morning, sir."

The third H. turned out to be Howard, who greeted me effusively when I said I'd read his book and was, er, challenged by his theories. "Well, well, well! How did you find me?"

"Actually I'm looking for Charlie Vanpool's brother-in-law. Is that you, sir?"

"Yes, indeed. Poor Charlie. We never saw much of him, Irene and I. The police asked about him and really, we couldn't help them at all. Charlie was pretty eccentric, you know."

"Sir, Charlie was found dead in one of my bungalows and I'm just trying to find out how he might have ended up here."

"I see. Well. I don't know how I can help you."

"Where did he work?"

"Now that's an easy one. He is, or was, a cook at an Armenian restaurant in Hollywood somewhere. Made a great shish kabob, Charlie did."

"King Leo's?"

"I think that's the place. Sorry he's gone. He was certainly eccentric. Irene and I always thought he smoked reefer, you know, like a jazz musician. Up in smoke! Wish I could help."

"You already have, Dr. Bernard. By the way, what do you doctor?"

"What do I . . . ? Very funny! I'm a CPA. I doctor the books! Do have a good day, sir."

The next call was to Sgt. Cummings who told me to expect his team to arrive in a couple of hours to investigate the garage and find the hidden entrance. I should give them the key or they would tear the hasp off the door.

I made coffee and thought about our bizarre experience with the Hydells. Kat and I hadn't even talked about it yet — where we went and if we were together and how we ended up at the motel. I sure didn't want to retrace my steps, but I'd like to see where hers had led. There was something about all three of the saucer people being small that made me think of a certain small window out of which something small must have been taken.

Suddenly, I knew what it was. Tape recordings — a life's work of them — packed in a deceptively large box in order to fool — somebody. Maybe just a handful. The two sisters could have done it. Did they wire up the furniture first?

And the Major wanted me to prove that one of the Others — Coopers, Baileys, whoever — had killed Wispell. He wanted me to believe my Court was being invaded by a Church of Science Fiction. The whole thing began to sound like Lord Buckley's version of the Crusades!

I watched as Kat came out of her bungalow, looked across at mine for a moment, then quickly left for the Hollywood bus. Something's the matter and maybe we should have dinner tonight. Maybe at the King Leo Café. I'd call her and make the date.

But what I really wanted was a copy of "From Saucers to You," Wispell's LP. One of the boys at Mixville Pictures had kept a copy for himself. I'd drive up there and borrow it. If they were writing a movie and scrounging an office to do it, I expect they'd be sleeping on the couch.

Actually, they weren't sleeping at all. A note on their office door said "At the Studio," which I took to mean the old Mack Sennett lot, much of which was still standing empty. This part of Los Angeles, just west of the old City limits, hilly, mostly barren, lightly populated at the turn of the 20th century, hosted several movie studios — Selig, Tom Mix's miniature Wild West called Mixville, and Keystone, where the Chaplin shorts were made. Edendale, the district was called, and it really was the birthplace of movie comedy, not that anybody in Hollywood cared a rap about day before yesterday.

Phil and Dave were just cleaning up after a dawn shoot. I caught up with them in a run-down corner where one of their girlfriend co-stars was supposed to be waking up after a night spent hiding from spooks in a vacant building. The girlfriend, Katie, looked awful, which had taken some doing. Maybe their little 16mm epic would land one or two of them real jobs in the industry. I tried to remember what a "real job" was, since it was all piece-work to me.

Phil and I drove back to their office and he retrieved the LP. I assured him that I'd return it safe and unscratched.

"The other rooms are still empty? Nobody's come back from the bus trip?"

"Nope. I hear the phone ring, that's all."

"Funny. I talked to Mr. Bailey yesterday. He had a script of mine somebody handed in as theirs. He was going to leave it with Andromeda."

"Nope."

"Good luck with the picture."

"Yeah, well, thanks. We're wrapping it up next week and we'll be out of here. I still want to check the space music out myself, so I wrote my phone number on the album, OK? Give me a call when you're done."

I took the "From Saucers to You" out of its sleeve when I got back to the Rose-Bud. The vinyl was blue. I put it down on the turntable, set it spinning and put a fresh Walco sapphire needle on the opening groove.

It started abruptly with a whistling tone. The spacy hissing of long-distance short-wave radio was a steady background, like a far-away waterfall or beehive. The whistle dropped in tone and became nearly musical. It stayed that way for a while before becoming two trumpeting pitches, high and low, speaking together like a man with a woman. Almost words. Exhorting. Instructions, maybe. I thought I heard "not ready." A barrage of muffled drum-beats or heart-beats and a clear bell-tone. This stuff is putting me right to sleep.

Every step you take is part of our plan to further progress. We know what is in your mind. Do not think of us as Gods. The Great Awakening is here! Remember, with a crystal miracles can be performed. You must be of one mind with us. Join us now. Join us or perish.

The needle was tracking around in the center groove. If the flip side was more of the same, the pit-band at the Follies was a big improvement, so I shut the turntable off. The Court was quiet. Very quiet. Too quiet.

How could that be when it was filled with extremely tall alien people with blue skin and what appeared to be eagerly displayed if strangely shaped sexual parts? These must be the Venusian nudists, booked through the Palmer Agency. Hello, friends. Earth welcomes you to the Rose-Bud. Why not settle here? I have so many free bungalows. Move in. Sorry about the low ceilings, ha ha!

The blue people vanished into each of the bungalows. Bugs Bunny popped from a hole in the lawn and said, "What's up, Doc?"

I must have slept for a second. The needle was tracking around at the center. I thought I'd turned it off. Lack of food and no water at all. Dehydrated, that's what the matter is.

I carefully removed the LP and returned it to the sleeve. *UFO's — Threat or Welcome Visitors? Listen and Make Up Your Mind.* Well, I guess it worked. I'd welcomed those Venusians in all right. Wow! What was that all about? Dreaming or passed out or something. La Glorieta Mexican Restaurant was two blocks away. I felt like I had a hangover that needed *huevos rancheros.*

Yesterday's *Mirror* lay as close to my porch as the bicyclist seemed to get it. Unfolded, the headlines proclaimed **BOY WATCHES DAD KILL MOM.** I folded it back again and left it behind.

The Death Squad was still busy in the garage when I returned and they'd opened an entrance in the back of the bungalow that led into that empty closet. Sgt. Quijalda took me aside.

"Look, Mr. Tirebiter, just between you and me, this tenant of yours must've known his bungalow was open for business."

"He might have, I certainly didn't. There was a director who had the place once, but that was before my time. Second-unit guy named Flax. Maybe he made some alterations."

"I'd say this place was used mostly in the Thirties. As a hideout, maybe. Maybe a little afternoon delight, midnight gambling. Weekend affair nobody could know about. There were semi-empty apartments like this all over L.A. I'm surprised there hadn't been murders here before."

"You'll seal it all up now, I hope."

"Sure, sure. Oh, and something you should know — it looks like Vanpool was brought to the apartment in that Ford. We're getting ready to haul it Downtown. You said whoever got away from you was going too fast to latch the garage door, right?"

"Either that or they wanted to lead me into it."

"Interesting angle. Should be quiet around here now, for a change, soon as we pack up."

I called the King Leo Café and made a reservation for 6:30 and hoped that Kat would come with me. I knew I shouldn't be too anxious about it when I called her at work.

"Hello, George. I'm really rushed . . ."

"Right, sure. Listen, dinner tonight in Hollywood? Armenian cuisine? I'll pick you up, OK? We do have things to catch up on."

"I have to talk to you, George, but not now. See you."

I wasn't sure if that was a yes on dinner or not, but I hoped it was.

CHAPTER II

U. S. PULPITS SLAP KINSEY

"ASPECTS OF SEXY DIME NOVELS SEEM TO BE INVOLVED," SAYS RABBI. DISAPPROVES OF "SWEET MORSEL" ASPECT OF MAKING CONFIDENTIAL INFORMATION PUBLIC

I was seeing blue Venusians everywhere. Well, not everywhere, but occasionally, every once in a while, out of the corner of my eye. They were big, like Harvey, the invisible pooka with Bugs Bunny ears.

Nope! None here! The Rose-Bud was empty. Kat's bungalow stared at me with downcast eyes as Tennyson might have said if he had been indulging in the pathetic fallacy. I certainly was.

The co-eds still hadn't come back from wherever they'd gone. Oceanside or La Jolla or Huntington Beach probably. The Bobs were apparently never to return, except to pick up their athletic wardrobe, which is about all they ever put on. Both bungalows were looking lost.

The former love-nest and safe-house appeared under construction. Maybe I could open it up as a curiosity, with a secret panel in the bedroom and a gift store in the garage. Call it the Church of Science (comma,) Fiction, ho ho ho! Punctuation is everything!

Mr. Wispell's brother should be along any day now, if he could book a trip from Salt Lake, he told me on the phone. There was hardly anything in his bungalow to pass along. Of course we took the stone and the crystal and they're both gone. "Saucer detector" Kat had called the crystal when it went off in Mecca. "TV prop!" But the fact was that the crystal did pull in some kind of frequency and start to amplify it. It was glowing when we left the ranch house and maybe it was picking up the vibrations of the saucer people who abducted us. If that's what happened.

The United Parcel man came with an armful of packages. Two were addressed to Mrs. Whitmer, one from Redeemer Universal

Supplements in Kansas City, which rattled like Vitamin C, the other from Harmony Products, West Covina, California, which looked like it contained a vibrator.

Audrey Gage's slightly larger box came from Frederick's of Hollywood. Something flimsy. A dozen pairs of black stockings, maybe. There was a box for Mr. O'Toole, from Archer Tobacco Products. A few ounces of his navy-cut.

And there was an envelope for me, from the Palmer Agency. The motherly secretary must have sent it, enclosing an 8x10 glossy photograph of the Coopers, looking for all the other-world like a pair of Baptist ministers sent to convert the benighted heathen Aliens. It took me a few moments to realize that I had given my name in German — Rieffenbissen — and that she shouldn't have known where to send the photo.

On the reverse, neatly written, was "You can contact the Coopers at HO 3-7373. They will be getting back to you on their return. Velma." Was that ominous or not? I needed a Bernard Herrmann underscore here to give me a hint.

I knocked on Audrey's door on the chance she'd be home. She opened it with a dazzling smile. "Hi, Mr. Tirebiter!"

"Just delivering a package, Miss Gage."

"Ooo! It's a baby-doll with feathers. Would you like to see something?"

"What have you got?"

"Come in." Audrey was wearing a modest yellow dress and her living room was pleasant, with a plant or two, square-cornered couch in rustic tweedy green with matching chair and ottoman, a Magnavox record player and a large, framed bullfight poster from Plaza Mexico. Arrayed on a cocktail table were a half-dozen black-and-white photographs of Audrey.

"These are all Ken's. What do you think?"

They certainly had the common touch. Audrey was posed kneeling on the living room floor by the phonograph, gazing warmly at a Sinatra album cover, and on her stomach on the couch, reading *LIFE*. In both she wore a silvery set of fairly modest underwear and an inquisitive smile. In two more she stood nonchalantly with one foot up on the ottoman, winking, wearing only tall black stockings. The last pair showed her in her dominatrix outfit, with the corset, whip and an evil grin.

"You look great," I said. "You're very photogenic."

"Thanks. I just like to take my clothes off. And I can make my little outfits, too. Ken's sold almost all of these, and he gives me a cut. These are for *Spank* and this one's for *Eyeful.* The really naked ones, those are sort of under-the-counter, I guess, 'cause you can't show pubic hair or you'll get busted. Isn't that crazy? Everybody's got it. I got a lot! Well, that's what you're missing on Tuesday nights, so get out that camera and join in. I only charge $5 a session."

"Maybe I will."

Audrey went from sweet to lustful to happy in a couple of seconds. "Hope so. Have a good Saturday, Mr. Tirebiter."

In order to think about something entirely different, I thought about Gideon Selz, who had told me he knew Charlie Vanpool. What a coincidence, sure . . . Charlie had been a recording engineer. But according to his Flat Earth brother-in-law he had been a cook at King Leo's. Most likely he was both. He wouldn't be dead now if he hadn't recorded something important or secret or both. I didn't suppose I'd find out much about Charlie at the restaurant, but it was handy to KTTV and I hoped the place had a quiet booth for whatever we needed to talk about, Kat and I.

Hollywood was busy with Saturday evening traffic. Lots of big movies playing on the Boulevard, José Greco would be flamenco dancing at the Bowl and, if you liked musicals, "Kismet," starring Alfred Drake, was premiering Downtown at the Philharmonic.

It was still early. I'd park near the restaurant and then walk over to the studio where they did "Hot Date." It seemed almost normal to see two very tall blue Venusians strolling down Ivar. No one seemed to notice them but me. Me, they noticed. Each seemed to be saying something like "breathe" or "swallow" or "you know what to do."

When I realized that couldn't have happened, I was in front of King Leo's. That night we were promised entertainment, Ali Rabab and Yasmina. I remembered their picture from the wall at the Palmer Agency. Authentic Middle Eastern Dance, direct from Fresno.

Kat wouldn't be off until 5:30. That gave me the rest of an hour. How about a beer at King Leo's bar?

The dining room had a grand mural of Armenian mountains and another of a dancing couple and a boy with a flag. The place was tile and brass heavy, but had its charm. Half a dozen people occupied stools at the bar. Dinner service didn't begin until 5:00. The barman looked like an old pro and most of the customers like regulars. He was chatting up an older couple, very well-dressed, before he got to me. King Leo offered Greek beer, so I ordered one.

"Can I ask you something?" I said, when he brought the bottle and glass.

"Everybody does. Something about Hollywood? Movie stars? John Carradine drops in before his show most nights."

"No, I'm good on local history, thanks. But you might know something about a fellow who used to work here? Charlie Vanpool?"

"Sure, Charlie? Wierdo. He cooked here sometimes, I guess you know. Haven't seen him in a couple of weeks. Why?"

"He was found dead in one of my rentals. Don't you read the papers?"

"Nah, not really. I got a daytime job too, so mainly I sleep. Sorry about him being dead. What happened?"

"The cops think he was murdered?"

"Holy cow! That weirdo?"

"He seems to have also had a job as a recording engineer someplace. Know anything about that?"

"Nah, not really."

"I thought I'd ask anyway. How's the food here?"

"It's . . . Armenian, I donno, lamb's real good. Check out the menu."

"I'm coming back for dinner later."

"OK, right. Say, I do know something. Wait a second."

The barman opened the cash register, rummaged in the back and came up with a card.

"This is him. His home number just in case, he said. It was months ago, but maybe."

Charlie had written his name and a Glendale phone number on the flip side of a business card from Record Magic on Figueroa St. The same place that pressed Wispell's vinyl albums.

"This is perfect! Thanks for your help."

"Poor cuss. He was weird, though. Always wore safari clothes, donno if he ever changed 'em, stayed up late he said, playin' checkers over the ham radio."

I finished the beer and set out for the studio.

Kat came out the stage door, saw me waiting and said, "Dinner? Close by?"

"A short walk. Mid-week blues? How's the show going?"

"It's not magic."

"I thought you were promoted to floor manager."

"Oh, boy."

"'Hot Date' is so silly, you wonder who watches it."

"Silly sells Lady Esther Skin Crème."

We walked a block or so silently, then Kat stopped and looked at me, "Strange things are going on, George. Ever since Mecca. I've tried to remember what happened before we woke up in the motel, but there's nothing there. And I'm hearing voices, or I think I am. About the blue crystal and the — the Mission. I have to know what happened."

We walked on. I didn't really know what had happened. Besides, Kat looked wonderful and I was thinking I'd say something about it.

"Is this it?"

"Right, we're here. King Leo's. I picked it because Charlie Vanpool worked here. Talked to the barman, got Charlie's card and now I know where else he worked — the studio that made Wispell's album."

The restaurant was as before, with a sprinkling of tables taken and the same regulars at the bar. I gave the barman a wave and he gave me an approving wink.

"What was that all about?"

"I think he approves of my date. So do I."

We ordered Manhattans and a plate of appetizers — grape leaves and cheese-stuffed pastries.

"Two things, George. No, maybe three or four things. First, tell me what happed to you in Mecca."

"It seemed as if I was abducted by aliens. Since that obviously couldn't happen, something else did. And I've been seeing blue Venusians in the street and they talk to me."

"Oh, God! What about?"

"The Mission, I guess. Same as you?"

"What the hell?"

"I think we were drugged, Kat. I think we got sacked on the doorstep of that ranch house and got hypnotized or mesmerized when we were under the drug. I think what we're seeing or hearing now is some sort of after-effect of the hypnosis. I mean, maybe these saucer-fanatics are trying to get us on board in another way."

"They want us to believe them. Maybe believe *in* them. What are we going to do?"

"Have another Manhattan, why don't we?"

"What about the Motel and your car outside?"

"I think someone rescued us, drove us there and tucked us in. Someone led me to the secret door in the garage. There are two factions in saucerville, which Vanpool explained to me — the believers and the de-bunkers. Somebody's on our side."

"So I shouldn't pay attention to blue Venusians?"

"You're seeing them too?"

"If that's what you say they are — about ten feet tall and, ah, naked, I think, if that's skin, and blue."

"I think they're here for the sex."

"That's what I thought."

The meal came- moussaka and a lamb and eggplant stew. Kat ate for a bit, then looked up and said, "Did you see the afternoon headlines?"

"Nope."

"The last of the POW's are going to be freed, including the ones the Koreans had in prison. It's really all over, I think, as far as my brother and my husband are concerned. I've known it all along, but Mother always keeps her hopes up." Long pause. "We only had two years."

"Two years can be a couple of lifetimes. Or, not nearly long enough." I was struggling. "Or, maybe too long."

Kat looked at me with a story behind her eyes she wasn't going to tell me. I wasn't going to ask. During the pause, Eddie Haroot appeared in the dining room, suited in a dark pinstripe and modestly hand-painted tie. He looked around, saw us, and his smile widened under his substantial nose and bushy moustache. In a moment he stood by our table.

"Mr. Tirebiter! Welcome to you and your beautiful companion. How is your dinner?"

We nodded approval. I introduced Mrs. Music.

"Madame, enchanted." He checked our plates. "Lamb and eggplant stew. Strictly Armenian! Excellent choice. Tell me, have you found Mr. Wispell's recording?"

"Yes — he had records pressed himself and they ended up with some saucer fans. I listened to one side. Put me to sleep."

"I'm glad I didn't speculate then. You like jazz, Madam?"

"Sometimes," Kat said.

"I have a new club in the Valley. Astor's. Ventura near Vineland. Jazz only. Chico Hamilton is playing. I'd like to book Lenny Bruce out there after his gig at Strip City is done. He deserves a little more class, don't you think?"

"A smarter crowd would help," I said.

"Ah! That reminds me to tell you something. Mr. Wispell wanted a wide distribution of his record and I explained that a jazz label such as mine has only a small market. Smart but small. He said to me that everyone has to hear this recording because it will change their lives. Really, I said, how do you know? And he said, the saucer people told me so. I said, try Folkways."

"Thanks, Mr. Haroot. That's actually very helpful."

"Happy to be of service. Remember, Astor's on Ventura. The jazz is top rate. An honor, Mrs. Music." He bowed and left us.

"That's interesting. Leads me to think there *is* a message in all that random sound. May have put me to sleep, but maybe that's the point. How about we go back and I'll put the record on and we can see what happens. Some kind of hypnosis? I'll watch out for you and you watch out for me. Nick and Nora on the trail for clues! What a team!"

Now there was another long pause. Then a long sigh. Kat reached out and laid her hand on mine.

"I can't . . . Oh, George. I really, really do like you so much, and . . . this is so nice. You cook for me and take me to dinner and the Bowl and Mecca and Outer Space. But I think you want a relationship I can't have right now. Right? You do. I can see it in your eyes."

"Straight into the soul, they say. Oh, I would like that relationship very much, Kat. I really am head-over-heels."

"Look, let me tell you something else. I am being heavily pursued by Johnny Bennett and he's my boss. We're doing 'Hot Date' in Vegas next week and there's only the two of us going, the rest of the crew is local. He would like it to make it more than a business trip, and I don't . . . I don't know why I'm telling you this. Sorry."

"No Nick and Nora?"

"No Mr. and Mrs. North."

"I thought we were making a great team. Intergalactic sleuths."

"This Vegas weekend is going to end up with me sleeping with Johnny. It's not the first time, George. Probably not the last. Sorry, sorry. I know what you're thinking."

"I'm thinking rosewater pudding."

I ordered dessert as the belly-dance performance began. Kat looked at me with arched brows. I shrugged. There was an oud player and a drummer and before long the dancer shimmied out, sequined, veiled, and worked the room. We ate the pudding with two spoons. How could Johnny compete with romance à la Tirebiter? On the other hand, how could Tirebiter keep pushing romance with Johnny on the spot?

Yasmina was collecting dollars in her girdle on her last tour around the room. She gave us a special "date night" belly-roll. I tucked in a buck. She winked at us. I smiled back even though I didn't feel like smiling.

On the way home to the Rose-Bud, Kat said, "I'm dealing with one thing at a time, George. Bear with me. We can still have fun, I hope. We're still friends, I hope."

"Tell you what. Will you kiss me goodnight?"

"I'll do that. And then please go home."

The kiss was worth waiting for and it went on for a long time. I think we both realized we probably shouldn't have done it, but it had been coming along for weeks, anyway. Kat said good night quickly and firmly, yawned extravagantly, unlocked her door, went inside and turned on the light. I was halfway across the Court when she screamed.

I was there in a second. Kat grabbed me when I met her at the door. "Oh God oh God oh God . . . !"

Sitting like a large stuffed animal in her comfy armchair was Major Hydell, late of Rancho Tres Palmas. He was open-eyed and dead and like Charlie Vanpool appeared untouched by human hands.

Chapter 12

All GI POW's to Be Freed
Includes Criminals and Men Convicted of Germ Warfare Seven Southland GI's Freed by Reds Today

"At least there's no secret passageway this time. The kitchen door is open and the lock's been jimmied. Don't touch anything, Kat!"

"Not the way I expected this evening to end."

"Let's go back to my bungalow and I'll call the cops. You can stay there, obviously. Take what you need."

Kat grabbed some things from the bathroom and a small bag from under her bed. "It's my overnighter. You never know. This is really awful, George, and — thanks. Let's go!"

The Rose-Bud bungalows were dark, the mocking bird silent, the distant boulevard traffic steady on a Saturday night.

"I'll go in first, just in case."

The living room was empty, at least of visitors, aliens and/or murderers. I checked the bedroom, bathroom, kitchen and the kitchen door. Nothing out of order.

Kat was shaking. "Why are they doing this to us? What's that man doing in my house? What the hell?"

"I don't know. Why kill him and dump him here? Why your place and not mine? It does seem like Wispell and Vanpool and Major Hydell were playing on one side together. The other side must be killing them."

"The other side of what?"

"Maybe the Church of Science Fiction is the other side, like Hydell claimed. That takes us back to Selz and the Coopers and that strange crowd."

"Are you going to call your cop friend?"

"I seem to be the major source of employment for the Death Squad. They love me down at the station house. Sure, I'm going to call."

"Is that the Space Music record?"

Kat pointed to Wispell's album jacket that I'd stood by the phonograph.

"Yep."

"Did you play it?"

"Only one side. Didn't I tell you?"

"Why don't you play it?"

"You mean now?"

"Why not now?"

"I've got to call Sgt. Cummings and report a murder. Or a strange death or whatever this is. You want to hear it?"

"I think we should."

I put the record on the turntable, set it spinning and put the needle down. There was the ham-radio hiss, the whistle, the conversation between high and low tones.

"Won't be on next week's Hit Parade," I said.

"Shhh."

There were the drumbeats and then the bell rang.

"I remember this," said Kat and closed her eyes.

I thought I'd better call in to the police and get the investigation rolling and solve the murders and get rid of Johnny Bennett and lie down.

Kat flies with me for an infinite while over a blue planet. There's nothing to be frightened of she says as she vanishes into a flaming sunset bank of cloud. I see that an Alien guides me into the spinning vehicle where I can rest and prepare to receive instructions. These are the Visitors and they wish to rid us of atomic weapons. I will be a leader, readying the world to awake to these Teachers and bring the people to them so that we all may join in the Oneness. I feel a stimulation that surges toward it.

The Voice says I can help them, the Visitors, I can find them and show them to the world, I can make Believers of many, I can present

miracles to Witness. I have Power to bring people to the Oneness. I feel a stimulation that surges toward it.

I am before the Conclave. The Coopers are enthroned and washed in pearly light. The Baileys bring me forward. The Coopers speak together. They say we are One now. We are at Home now. Together we will serve the Star Beings.

Because I am a woman I can serve best. I have the power of the orgasm. I will know when to use it in service of the Visitors. I am ready for the next Instructions.

I am ready for the next Instructions. The other side of the record. Instructions on the flip side. Turn it over. That's easy. That's the easiest thing.

"George?"
I thought she could help me. Help me turn over the record, Kat.
"George!
The needle is going around in the center of the record. Don't you hear that? We need to lift it off and then turn the record over.
"George! For heaven's sake look at me!"
"I need to turn the record over, Kat."
"No! Stop! Look at me!"
I did, finally. She was beautiful. She was scared.
"What just happened?"
"We were listening to the saucer record," I said.
"We were having the same dream." She closed her eyes.
"Maybe. We you just abducted?"
"They want me to work for them." Her eyes still closed.
"You mean, put them on television?"

"Maybe. Just don't turn the damn thing over. That's what they really want. It's some kind of hypnosis. Oh, God! Did you ever call the police?"

"I don't think so. Wait a second, Kat. Did we really see a dead Major sitting in your living room?"

"I sure as hell did!"

"I'm not so sure. And I'm going to check."

The Major was still occupying the best seat in the house. Everything was as it had been before. There was no reason not to call in to Sgt. Cummings. How he'd love this one!

The Death Squad was about its business most of the rest of the night. I put Kat to bed in my room, made coffee for anybody who might need it and made a statement to a sleepy young officer. The Sergeant would be around in the morning, I was assured, as the Major's body was carted off. This time I hoped he'd believe that flying saucers are real.

The coffee wore off about 3:30 in the morning. I shut the front door against the murmur of police coming and going and stretched out on the couch. The record album cover, with its amateurish Alien oasis painting stared at me from where it leaned against the hi-fi speaker. I got up and looked at it more closely. It was a signed original! "A. Selz '53" was lettered on a little plaque in the corner. "Abigail" ya think?

The blue vinyl disk made every effort to jump out of the sleeve and onto the turntable. I resisted and slipped it in between records on the shelf below the hi-fi. Right between Beethoven's 5th and Stravinsky's "Rite of Spring." Two heavyweights to hold it down and keep it from working its potent magic while I slept. Which, gratefully, I did.

It was Sunday, a workday for Kat, doing double duty on "Hot Date!" and the new quiz show that I was supposed to audition for on Monday. She got up early and quietly, dressed out of her weekender bag and put on the coffeepot.

"Morning, George. How did it go last night?"

"Good morning, Kat. Your place is sealed, I'm afraid, at least for a couple of days. You can stay here. I'll move into Wispell's."

"There's my mother's."

"Too far. Look, Kat, things'll be better. I won't tell you I'm in love with you every time I see you, OK?"

"Don't."

"You still want to live at the Rose-Bud?"

"I'm not sure, especially now. Look, coffee's made and I'm going to catch the bus. You'll be OK?"

"I guess so. I'll stick my head in the sand of writing and try to invent something for the Smartee Boys. Or, I've got an idea for a movie about a space-pilot who's been gone so long on a voyage to — I don't know — Planet X — that when he comes back to Earth nobody remembers him or cares what he did."

"That's got possibilities. I'll call you later. Don't forget about the audition — tomorrow at 12:30."

"Can't wait."

"You'll be very good and it's a steady job."

"Thank you, Kat."

"Oh, George!" She gave me a very brief kiss on the cheek and left.

Cummings rolled in at 9:30. He looked at me and shook his head. "Shall we just move the morgue over here, Tirebiter? Lot less drivin'. And yer coffee's better."

"I know for sure who this guy is, Sergeant. He's a Major Hydell. We met him at a place called Rancho Tres Palmas down in Mecca, near Indio. He's married to an Effie Hydell. They lured me down there and tried to convince me that a cult called the Church of Science Fiction was taking over the Rose-Bud Court. And maybe that's true. Take a look at this!"

I pulled the LP from its classical prison and handed it to him. He looked at both sides. "This is a joke, right?"

"I think if you've been properly prepared, and by that I mean drugged with some jungle potion, listening to this record will put you into a hypnotic spell. I think it's a recruiting tool for the Science Fiction Church thing."

"Wispell recorded this crap, excuse my French?"

"So it says. I think Vanpool was in on it and the both of them were cancelled out. Major Hydell must have known too much, so he had to go too."

"Why here?"

"Gideon Selz. Have you spoken to him?"

"Gave a statement to the P.S. Sheriff. Just larkin' around in the sunshine, he said, don't know anything about saucers or secret doors."

"He's behind this, I'm sure of it."

"Somebody's behind three murders and the Chief is goin' stark ravin' that I don't have a suspect."

"Don't you?"

"I'm workin' on it. Stay home, Tirebiter. No outta-town joy-rides. Say, does anybody live here anymore?"

"The ones that do seem to have gone away for the weekend. Mrs. Music is staying here and I'm going to camp next door at Wispell's. The young woman in 627-and-a-half works at the Auto Club. The murders don't seem to have ruffled her feathers at all."

"Yeah, we talked to her. Gave me to understand she was a religious-type person and spent her time serving the under-privileged."

"Harmless."

"Good lookin'."

"Town's fulla good-lookers."

"So they say. The Riverside County Sheriffs have been informed about this Rancho and they will contact the relatives. They will regret the death of Major Whatsisface, but they will also find out something out about the Church and the saucers and the hypnosis and the three dead bodies! I'm goin' down there today and question 'em myself!"

"Get some sun."

"That'd be a laugh. There's a man on this place for whatever good it'll do."

"And while you're down there, look out for an old yellow school bus full of saucer people. One of them just might be the murderer you're looking for. It's probably parked by the lake-shore waiting for the Aliens to show up."

"Are you hustlin' me?"

"I'm only trying to help, Sergeant. Only trying to help."

Cummings was still shaking his head as he walked out the door. I followed along and caught the screen before it slammed.

Great!, I thought. L.A.P.D.'s own "Mask of Death" cop is on the job with the nut-bars at last. The answers to this case are down in the Valley of the Saucers, if only he can pick his way among the crazies and grab onto the one who's not.

The LP, which Sgt. Cummings had left on the table, needed to be hidden away again because of the way it sirened me. I could hear the plunk of strings and palm fronds rustling and the song of the almond-eyed Alien set to the rippling of water. Side Two wanted to be played so the song would continue . . .

I forced the damn thing back into the record-stack and the song faded away. Compulsion! It was unnerving to be yanked so easily into — into a cult. Into the Church of Science Fiction.

The phone rang. It was Phil, who let me know that the school bus had returned and was parked in the lot. Nobody in the New Age offices yet, but he thought I should hear about the bus.

"We're done here," Phil said. "Got a garage on Alvarado Street we can convert into an editing office for a while. Are you finished with the record yet?"

"Not yet. I've only heard one side. Can I hold onto it for a little longer?"

"Sure, that's fine. My number's on the back."

I hung up thinking it's most likely that this record is going to end up as evidence. And I wasn't going to listen to Side Two. The phone rang again.

"Hey, Tirebiter! Ken Adair! Listen, you mind if I drop in with Patty O'Duff tomorrow? She's gonna do a feature on the place and she thinks you're the main interview, right? Couldn't hurt. And listen, that Selz character? Writes movie music? That what he told ya? Lotta b.s. so far as I can tell. Well, see ya sometime tomorrow mornin'!"

More Press. Just what the Rose-Bud needed. Maybe I should turn the whole place into a haunted house, corpses everywhere! Every day is Halloween! Don't be scared! It's only Cap'n O'Toole, the Stinkin' Pirate! There lurks The Crazy Lady! See her eat raw yogurt! The Insane Painter! He lives on Jupiter! Have your foto taken with our own gorgeous Nudist Model! Meet Me In Person! Postcards available!

There was a half-cup of coffee left in the pot and I poured it into my cup and would have gone to sit on my porch but the phone rang again. Busy Sunday!

"Mr. T., Shifty. Here's the thing. Mr P.'s sayin' 'I need a drive,' and you know that means he wants ta meet ya in the parkin' lot by the Culver Hotel. Make it soon, 'cause he's got about a hundred itches ya need ta scratch. OK? OK!"

Pingo was waiting for me in the donut van he sometimes drove around in. The lot was otherwise empty, but he pulled the hood of his jacket around his face for the few feet between the van's door and my Mercedes. I'd kept the top up, which is mostly how he liked it, at least when we were in the city.

"Tirebiter, good," he said. "P.C.H. north, OK, swell."

Traffic was light on the way to Santa Monica and Sunday beach-goers would wait until the overcast lifted, so the highway was open.

"Things. I've been thinkin' about the next big thing. Drivin' me outta my house! What about this door Shifty told ya about? Anything to it?"

ROOSEVELT HIGHWAY AND BEACH SANTA MONICA, CAL. 554

Pacific Coast Highway way back when

"The one I know about is really a sort of dada art-work."

"If it's art I can buy it."

"Well, Mr. Pingo, the thing is that the door exists but nothing else does. Or else it's just empty doorways going nowhere."

"Would kids like it?"

"I suppose so. Until they got tired of it."

"Artist make anything else besides the door?"

"He mostly finds things. In the future, maybe artists will only find things lying around and make poems out of them."

"Um, poetry. Donno about that. Keep drivin'."

It was a pretty day for a drive. Between Pingo's bursts of words, I thought about Kat. She looked wonderful in the morning, wearing my bathrobe.

"See that murder-trial wire-recorder? Front page. Size a pack a Camels. Dick Tracy. Wrist radio, see? Changes everything, you can carry it around. It's gonna happen with this rock 'n' roll bomb and we conquer the Universe, you get that dontcha?"

Zuma Beach opened out to the Pacific and a light surf. Catalina and the Channel Islands gave the impression that California refused to end and that its desertscape continued on beyond the blue horizon.

"Howja like to own a radio station, Tirebiter? Know anything about FM?"

"Inventor named Armstrong. Short broadcast reach but a very clear signal with no static. Aren't many people doing it. Everything's all wired up by phone lines and the big AM's — you can hear them for five hundred miles. What's the point?"

"Yeah, well, what's the point, what's the point? Own a radio station makes you a rich man. Makes you a rich man if you own the right one, see what I mean? FM. No competition. Next big thing maybe. Get in on it."

We rolled through Ventura.

"I got my eye on you, Tirebiter. What's with the murders at your place? What the hell?"

"The cops are working on it, Mr. Pingo. It's got something to do with flying saucers. Bad publicity for the Rose-Bud."

"You crazy? No bad publicity. You could maybe run for City Council or somebody. You gotta get outta this Rose-Bud rut, get back to bein' a star. You'd look good in politics. We could use ya!"

The very tiny beach town of La Conchita was a mile or so ahead.

"Let's get some fried clams up there. You can take the top down. You know who's the murderer yet? I hear because I hear things. Shifty hears things. They add up. Small fry add up to Mr. Big. What do ya think, Tirebiter? Mass hallucination? What if ya could hallucinate everybody? Maybe TV, maybe that'd do it. Could be as easy as teachin' your canary to sing."

We pulled into the wide spot under the bluff that was La Conchita and found the Clam Shack. What if that's it? Hallucinate everybody!

I ordered and waited while the owner, a broad guy with the look and Southern Pacific logo tattoo of a retired railroad worker, plunged it into the hot fat.

First thing through this part of the coast was the railroad. Before that the bluffs just slumped down into the sea. The rails and the highway hadn't stopped the slumping yet.

A late-model Buick pulled into the lot and parked a couple of slots away from the Mercedes. The couple inside I recognized immediately — the Coopers, no doubt on their way back to L.A. from their performance in Santa Barbara. Bill Cooper, looking very astral, got out and walked up to the counter. He nodded. I nodded back.

"You look familiar," he said.

"Maybe from the saucer convention. I attended your wife's presentation. Fascinating."

"Yes, our experiences have been both fascinating and life-changing." He pulled something from under his shirt and showed it to me. "Souvenir."

The blue Venusian served up my order. Another one. They *are* everywhere. Cooper was looking at me curiously, the shiny medal reflecting the sun into my eyes.

"Yeah, well. Nice running into you. Gotta take my clams now."

"Certainly. We could meet any time. Any time at all."

I turned back to my car and felt his eyes on me, and from the front seat of his Buick, Mrs. Cooper watched me and smiled a thin smile. I didn't like turning my back on them, but I did, and handed over the clams. Mr. Pingo took one, dipped it in ketchup, ate it and said, "Don't like them."

"The clams?"

"Them. In the Buick."

"They're in this murder thing up to their lousy haircuts."

"Go back to Culver. I gotta talk to Shifty."

Cooper watched as I backed the Mercedes out, turned and drove toward the highway. In his hand he held up his shiny pendant. It winked fiercely in my rear-view mirror.

Mr. Pingo was silent, mostly, on the way back to the parking lot in Culver City. He spoke three oracular statements in the way he was prone to do: "Buy Dada." "Run for President." "Saucers, Go Home!" Between each oracle he thought, almost audibly, before pronouncing his wisdom. When I dropped him off at the donut truck he said, "Inspiring drive. I trust you, George, trust your ears. But don't trust your eyes. Don't. I'll call."

I put the car away behind the Rose-Bud and walked around to stand in the entry and look at the bungalows. All's quiet at the Spook House.

As I walked up the steps, my door opened in front of me. There stood the Old Prospector, bushy-haired, grizzly-bearded, tailored in coveralls. He smiled like a carnival freak show barker and said:

"Well, well, 'bout time ya got home! C'mon in! Got some outta this world recordin's I'd like ya ta hear!"

CHAPTER 13

MAFIA TERRORISTS HELD IN L.A. PLOT

$1,000,000 SHAKEDOWN CHARGED HOODLUMS INCLUDE JIMMY (THE WEASEL) FRATIANNO

What some people believe! What spell creates a suspension of disbelief so profound as to merge with madness? Why was my living room occupied by dancing blue Venusians? Music was playing from my hi-fi. Side Two.

"Great ta finally meetcha, Tirebiter! That radio show you had? Funny stuff! Not workin' much anymore, eh? That's show-biz, yes sir! How ya feelin'?"

I feel as if the roof has faded off my bungalow and galaxies of stars are rushing by in clouds of Metrocolor bursts.

"Bon voyage!"

Knocking at my door. The Venusians stop dancing and stare. Knocking. My door opens.

"My God, George! What in hell is going on?"

"I'm losing my mind."

"Join us, young lady! Join right in! Welcome to the Church of Science Fiction!"

Yes, I understand, the Plan is to get you on TV. The saucer-people represent the Universe and the message of the Planetary Conclave must reach America before the Aliens destroy us. The Ambassadors will care for us after the Church is established. To join this Church we must take the Sacrament which opens the Universe to us. Here's the number to call . . .

They've got Kat! That's nice, we can travel together. She's home from work just in time. The blue Venusians like to dance and see? Kat's with one and they're spinning at 33-and-a-third just like the record on the turntable. I'll cut in, that's easy. The Venusian is an It. In the future all earth beings will be Its. Only by breeding with an It can we keep America great. Welcome to the party, Kat! Remember Fred and Ginger . . .

I can use my Power to get your story to everyone. Sex is everything. I can use that. I understand. We'll take a meeting. Hello, George, imagine seeing you here! It's my job and you may not like it, you especially won't like it. I don't think we can do this together. Maybe later. Nightmares, I don't want them. Mike and Dale blown to pieces so the pieces can't be found and they've vanished. Just boys. Stupid boys. Over and over, the nightmare circles around me like a silent creature waiting to attack, waiting to blow me to pieces. I can't dance, George, don't make me . . .

The last time the Venusians came to visit, I gave them the Rose-Bud. There's one of them in each bungalow now. Moved in and made themselves comfortable. I'll keep it that way. No sense in renting the places out if they're occupied. Spook House or Church? High Priest or Ghoul?

Priestess. Goddess, even. This is a million-dollar deal! Here's the numbers to call! Buy one now, Rotomoto-head-spinner with new energizing drink inside! No lines, no waiting, slavery is only a swallow away! Say hello to today's guests!

A big door in the Universe opens and the astral bodies of Bill and Alice Cooper drop in, wreathed in white roses. What's not to like?

Roses? The Rose-Bud has a radio tower. The police didn't haul that away. Pingo told me to get into FM. Easy as A-B-C. Alien Broadcasting Co. Deliver the Message. Rent to Church members. The others will have to go. Intergalactic Headquarters of the Church of Science Fiction right here! It's a Miracle!

I love these new people. White roses. I should work for them. They've got the right connections. Both of them have mated with the Aliens. We all must mate with the Aliens and give birth to the New Human Order. Poor George. Here he is and he wants the Impossible Me . . .

It's a deal . . .

When we wake up we won't remember anything but we will act upon what we have learned . . .

I woke up with my head on my dining room table. My typewriter was in front of me. On a piece of yellow paper rolled up in it for me to see was typed: "Sales Agreement: I, George Tirebiter, agree to convey the property known as the Rose-Bud Bungalows to the Church of Science Fiction for the sum of one dollar." There was a line for me to sign. I hadn't signed.

Kat lay on the couch, wearing my bathrobe, asleep. We'd both been drugged again or — can they do this? — triggered into the same drugged state. Kitchen clock said 8:17. Must still be Sunday night. The place was empty, of course. No evidence that anyone had stopped by to recruit us to an Alien cause.

I looked outside, heard the mocking bird brushing up on his act. There were lights at Audrey's, and the co-eds seemed to have returned too.

"George?" Kat's voice from behind me, suspicious.

"How are you feeling, Kat?"

"How did I get here?"

"You came through my front door and the Venusians grabbed you. Don't you remember?"

"It wasn't you that grabbed me?"

"Unfortunately, no."

"Why," she said, sitting up and suddenly aware, "am I naked and wearing your bathrobe?"

"I don't know. Don't you remember?"

"This is stupid!" She got up and stalked into the bedroom. "My clothes are in here," she said. "This is weird, George."

"I don't know what happened to you, but I think I just about sold the Rose-Bud to the Church of Science Fiction."

"You didn't really?"

"I don't think so. Anyway, we were drugged."

There was a long silence from the bedroom, then, "I may have had sex with one of the Venusians."

"Do you remember doing that?"

"It's not that I remember, it's that I kind of know it happened. I can sort of feel it."

Kat reappeared, dressed in her working-girl outfit. "You know, George, it might be fun to really do that para-normal show we thought up as a cover story. Great place to start, right here. Bring in the camera crew, find those Cooper people and whoever else might be available, let them talk about the flying saucer congregation, it'd be good entertainment."

"A *Mirror* reporter is coming by tomorrow."

"That's a start. Don't forget the audition. Twelve-thirty. Your call is eleven for make-up. You can read over the prompter copy then."

"What did you mean, about sex with a Venusian? There are no such things. I know, I saw them too, but they're illusions! Were you — were you molested?"

"I think I was admired and absorbed, George. That's all I can say. I'll see you tomorrow."

"Remember, Kat, you can't get back into your bungalow. You were going to stay here and I'll move next door."

"See you tomorrow."

With that, and no smile, Kat left. She had been absorbed, alright. Something in her sweet face was gone. Whatever had happened, and I remembered some of it, when we traveled together, I could feel a matter-of-fact part of my mind holding on to the knowledge that there are no Aliens, no saucers, just this drug-induced illusion that almost bought me out for a buck. Hold on to that thought.

I saw that the saucer album was gone. The disk was off the turntable and it wasn't in with the other records. So much for evidence. There was my unsigned bill-of-sale, but I could have done that as a joke, so far as Sgt. Cummings would be concerned.

I made coffee and realized I'd never eaten. After I drank a cup I figured it was nine o'clock on a Sunday night and no place local was open. A car stopped in front of the bungalows. Someone else must be home at last! I looked out to see who. I was pretty sure the nice Lincoln that pulled away was Johnny Bennett's. Well, of course, Kat hadn't eaten all day either.

There was a diner that I liked, Simon's, out West on Wilshire Blvd., so I drove there and had time to think. Mr. Pingo said I ought to get into FM broadcasting, own a station.

The saucer-people want a voice, like a few other churches around town. Maybe some sort of FM station could broadcast using Mr. Wispell's antenna. All they'd have to do is put on the hypnotic album, invite in the curious, dose them somehow with the outer-space chemical and they'd become followers. Followers of a freak-show barker who could sell you a ticket to see the Alien Pin-heads and of the Astral Couple who run the show and appear and disappear like cotton candy.

They killed Wispell for his antenna. No one would really notice if it got modified to broadcast the Alien Gospel. What's more, none of those saucer people knew enough about it to wire up the rig to electrocute the poor guy. That might point to Charlie Vanpool.

Charlie had acted innocent as baby food. He told me he'd expected Wispell to show up at the convention with some damning information about the saucer cult and especially about the Coopers. That was before I knew he had probably recorded the Cooper's hypnosis LP.

One murder solved, maybe. Two more to go. Sgt. Cummings won't tell me what the coroner found, but it must have been some sort of heart-stopping poison. Or drug.

Before I knew it, the Simon's Classic Burger With Salad and Fries was gone. I padded dinner out with apple pie à la mode. Better late than not at all, I thought. Traffic was thinning along Wilshire's Miracle Mile. Stores closed, no mastodons hulking around in the La Brea Tar Pits. Time to go home to the Rose-Bud, put my head under the pillow and figure out how to evict a party of Venusians before they evicted me.

Only Audrey's lights were on, and mine, which I'd left blazing. No more visitors. Only one. Sgt. Cummings rose from my porch and put out his cigarette.

"'Bout time. I been here maybe twenty minutes. You and me keep damn funny hours. Thought I'd have a cup a coffee and have a little chat, since maybe you've been right about this thing from the beginnin'."

I made the coffee. Cummings looked at the unsigned bill-of-sale and shook his head. I'd gotten used to the head-shaking, which had a whole vocabulary of its own. This one seemed to mean I was back to being a nut-bar.

"That Rancho you met the dead so-called Major at? Nobody there at all. Owner lives in Palm Beach, house is closed for the Summer. Hired hands take care a the dates. Wha'dya think?"

"I think I — we — were lured down there so that we could be dosed up with whatever drug they're using to indoctrinate true believers. At the time, I thought those three — the Major, his wife, Kaawi — were part of the de-bunkers, trying to expose the Church of Science Fiction as a fraud."

"They're all nut-bars in it together."

"I'll tell you, Sergeant, I think we were given something in the gin-and-tonic that immediately appeared when we arrived. We figured something was off and tried to leave in a hurry, but we were lifted into Space before we cleared the porch. I think they took us down to the lakeshore just in time for a mass hallucination."

"You're right about the campin' place on Salton Sea. Lotsa saucer-people out there every week, waitin' for a sight. All bunco. Tried to track the Major down. No trace on him in the Armed Forces of the U. S. of A. The wife? Quit her job at the Oasis Café after workin' there a week. The other one? Nobody in the area remembers a midget or a dwarf, if that's what this Kaawi is."

"I don't know that she's either. Small, though. All three were pretty small."

"Gotta bulletin out on the two women. Major's in the morgue. You say the Doc should check on some kind of overdose, like with H?"

"I'm sure that's the cause. Believe me, Sergeant, I have been under that stuff, whatever it is, and it'd scare most people to death. You're wide-open to suggestion. They almost got me to sign this place away, but maybe they haven't figured out the right dosage yet. They do know it kills people."

"So far, so good."

"Here's farther. Late this afternoon, when I came home from a little drive up the PCH, I was met at the door — my door! — by Mr. Bailey, from New Age publishing. He goes around looking like an Old Prospector. I came inside — no choice — and this room was filled with dancing blue Venusians. Mrs. Music arrived some time later — I can't remember — and they got her, too. We woke up maybe a couple of hours after that. Nobody here, the note in my typewriter."

"I'd like to have a talk with Mrs. Music about what she saw, like Aliens for instance."

"I'm not sure she wants to talk about it. Anyway, she's not at the Rose-Bud. I think she may have decided on a hotel. She works tomorrow at KTTV. So do I, come to think of it."

"You think Vanpool killed Wispell?"

"He probably had the technical skills."

"Why?"

"He recorded, or was in on the production of that record album I showed you, which the Old Prospector stole, by the way. Since they want to sell the thing as really coming from outer-space saucer-people, it helps not to leave the guys who know better alive — Wispell and Vanpool."

"Tell ya somethin' about Vanpool. Reefer-head."

"That's what I hear."

"Ya hear he's a big-time connection in the jazz trade, the burly-Q trade around town?"

"I thought he was a part-time cook."

"That's it. He worked at Haroot's dinner joint. Haroot owns a jazz club. He's got a piece a Strip City. I'm not sayin' Haroot ain't a straight businessman, just there usta be lot a reefer in town, especially around his places and things've gone dry since Vanpool got laid out."

"Anything else you can tell me, Sergeant?"

"Paid a call on your Mr. Gideon Selz on the way back here, up above the Springs in the glass house with the view. Just him there, in and out of the pool, great tan, offered me a drink, I didn't take it, he said how sorry he was about how his nice little apartment here was gettin' torn up. Lookin' forward to movin' back in, he said. I said, it needs some fixer-uppin' since we found the secret entrance. He didn't seem surprised at that, said it'd been there since the place was built. Movie stars used ta use it. Told me a dirty story about 'Jack' Barrymore. I s'ppose he meant John."

There were more ghosts resident at the Rose-Bud than I ever imagined. I was doing my imagining at the Witching Hour, wide-awake and feeling fine. Two years before, when I bought the Court from Oliver Tulley with what I had left over from my divorce, he'd given me a file of documents concerning the place. I was imagining that now was the time to see if there was anything there that might reveal the original construction plans and the secret entrance, if it had in fact always been there.

I had kept Oliver's stuff in a hatbox with tax records, birth certificate, Social Security card — that kind of thing — under the bed. It looked untouched by Venusian tentacles.

There were more papers in the file than I had remembered, some poking helter-skelter out of three grimy oak-tag folders. I began laying them out on the kitchen table.

Graylow & Pitcairn were the architects, back in 1927. A nice little wash drawing of the Court was included, to show what it would look like when built, along with a general ground plan. As far as I could see, these are the cottages I know. Original owner, said the plan, was Desmond deMonde, a cross-dressing silent film and vaudeville performer best known for his version of "Carmen."

A blueprint of the back half of the Court had been folded in quarters and was crispy along the edges. I opened it up as carefully as possible. Bungalow 7 was there, along with its opposite counterpart, Number 4 and the rear two-bedroom units. The plan showed an inked-in "Houdini Hatch" at the rear of Number 7, linking the building with the garage. An arrow pointed to the back wall of the rear units and, inked-in, "existing wall."

The numbering must have been before the post-office insisted on fractions. Counting left-to-right, Number 7 was the Selz bungalow.

There were a bunch of news-clippings in a folder with "Goldwin Studios" printed on the front. **ANOTHER SENSATIONAL MURDER!** hailed the top one. "Hollywood, already scandalized by a series of deaths due to drugs and alcohol, has another. Desmond deMonde slain by jealous husband in frenzy over wife's infidelity." The murder had happened at this address, Apartment 7.

The next clipping was headlined **BANK ROBBERY SUSPECT CAUGHT IN PAL'S HOME.** It was 1934 by now, and the new owner, interviewed for this story, was another faded actor, Gordon W. Maxwell, who played the occasional meek bartender or desk-clerk on Poverty Row. The robbery suspect, who was caught with the cash in a bag, hiding under Maxwell's bed, was his "good friend," Butch Vincent, a "hoodlum well known to the authorities." Maxwell, who lived in Number 7, said he knew nothing about the theft.

In 1943 another clipping proclaimed **SÉANCE DENOUNCED AS FRAUD.** A Mrs. Shelly Hartle complained that she had been parted from one hundred dollars of her savings by a self-described "medium," known as "Madame Arcadia," who conducted her business at this address, apartment 7. "Mr. Hartle never showed up or spoke to me," Mrs. Hartle complained to a *Mirror* reporter.

The last of the crumbly, deeply-tanned pulp-paper clippings said, **RED SPY CAPTURED.** It was in 1947. The spy's name was Conrad Rich and he was reportedly sending secrets to the Kremlin that he had uncovered in his job as a statistician with the Department of Agriculture. Of course, he was arrested in his bungalow, Number 7.

It was obvious that Number 7 had long been a place with secrets and that the secret entrance, which could have been used for endless unseen comings and goings, had been there almost from the beginning.

In a clutch of random items, there was a snapshot from the 40's, with the Levy's posed beneath what looked like the brand-new wrought-iron "Rose-Bud" arch over the front entrance. They were holding hands and smiling.

A small handbill advertised "Spiritualism, Ouija, Palms, Crystal Orb Science From Madame Arcadia, No Appointment Necessary." There were business cards from a plumber, a window-washing concern, a veterinarian and two different gardeners.

Finally, a black-and-white postcard photograph of a deep, almost formal garden, a fountain half-way back and a couple of weeping willows bent over a stone bench set against a six-foot brick wall at the rear. On the back was gracefully written "our garden across the street." Under that, in a much sterner hand, "sold 1925 for development."

The last folder contained the bill-of-sale for a lot "previously in use as a vegetable garden plot opposite 628 30th St, Los Angeles." The seller was Mrs. Albert Montrose. The buyer was Emil Selz. It was clear the Rose-Bud Court now occupied the former garden of the aged Victorian with the three-story cupola right across the street.

And just who was Emil Selz?

In the light of Monday dawn, which came on pretty strong, with gusty down-canyon winds, I rubbed my eyes and sat up from the couch. Coffee was important, but the first thing on my mind was Emil Selz, who owned the land, but apparently not the Court. Given the date of sale in 1925, Gideon would have been in his mid-twenties. Emil could easily have been his father.

As a matter of fact, Desmond deMonde may never have really owned the Court, but fronted for Selz after it was built. Perhaps the same was true for Maxwell. Bungalow Number 7 allowed the selected residents to have their very private lives and eventually son Gideon took it over. Now he wants the whole place.

I carried the cup of coffee I'd made and stood outside looking at my own private little neighborhood. It was a nightmare. Mrs. Whitmer ought to be back today, maybe the co-eds would show up. Kat's door was firmly padlocked. I wondered if she would ever come back and gasped with a sense of loss that surprised me. Maybe I'd never see her again after today's audition which, I was convinced, was set up by Johnny Bennett to make me uncomfortable in front of her. Which, I determined, wasn't going to happen.

"Mornin', Mr. Tirebiter!"

The Court was almost the first stop for the U. S. Mail and our regular carrier was Mr. Ballard, who'd been on the job since before the war.

"Tell me something, Mr. Ballard."

"What's that, sir?"

"The people who owned the house across the street, before it turned into student housing, do you remember their name?"

"Sure. Montrose. Mrs. Albert Montrose. She used to own a lot of rental properties along University Street. Her husband passed away sometime in the Thirties. He was a watchmaker, I think, anyway she was very well off. Got checks regular from a mining company in Idaho, Sawtooth Metals. Passed about five years ago."

"She used to own this property too. It was a formal garden back when that monster across the street was in style."

"Sorry to say, before my time. I started delivering about when Mr. Oliver Tulley moved in here. Your place."

"Who else?"

"Lived here? Shoot, let me think. Mrs. Whitmer's been here since Methuselah was a pup, I guess. Mr. O'Toole too. Couple a actors, kinda fay, know what I mean? Mr. Selz came in soon after I started on this route. Across the way from you, a County Sheriff lived there a long time. Sheriff Jim Brisket. Got a lotta mail, he did. Stamp collector maybe. Envelopes and packages from all over the world. Students usually in the other bungalows. They don't stay long. Say, this one's for you. You have a good day now."

The envelope was from Andromeda at New Age Books. It contained my purloined manuscript and a note written on Palmer Productions stationary: "We will waive our usual fee to speak at your Church event. For a dramatic offering, we suggest an outdoor program at the Rose-Bud bungalow court tomorrow evening, when we can promise celestial fireworks. We will arrive promptly at 6:30 with our books, refreshments and slide show. I hope your entire congregation will attend. Thank you for the opportunity. The Coopers."

"Good Lord!" as Capt. Hastings says with amazement at least once in every Hercule Poirot novel. I believe the spiders are building their web for us flies.

OK, I thought. Let's pit the forces of weirdness and evil against our own free spirits. They'd drugged me, but they hadn't killed me or convinced me to sell them the Court. I'd wanted all my tenants, all my neighbors, to have a happy home here, each in his or her own way. Some fact eluded me. Something hidden. Behind a wall.

A brick wall? The blueprint I found had been marked with the "Houdini" door and the "existing wall." That wall was now mostly hidden behind the alley garages on the outside and long since incorporated into the two rear bungalows, which were actually one architectural unit, on the inside. What was it about "existing wall" that meant as much as "Houdini" door to be noted on a blueprint?

I speculated on that question until the phone rang.

"Hey, Tirebiter, Ken Adair. Look, Patty's got this human interest with the boy that his dad killed his Mom and then himself in front of him. Horrible. Kid's right where Patty wants him for the story. So, look, let's make this thing happen tomorrow, if that's OK. OK?"

"You bet, Ken. It may be a much better story tomorrow anyway. Come early, stay late, the Church of Science Fiction is having a party."

"Who's that? Doesn't matter, party's a party. Tuesday? Be there around six. Mind if I bring a friend?"

"Not at all. Lots of room."

"OK, well, see ya then!"

Chapter 14

Oh Boy! We're Back at That Good Old "Time for Beany" Time!
KTTV – That Good-Looking Channel Eleven!

I sat in the makeup chair in one of a warren of assorted backstage rooms, housing, separately, the Santa Monica City College Jazz Band, three boys from ditto and three girls from Fullerton J.C., plus the host's "star" dressing room, a Green Room and production offices. Beyond, lay the small auditorium stage, set for "Hot Date!"

Things were on a break after what seemed to have been a messy run-through. I'd found my way to makeup without seeing Kat and introduced myself to Milton, who lavished me with pancake. "Were you here?" he asked.

"For what?"

"Big explosion on the floor. Writers called back in, all four of 'em. Garnett hated his jokes. Tad Garnett. He's the M.C., you know that. You watch this show, Mr. Tirebiter?"

"I don't own a TV. That's why I'm auditioning to be a TV host."

It took a second. Milton snorted and said, "You're from radio, right?"

"Yep. No makeup required, except for photo shoots when I had to be aged for my character, who had twenty-five years on me."

"Lotta talented radio people on TV now. 'Course all the top radio series are marchin' right on to TV every year. All the junk too, ya ask me."

"You know anything about 'What's My Name?'"

"In the line-up for the two o'clock slot, replacing 'Chef Milani.' You up for that?"

"Since it was arranged for me, I'll give it my best voice."

"Well, you sure have a different personality than the other guy!"

"Who's the other guy?"

"Real card named Bob Carney. Came early. Friend of one of the producers. Well, you're done here. Haffta wait until lunch break is over now."

Bob Carney! I sat back in my comfortable seat and drank a cup of studio coffee — always on, always slightly burnt. I looked at myself — nice suit, nice tie, neat moustache and haircut. Behind me I saw a John Lund-lookalike come in with a smile as genial as he could make it. His hand was out.

"George! Great to meet you at last! Kat sings your praises. Johnny Bennett. I'm the producer."

I swung around to meet his fake smile with one of my own. "I hear you've had some star-trouble this morning, Johnny. Hope it's settled."

"Sure. These 'Hot Date!' shows are always a little crazy. Tad wants to keep up with funny headline stuff for his monologue. Can't blame the man. Otherwise the show's mainly hormone-driven teenagers ogling each other. So, Kat's working with Tad and the writers on a few new lines. Thing is not to come off as a parent-type, but still get the best answers back from the kids. Oh, yeah! This is your audition script. It's all on the prompter except for the first couple of pages. We'll rehearse once after this break and shoot right after that. Gotta finish tomorrow's 'Date' show, ya know. The winners are going to Las Vegas, have dinner, see Sinatra. I get to go chaperone with Kat. Perks of the job. Well, see ya on the set. Gonna be lots of fun!"

Long speech, nervously delivered by a real s.o.b., that's how much fun I was having. Johnny gave me a parting thumbs-up and left me with Milton, who poured me more coffee.

"They got something goin' on today, too. Johnny and Kat Music. Usually, they're heads-together on the show and, really, she does all the kid-wrangling. Been on opposite sides of the stage all morning. Maybe they've got something goin' and it ain't goin' today. Studio gossip, pay no attention."

"I'll just read the script, Milton. Maybe I'll read it as if I was Bob Carney!"

The M.C. (me) is to enter through the curtains, blindfolded, walk exactly six steps to the front of the stage and demand an answer to the question, "What's My Name?" The audience, trained in advance, will yell back "George Tirebiter!"

Then I say, "How right you are, ladies and gentlemen out there in our studio audience. I can't see you, but you can see me, and that's the way our little question-and-answer show is going to go today, with musical clues from Ralph Day on the Wurlitzer. Fortunately, Ralph can see!" (Little laugh here.)

"Our blindfolded contestants are dressed as famous historical figures and each will have to guess who the other is inside a two-minute time-limit! The winner goes on to the next round and the victor of the final round takes home one hundred dollars! Welcome please our first pair of colorful characters and remember, absolutely no hints about their identities from the audience!"

Then the M.C. (me) "whips off his mask," shushes the audience and brings on a pair of bozos dressed as George Washington and Charles Lindbergh. They weren't actually going to be at the audition, which would now be over. My entire script may have been on the teleprompter, but I was going to have to memorize it.

A production assistant came by and asked, "Mr. Tirebiter? Fifteen minutes."

"Shall I put the blindfold on you now?" Milton held out a folded black handkerchief with white question-marks printed on it where the eyeballs ought to be.

"After I read this stuff through a couple of times."

"Right. I'll follow you out and do it before you go on."

"Great. Oh, hi, there. Yes?"

"Mr. Tirebiter! I'm so sorry, so, so sorry! I'm Jim Drake, I direct 'Hot Date!' and now this audition piece for 'What's My Name,' which they really just threw at me. So . . ."

He paged through his notes.

"You're supposed to have organ theme music, but we don't have one on this show, so Marcy, my assistant, is hunting up a library cue that'll bring you out. You're walking into Camera 2. Six steps. I'm next to it. I'll throw you a hand signal . . ."

"I'm blindfolded."

"Right, but you start behind the curtain. Somebody taps you at the right moment, out you go. Six steps straight out. Camera 1 to your left is on the house when they yell 'George Tirebiter.' You quarter-turn right to 3 after 'Ralph can see.' You're on 3 until 'five hundred dollars', then turn to your left, to Camera 1 for the rest of the script, then, when you take your mask off with a big flourish you're back on 2. That's the one in the middle, remember?"

"We'll both do our best, Jim."

"Oh, and I hope you don't mind but I'm doing Bob Carney first. He's got a job to go to I guess."

"He sure does. Strip City. Western at Pico."

"Well. Old time comedy. Have fun out there, Mr. Tirebiter. It'll be all over in a few minutes."

I wasn't worried. It was only junk TV. It wasn't going to elect a President. Not for sixty-three years.

I listened to the rehearsal of Carney's version of the Text. First, the music cue came. I recognized it — Major Sound Effects, Big Quiz Show Opens, Vol. 1. There was a fanfare that led into a few transitional bars — Question — then a splash chord — Answer — then it faded out and another cue, Bouncy-Silly Number 5, faded over it and would stay under until the bit was over.

Carny came on doing the sly fox in "Pinocchio" — Honest John Worthington. "What's My Name?" he boomed. Since there was no audience, the crew boomed back. I could hear Kat's voice loud and clear.

The sly fox ran through the material quickly and with oodles of oil. The actual take followed almost immediately. A scattering of applause, murmurs of thanks and Bob came cheerfully out the stage door.

"Say, damn, George. we run inta' each other in the damndest places! Who're you followin' this time?"

"You, Bob."

"I heard that. Piece o' cake. Go kill 'em!" He marched off to the john down the hall.

"Ready for you now, sir," said the production assistant. That was the way Kat had started, like the p.a., doing things for the important men, keeping her eyes down, like a Saharan wife, until the Christmas party and as much as you can drink, cutie-pie.

The curtain that was the standing set's backdrop was my entrance point. Milton had the blindfold, the p.a. held one side of the curtain, ready to pull it aside.

"Rehearsal!" A beat. I was ready. The fanfare struck. Can't wait too long. Go!

Take six steps, lift those invisible eyebrows! Smile that oh-if-it-were-only patented smile. I had decided I'd do my best Steve Allen impression and whip on my own black-rimmed glasses to replace the blindfold.

I got through my lines with a few seemingly (and actually) improvised moments, delivering a somewhat better product than the one I'd been given to read.

"Thank you, George," said Jim Drake, standing in front of me, back of the big studio camera. "Let's take this so we can kill the lights for twenty minutes and feed those kids some pizza. Places, please."

"Just a second, Jim." It was Johnny Bennett from the booth. "I think drop that glasses bit at the end. Makes you look like Steve Allen. Don't need it. Want another rehearsal?"

"Let's just do it."

"Happy to oblige."

"This is a take. Places, everybody."

Why don't I just make like I really don't know the answer to the question? So instead of six lonely steps into Camera 2, I entered at the top of the fanfare to gain a few seconds and looked blindly around, stepped a drunken couple of steps sidewise. Looked around, still blindly, and made an imploring, prayerful gesture, gazed upwards and dropped to my knees, hoping one of the three cameras would be on me.

"What's my name? Can anybody help me?" I pleaded, voice breaking.

There was some choking laughter from the crew and haw-haws from whoever was in the audience seats. A few voices, Kat not among them, hailed back "George Tirebiter!" I rose to my feet. "How right you are, ladies and gentlemen." Sincere, but building up to "five hundred dollars." I clapped my own hands to get the applause going for the uninvited guests, whipped off my blindfold as directed, gestured wide to both sides of the stage and bought on, from the right Mrs. Kat Music. She stepped forward a couple of paces, gave me a brief smile and nod and retreated into the wing. From the other side, the John Lund look-alike came forward.

"That's it, folks, take twenty. Swell job, Jim. That was funny stuff, George, that unrehearsed shit at the top. Big surprise. 'What's

My Name' is not a comedy show, just plain old give-away for housewives, you know that, right? We caught the rehearsal, so I can show the Veeps the Steve Allen version if we like it better. You look great on the tube."

"You saw my face for five seconds."

"Looked great."

"Is Kat around? Like to say thanks."

"She's getting pizza, sorry. For the teen lover boys and girls. You want to stay, there's probably enough to go around."

I thought, I hate you, John Lund look-alike. The real Lund was currently co-staring with Ricardo Montalban in "Latin Lover," both of them eating their hearts out for Lana Turner. Lund looses Lana. Lund not star material.

"I can see she's got a lot to do. Thanks for the opportunity. Good luck with the program. Both programs. I don't have a TV set, so I won't be watching any of them."

Good enough comeback? What the hell.

I got out with my makeup still intact, found my car in the studio lot and had it wheeled around to leave when I saw Kat coming in, driving a Lincoln. I pulled up next to her and we rolled down our windows.

"Why did you do that, George?"

"Because it just came over me, Kat. Sorry. You tried, but you were trying to convince your boyfriend about how wonderful another man was. He doesn't like me. I don't like him either. MGM's Technicolor threesome we are — Lund and Montalban and you make an adorable Lana."

"Don't."

"Tomorrow night, big L.A. premiere at the Rose-Bud! The Church of Science Fiction in a 3-D outdoor saucer-service! All your favorite Venusians will be there. Hope you might show up too."

"Are you kidding?"

"The game's afoot. Maybe a-tenticle."

I didn't know what more to say, so I looked straight ahead, drove out of the lot, and thought that I might never look back.

But I returned to the Rose-Bud instead. The Court was quiet. On my door was tacked a small sheet of cop's notebook paper: "Call me. Cummings, Badge #3412" was penciled on it. I did.

"Tirebiter! For a man who's supposed to be poundin' a typewriter, you spend a lotta time outta town!"

"I was only over in Hollywood. What's up, Sergeant?"

"Got some info you might help me deal with."

"Well, I have the same for you."

"Coffee?"

"Good to the last drop."

"Save me a cup."

I made coffee, but popped the cap off a bottle of beer for myself, turned the radio on, sat at the table and looked over the old Rose-Bud files and clippings. KFAC stopped the music to advertise "King Leo's Armenia" with its "succulent lamb kabobs" and moved on to a Slavic kabob of "Polovtsian Dances" and "Pictures at an Exhibition."

I wondered about Sawtooth Metals, somewhere in Idaho. Was it still in business? Long Distance in Boise gave me the answer, yes, if it was now known as STM and had an office on State Street. She rang me through.

"STM, good afternoon, who did you wish to speak to?"

"My name is George Tirebiter. Do you have an employee there who might be a historian of your company? It used to be called Sawtooth Minerals, I think."

"That was back in the 1930s. You are?"

"I'm a writer, doing some research about gold mining back in the early days. Also, I believe you had some interesting characters among your founders."

"Sure did. But look, your name, you said George Tirebiter? Didn't you have a radio show back in the 1940s? 'Hollywood Madhouse'? My parents loved it!"

"That's me."

"You sound much younger than I remember."

"That's because I did the character like this," I said in my own voice and then, "For heaven's sake, Lillie! What are the Bulgarian jugglers doing in the living room?" in the Old Man Voice.

"That's him. That's you?"

"Believe it or not."

"I'm Janet. Say, I know who you should talk to and I'm sure he was a fan of your show — Mr. Austin. He's retired, but still keeps his office here and he's in today. I'll see if he can take your call."

The long-distance dollars sped along in silence. Then Mr. Austin connected.

"Mr. Tirebiter. Paul Austin here, how can I help you?"

"I live in Los Angeles, actually on a property that was once owned by Albert Montrose. How might he have been connected to Sawtooth Metals?"

"One of the founders. Stake-holder in the first strike. Sad story about him, though, very sad. He was accused of embezzling a small fortune from the company but died suddenly before he could be put on trial. The gold he stole, if he stole it, was never recovered. Left his Sawtooth shares to his widow."

"Did a man named Emil Selz work at Sawtooth?"

"Name's familiar."

"How did Montrose die?"

"Heart attack. Fell off his roof."

"Well, Mr. Austin, thank you. It's all very interesting."

"I remember something about your Emil Selz. Metallurgist. Checked out test-bores, probably, back when Sawtooth Number 3 out near Gimlet was opening. Picture of Selz and Montrose at the mine in 1933 has been on the memory wall in the board room forever."

"You're a gold mine of information, sir. Thanks again."

"Always wondered what happened to the money he stole."

"Maybe I can find out."

"You find it, you can keep it. It's nothing to me. Goodbye, Mr. Tirebiter. Or should I say 'Max Morgan'?"

"You heard that show? Glad somebody did."

"It was good fun. Those radio-program days are over, I suppose."

"True. Thanks again."

I tried to add two and two together for the next few minutes. Both twos refused to line up. Sgt. Cummings' arrival saved me from add-itional confusion. He settled in with a fresh cup and opened up his note pad.

"There was a murder here after all. Checked the morgue a little deeper. Swish actor named Desmond deMonde, you can believe that!

Got whitewashed by the studio to protect their investment. Killed by jealous lover. No wife involved."

"Seems like more than one of these bungalows was home to homosexuals back in the day. Probably felt safe here."

"Also, you know about an unsolved murder across the street?"

"I know Albert Montrose fell off the roof."

"Got put out it was an accident. D.A. was about to indict on a grand theft charge, wham! Montrose hits the back terrace. Couldn't prove it was murder, but everything pointed that way."

"Here's one for you, Sergeant. I think Emil Selz — Gideon's father — was the original owner of the Rose-Bud. He was a business associate of Montrose. Bought the lot right after Montrose died, then had the Court built a year or so later."

"Anything illegal in that?"

"No, but there might be something else going on. Check the blueprint, where it says 'existing wall'."

I passed the blueprint across. Cummings pointed.

"Houdini Hatch! That's a hoot! So what's it about this wall?"

"It's the original wall from the old garden, see? Goes all the way across the property. Still does. It, or most of it, is part of the rear wall of the back cottages. What do you think?"

"Possible Emil Selz disposed of Montrose to gain control of this property, that what you think?"

"Why would he do that?"

"Money Montrose stole coulda been in cash. They never found it."

"Could have been in gold."

"Brother!"

"Could still be hidden here."

"Talkin' about gold, I told ya we were lookin' inta Wispell's denture business? When you caught me sittin' in his lab I about had it figured out. You look close at those teeth you can tell they aren't solid gold. Not heavy enough. He was skimmin' a gram or so every ounce."

"Could he have been melting down old coins?"

"Hadda melt somethin' to make a gold tooth. This gonna be your treasure map, Tirebiter?"

"I think so, Sergeant. However, tomorrow evening everything may be different. Assorted nut-bars will be assembling in the courtyard out there to hear about saucers from two famous abductees, the

Coopers, who promise — who knows what they promise? It might be a good time for your forces to show up and keep an eye out."

"Wouldn't miss it."

Mrs. Witmer's sister dropped her off about four. She had her overnight case and a large grocery bag with "Queen For A Day" printed on it. I took both of the bags and carried them to her door. She didn't say a word until we got there, then there came a torrent.

"I'm just speechless. I am. I've never had such a good time! Jack Bailey came right up with his microphone and asked what my name was and where I lived and I said the Rose-Bud and everybody laughed. He said that must smell sweet and that he had a gift for me and look!"

She pulled two tins of Kraft Malted Milk from her grocery bag. Underneath was a cardboard box containing, apparently, a Dishmaster Deluxe, "World's fastest dishwasher," the package exclaimed.

"Oh, Mr. Tirebiter, you never heard such sad stories. I have no troubles at all compared to them. There was one woman who lost her train tickets and was stuck in Los Angeles with her crippled nephew. The other one had to have an emergency lobotomy or something and the one that won, she never did have a birthday party in her life and she was going to be seventy-two, so she was voted Queen For A Day on the applause meter and Jack Bailey was going to take her to dinner at Trader Vic's and then to a show — 'John Brown's Body' with Tyrone Power! She cried and the audience sang Happy Birthday. Oh, I'm so glad I went! Now I want to take some vitamins and just rest for a week!"

"It's good to have you back, Mrs. Whitmer. That prize you got, the dishwasher thing?"

"Oh, I hardly have any dishes. I'm giving it to my daughter, but I jut wanted to look at it for awhile, it's so modern and Mr. Bailey called me Rosebud!"

She picked up her bags and smiled goodbye.

A few minutes later, Audrey came into the Court and waved. I waved back. She did one of her quick-change looks, from girlish cheer to South Seas passion and back in a second.

Jack Bailey awards another Dishmaster (the blond's a prop)

"I might get a job in New York," she said.

"New York! What for?"

"Modeling. Ken showed some of my pictures off to a publisher back there. He liked them a lot and Ken said the man wished I lived there in Brooklyn and he'd use me every day. Movies, even, possibly."

"Maybe you can just work long-distance."

"Ken said he likes to personally direct the models. He's into spanking and girl-wrestling besides the nudey stuff. I don't know. It'd be a big move."

"We'd hate to lose you. Those of us who are left."

"Is anybody coming back to the empty places?"

"As soon as the police investigation is finished and I get the repairs done, I'll put them up for rent again. Get things back to normal."

"It's a little sad this way. Oh! You can cheer up tomorrow with the Camera Club! They want a lingerie shoot and I have that new baby-doll with the feathers, and a transparent shortie one too, like a Petty Girl. They're bringing a special strobe light."

I thought, should I tell her about tomorrow's Saucer Church Service? No, better to let all the Camera Clubbers loose on the UFOs when they land.

"I'll see, Audrey. I may have company tomorrow night."

She gave me a blazing pout, then grinned.

"Hope you're having a nice evening, Mr. Tirebiter. I'm going to make some macaroni and cheese."

Chapter 15

Fancy Meeting You Here . . .
Adlai Stevenson, Defeated Democratic Nominee, Gives President Eisenhower Report on World Tour
"Every American Responds to His President's Requests."

I got to thinking about the Sheriff that used to live across the way, the one who got mail from all over the world. Funny that a County law-and-order officer could be living in the same place as men who could be destroyed if their sexual lives were revealed. Where did he go?

Mrs. Whitmer's lights were on, so I thought it was OK to knock on her door. She answered, clutching a cotton wrapper printed with wild strawberries around her.

"Sorry to disturb you, Mrs. Whitmer."

"I wasn't really napping yet, Mr. Tirebiter. Is there some difficulty?"

"Just a question. Do you remember the fellow who lived down front — a Sheriff Brisket?"

"Oh, yes. I recall he moved out very suddenly. Ten years ago, I think."

"Did you know him at all?"

"Only to nod to. I think he must have worked at night, mostly. He had his Sheriff's car parked out on the street during the day. I suppose he was catching up on his forty winks."

"I heard he got a lot of international mail."

"If he did, he didn't share the stamps with me, and I used to collect them for a nephew who liked stamps, but then he liked baseball cards better."

"Well, thanks. I was just wondering."

"He was friends with Mr. Selz."

"He was? When?"

"They spent a lot of time visiting each other on the weekends. It was soon after Mr. Selz took the bungalow over from a boy who told me he was a set-dresser, whatever that is, and he hadn't lived there long."

"Brisket moved out suddenly, you say?"

"Right after that nice Mr. Tully purchased the Rose-Bud from the Levy's. I believe he joined the Navy."

I heard my telephone ringing and took my leave. When I picked it up, the voice on the other end slid sideways.

"It's Kaawi. I thought you'd never answer."

"Telephone demands it. Jobs, lovers, lawyers, bad news, good news, clues, mysteries. They're all on the other end. That's where you are. What the hell is going on, Kaawi?"

"I saved your skin, you and the Music woman, you should be grateful."

"You've been around a lot, Kaawi. Around the Rose-Bud. One question. Did you drop us off at the motel in Palm Springs?"

"Mr. Bailey said he needed both of you alive and well to advance the cause of the Church, so, yes, I put the two of you in bed together. Thought you'd like it that way."

"You work for the Bailey's."

"We all do. Did. The Major was poisoned by Aliens 'cause he knew too much about the research in Arizona. Mr. Bailey said it would get the Church on TV if they found him in the Court."

"Was Mr. Vanpool poisoned by Aliens too?"

"That's what Mrs. Bailey told me. They mean for it to be a Church sacrament if you only take a little sip, like Communion. Mr. Vanpool wanted more because of the visions."

"Did you steal tape recordings from a box sent to Mr. Wispell?"

"How did you know?"

"You're small enough to get in and out of the bathroom window. The box was big, but the contents little and light. You must've been waiting for him when he brought the box in."

"You don't think I could have killed him, do you? I am a person of the Light! I wanted to talk to him about what was going on, so I sneaked in and hid in the bedroom. I was about to come out and say hello when I heard the electricity. He had gone to eternity, I could see that. I knew Mr. Bailey wanted the recordings, so I picked up the box and carried it into the bedroom. Then you came in and went out and locked the door."

"So you had five minutes to collapse the box, remove the contents and shove them both, and yourself, through the window before anyone thought to look behind the bungalow."

"I had help."

"Who? Your sister?"

"Effie? She's not my sister. She's Mrs. Bailey's secretary. No, it was Sidney Carton. He has keys to the whole Court, or did, liked to burgle little things sometimes. Rearrange things to spook people. Nasty sometimes."

"Sidney have another name?"

"If he does, I don't know it. He wants to write science-fiction and stuff about saucers. Does favors for the Baileys."

"Why are you telling me this?"

"You're having the Church service there tomorrow night, aren't you? You need to know that none of us are murderers. The two bodies were simply settled right there where they'd be the most comfortable. As for the rest, live in the Light."

Kaawi slid sideways off the phone. Good news — none of 'em is a murderer!

Albert Bailey, no matter how Old Prospector he appears, is the con-man behind the Church of Science Fiction and with his various publishing enterprises looks to profit nicely from it. Only half-thinking, half drugged, I'd done just what he wanted — let the Rose-Bud become Church headquarters, at least for tomorrow night. All my bungalows suddenly home to strangely-sexed blue Venusians. Why here?

The phone rang and rang again. Now what?

"Hello, George," Kat said. "I missed our after-work chats. I thought I'd call. How are you? Are you writing?"

"Kat. Thanks, fine. I'm waiting for the saucers to land."

"I thought I saw a blue Venusian on the bus. Big blue Alien who wasn't there. It wasn't there again today."

"That's good. The stuff will wear off, eventually, I hope."

"Sorry to be mad at you about the audition. I know you didn't want to do it. You made fun of it and Johnny takes everything so seriously. Nobody knew what to say afterwards. Bob Carney was in the audience and laughed his head off, though, and it really was funny, what you did."

"Spur of the moment. I told you."

"He's not my boyfriend."

"No?"

"You said I was trying to convince my boyfriend how wonderful you are. Johnny's not my boyfriend."

"I thought you were going off to Vegas with him tomorrow."

"I am. I have to. Separate rooms at the Sands."

"Are you going to come back?"

"Well, I can't until the police unlock my door. Will you talk to the Sergeant and get him to let me in early tomorrow so I can change my clothes? There may be a Frock Sale at Bullock's, but I can afford only so many frocks, even at two dollars off."

"I think I can manage that."

"My call is noon, so sometime before then."

"I meant, are you going to come back to live here again? You'll have to get a new comfy chair, but otherwise . . . unless you're spooked by the place. I guess I wouldn't blame you."

"The Rose-Bud is perfect for where I am in the business right now. My bungalow has been perfect and you've been the perfect landlord and the perfect Nick to my fledgling Nora. I'm not perfect. If I was . . ."

"If you move back in, you'll still be living across the walk from me. Are you thinking that would be tough?"

"It might be. Probably. Hard to go back to my bed alone at night after you've gone all-out to romance me. Literally take me to the Moon. Then leave you to say goodnight at the door with those shiny eyes batting at me."

"Am I that bad?"

"You're wonderful. That's the problem. Lonely writer meets ambitious woman. Ambitious woman wants nothing in her way between now and the Network job that puts her in the same room with the men. Lonely writer doesn't even own a TV."

"I guess I better get one so I can follow your upward career trajectory."

"That was mean."

"Sorry. Snarky to a fault. Coming tomorrow night for the Church of Science Fiction's Old Time Alien Revival?"

"We leave for Vegas with the kids after the broadcast, so, no, I can't."

"Well, then, I'll see you sometime after ten so you can pack. I promise not to bat my shiny eyes."

"Goodnight, George."

"Goodnight, Gracie."

We hung up. My damn shiny eyes were batting like crazy. It was really going to be an awful thing, to say goodbye.

It was early morning the First of September, though in L.A. you mostly can't tell. Two weeks before Mr. Wispell was meeting his maker on an otherwise peaceful, if steamy, afternoon. Mr. Tirebiter's neighborhood seemed then as if it would stay the same way forever, with all its varied characters cheerfully coming and going, maybe only needing new red geraniums on every porch in bright Olvera Street planters.

I hadn't gotten around to the geraniums or the planters, so I sat solitary and coffeed-up on my porch and thought about brick walls. There were a bunch of them, including the back wall of the Court. If the old blueprint was a treasure map, then the gold pirated from Sawtooth Metals by Albert Montrose, maybe with help from Emil Selz, remained in or under the original garden wall, concealed there after the theft. In order to find it, you'd at least have to seriously damage the rear bungalows.

That, I thought, must be Gideon Selz' goal. He'd waited long enough for Mrs. Whitmer to pass away and she wasn't going anywhere, powered by fresh liver and Vitamin C. He'd kept watch over the Court from Bungalow 7, which had stayed in the family and which probably had brought in hundreds of off-the-books rentals over the past twenty-five years, as well as sheltering members of the film community who needed to have a congenial living environment.

If he could just buy me out Selz could have his way with the place.

A month or so before all this, a broker had called me from Golden Real Estate, he said, and wanted to know if the Rose-Bud was on the market. No, not at all, I'd replied. We have it valued at a very nice market price, sir, he said. Not interested, I said, and that, I thought was the end of it. Maybe instead it was only the beginning.

I called in to the Murder Squad and Sgt. Cummings said they were done with me and a deputy would be by to pull the seals and padlocks off. "Sorry about the mess," he said. That reminded me to call my regular housekeeper to scrub down Kat's unit and Wispell's. I knew there'd be nothing much in there whenever his brother showed up (his last call was from Topeka) and I was really sorry we'd lost the talismans.

How could the denture-man have owned such precious objects? The stone was a ritual piece, probably pilfered from a shaman's sacred pouch. Kat and I took it toward home and home it went. The crystal? I guess it must have come from, let's see — a flying saucer? Were they planted there for me to find? Kaawi again?

Morning evolved. Audrey appeared, ready to walk to the Auto Club.

"Morning, Mr. Tirebiter. Don't forget, tonight's Camera Club night, Greetings gate, bring your date, don't wait, 'round about eight, don't be late, mate, it's your fate!"

With each "ate," she gave me a different face and body position. At the end, she smiled sweetly as Margaret O'Brien and waved good-bye. As Lenny Bruce would say, "It ain't no submarine, but it's pretty nice."

A cop did come by, about eleven, and took away the padlocks. Kat arrived soon after and walked straight to her door. Bennett's Lincoln hovered out of sight as she went in, leaving the door open. I waited for her to come out, standing on my porch where it was warm in the sunlight. After a few minutes, filled with the annoying sound of the Lincoln's big motor idling on the other side of my hedges, Kat reappeared with a suitcase and relocked her door.

"Welcome home," I said.

"It's a mess, really. There's fingerprint dust all over."

"Veronica is coming today to clean it clean as a Dutch stoop."

That made Kat smile and she walked half-way across the Court toward me, smiling. She looked great.

"A Dutch stoop?"

"They keep 'em scrubbed, that's what I read in the *National Geographic*."

She looked at me. Nice eyes. "I'm staying at a hotel in Hollywood. The Hobart Arms. Since I couldn't come back home." She held her hand out. "I didn't want you to think I was boarding at Johnny Bennett's, George. I've been in a hotel."

I took her hand. She was beautiful.

"Not really any of my business, is it?"

"You're my landlord." She gave my hand a firm press.

"At least." I pressed hers in return.

"I'll be back. I'll call you." We both pressed.

"Things will be cleaner than the day you moved in."

"I hope so! There's a tin hatbox filled with stuff in the back of my utility closet. Never noticed it before and it's taking up space. Call that clean? I gotta go."

"Wait! A hatbox? You moved in after Dr. Mitchell and she moved in after Ollie Tully moved out and he moved his office over there after the Sheriff left. Must of been in the closet for years. You look terrific."

"Uh-huh. Thanks."

"You gotta go. Mind if I go in and get the hatbox?"

"I guess, sure. I'll call you. I'm sorry about this. Only the bad part, I mean. Glad about the rest."

Kat carried her suitcase out of the Court and around the hedge and out of sight. The Lincoln rumbled discretely and pulled past. The John Lund look-alike didn't give me a glance.

I gave him the finger.

The Court was quiet. After Kat drove away with Johnny, I felt bereft. Inside my bungalow, the typewriter sat ready for the next job. I parked in front of it, rolled in a piece of blank yellow paper and a carbon copy.

Fortunately a knock at my door saved me from further blankness. It was Milt Birnbaum from next door, his usually worried face more crushed than ever.

"Good morning, Mr. Tirebiter. You remember me, your neighbor?"

"Of course, Doctor. I'm sorry for what happened to you and Anna. Are you OK?"

"The FBI held us overnight while they searched our home. I don't know what they expected to find. *The Daily Worker*? 'Das Kapital?' Plans for the H-Bomb? Anna and I are psychiatrists, not spies. We quit the Party years ago, but we are anti-Fascists. The FBI is a fascist, racist, un-American threat to every citizen. That is how we feel, especially after being subjected to their questions. I wanted you to know that we are home and all is, at least for now, well."

"Things have been strange here. Since Mr. Wispell's death, two more bodies have been found in our bungalows."

"My God!"

"The police are working on those crimes and I expect they'll be solved soon, at least in some way. I do have to warn you that part of the solution means that I have to host some people who say they've been abducted by Aliens. It's tonight."

"Aliens? You mean from other planets?"

"Exactly."

"These people are possessed with serious delusions. You know that? Are you concerned?"

"The police will be here to watch over things. I think their delusions are fabricated to make a profit. I suspect these people are dosing their followers with a hypnotic chemical of some sort. They've given some to me and I thought for a while that I'd been abducted. Really. It's very spacy."

"I can help, perhaps. There is a psychiatric drug, very potent, called Delysid. It is derived from ergot, a fungus. It is possible to produce very real illusions, perhaps an hypnotic state. A drop is enough."

"Thanks, Doctor, that might be very helpful."

"Anna and I will be nearby in case you might need us. Well, Mr. Tirebiter, I have a class in ten minutes. Excuse me." He bowed slightly and left, looking concerned.

So there was a drug connection someplace. Of course there was! Vanpool was a seller of "reefer." Might he not also distribute other kinds of drugs? Might he have died from an overdose of this Delysid or whatever? If that's what Kat and I were given, no wonder we saw giant blue Venusians strolling along Hollywood Boulevard!

The blank page in the Royal stared blankly back at me. "The Smartee Boys and The Old Radio Station," that much I'd been given.

The brothers, Don and Rick, and their cousin Larry, 16, 17, 18, live in Indiana, and since the series has been going since 1928, it's still pre-WWII in Middletown. The illusion of blue skies, smilin' on me, in Middletown, where Pops is a lawyer and drinks (moderately) at the Country Club and Mom makes a heck of a Jell-O Pie. They solve crimes with a sort of teen-age deductive skill that baffles the local Police Chief. This one was supposed to take the boys into an abandoned Marconi radio transmitting site to do. . .what?

Since the answer to that question was mine to solve, like any experienced writer, I put it off.

Saved by another visitor!

"Mr. Tirebiter?" An authoritative female voice.

"That's me," I replied and opened the door on a woman as glamorous as opening night at the Mocambo, wearing a smile as wide as the Miracle Mile, her gloved hand held out.

"George Tirebiter? I'm Patty O'Duff from the *Mirror*. I'd like to ask you a few questions if you don't mind, about the Rose-Bud."

"Hello, there. I've read your stories. Glad I'm fully clothed. Sure, come in. Like coffee?"

Patty had her note-pad and pencil out as she smoothed herself into a corner of the couch. I put down the coffees and sat at the other end.

"You've had quite a lot going on here in the past couple of weeks. Three dead bodies, break-ins, one of the bungalows torn apart. How do you feel about it all?"

"Like we've been invaded by Aliens."

Her pencil seemed to have a life of its own. "Aliens," it wrote.

"I can see how you might feel invaded, George. And I know this Court has a history, which, I think our readers would say, was somewhat sordid. Do you know about that history?"

"I had no idea."

"You have renters who've lived here longer than you have, correct?"

"Certainly. A couple of them for fifteen years or more. They certainly have more history than I do. However, since I am a writer myself, pardon me if I direct your story toward the Selz's, father and son, who have rented the one across the way since it was built, and the land under it since before that."

"Why? Why would I be specially interested in them?"

"I think that Gideon Selz carries a secret with him that's wrapped up in theft, probably of gold, and death, probably a murder. He wants control of the Rose-Bud so he can hunt for treasure. I also think he's financing a pseudo-religious cult called the Church of Science Fiction. Interview him in Palm Springs."

The pencil kept up with me most of the way.

"Church of Science Fiction?"

"They're meeting here tonight, in the Courtyard. You're invited. Don't bet on flying saucers."

"Why do you think the two bodies ended up at the Rose-Bud?"

"Because the Church thought they'd be more comfortable here, that's what Kaawi told me. K-a-a-w-i."

The pencil spelled and paused. Patty waited.

"She told me that she brought the bodies here. She also stole a box Mr. Wispell brought inside just before he was electrocuted. She and someone called Sydney Carton had a master key, until I changed all the locks. They apparently roamed all over the place, turning on the TV, stealing things. You might see her tonight. She's about four feet tall and her voice sort of slides sideways."

"Do the police know about all this?"

"Talk to Sgt. Cummings of the Murder Squad. And sure, they know, and they know a lot more they're not telling you or me."

The pencil stopped.

"Really, I'm not on the Metro Desk. Ray Parker's the Editor over there. I'm supposed to stick to human-interest. So, do you think life in a bungalow court is very special to Los Angeles and do you think your personal contact with residents is different from, let's say, in an apartment house?"

Patty went on like that, and her pencil kept up with both of us as I repeated my wisdoms on the subject of my comfortable Court neighborhood.

"What about love life? Do people here have more of a chance to be with one another, so friendly relationships might easily take place?"

The pencil hovered.

"Could be."

The pencil still hovered.

"Everybody's very friendly. The college kids who live here date sometimes. Our older tenants are interested in, ah — different pursuits."

"You do have single women renting bungalows, don't you?"

"Certainly. They're quite comfortable here as far as I know. The Downtown and Hollywood busses are only a block away."

"You're an attractive man, George. You were in the movies, starred on radio — a prodigal youth, they say. I'm surprised you don't have a sign-in sheet on your door."

"That's very flattering. Thanks. I'm just a hard-working writer, Patty. Same as you. Not much time for a love-life."

Her pencil wrote, as if by itself, another thought, then another, as if pencils had thoughts of their own. Patty put the pad and the reluctant pencil away in her bag and held out her hand again.

"Pleased to meet you, George Tirebiter. I'm just going to wander around the Rose-Bud for a bit, make some notes. Don't mind me."

On the porch she turned and smiled the Miracle Mile Smile again and said, "I don't believe you."

"About?"

"About your love-life. News-hen's instinct. Bye-bye."

It was the size of a hatbox, but once taken down and turned around the faded label read "Magnus Brand Chocolate Cake Icing." It had once been filled with "a rich fondant." It evidently wasn't anymore, as the contents rattled around a bit when I put it down on Kat's kitchen table.

I saw her slightly faded daisy bouquet there, in a green glass vase on a square of Mexican tile. I'll replace the flowers, I thought, so they'll be fresher when she comes back home.

The tin box was old, maybe from the late 'Teens and had been dinged up in its travels. The lid was tight but not stuck, so it gradually turned and came loose. The interior wasn't chocolaty at all. There was a yellow silk scarf from the 1939 World's Fair's "World of Tomorrow" folded over the top.

I took the dozen objects out one by one and set them on the table where they seemed to belong, standing in for each bungalow's occupant, from whom they must have been lifted.

The signed five-by-seven glossy of Tempest Storm, holding a pair of six-guns across her ample chest, red hair glowing through the black-and-white print? That must come from Mr. O'Toole's museum of burlesque.

The "World of Tomorrow" souvenir scarf? Will Perry's no doubt, along with one hand-knit baby shoe and a 5-cent coupon for a can of Gerber's strained peas standing in for Sally and Little Joe.

Another photograph. Audrey, wearing a pair of black silk stockings, smiling as if she knew what I was thinking.

The Bobs were easy — a flattened can of Blatz and the Queen of Hearts, a bikini-clad blonde from a girlie deck. The co-eds? A 45 record of "How Much Is That Doggie In The Window?" by Patti Page and a test paper for Rhetoric 101, graded "See me."

Even easier was a three-by-five publicity card of my own picture, in costume as the "elderly" Tirebiter I'd played in my twenties, a white-mustached old grouch. It must have been slipped out of a scrapbook I kept in the closet.

The silver lily-pad-shaped earring was one I was sure I'd seen Kat wear. That must have really bothered her, to have "lost" that.

There were three items left, stolen from the Wispell, Whitmer and Selz bungalows. A postcard photo of a huge poster for "Cole Bros. Circus with Clyde Beatty," featuring a pair of little girls riding an enormous hippopotamus, plastered over a city wall; a CQ card from a ham radio operator in Yerevan, Armenia; and a carved ivory comb. It had a sinuous dragon etched across the top and a set of fine teeth. Very old. Valuable? I wasn't sure.

What about the tin box? It must be older than the Rose-Bud, as old as the classy garden across from Mr. and Mrs. Montrose of Sawtooth Metals.

I pondered the pieces. Sydney Carton, whoever that really was, had pilfered these things and kept them in this tin box. If the ivory comb was an heirloom of Mrs. Whitmer's, as I would hope, and the CQ card a remnant of Wispell's collection, that left the postcard photo of a circus poster. Was it stolen from the Selz bungalow? It must have been.

No one was in the picture, so I couldn't really tell the scale. It was probably taken back in the days when walls and fences would get randomly plastered with five-by-fifteen-foot panoramas of thrilling circus action. On either side of the giant hippo were decorative ovals containing flying Chinese acrobats and an especially fierce lion rampant.

Still pondering. I'm shown in disguise, the three females are more-or-less revealed. The two objects, an earing and a comb, are things the owners would hate to lose, as were the scarf and baby shoe. "See me," said the class paper. "How much?" queried Patti Page. "CQ" — "seek you" — asked and answered from Armenia. A circus. Were these found objects a set of clues or was I making this all up, seeking Unity on behalf of Sydney Carton's random thefts?

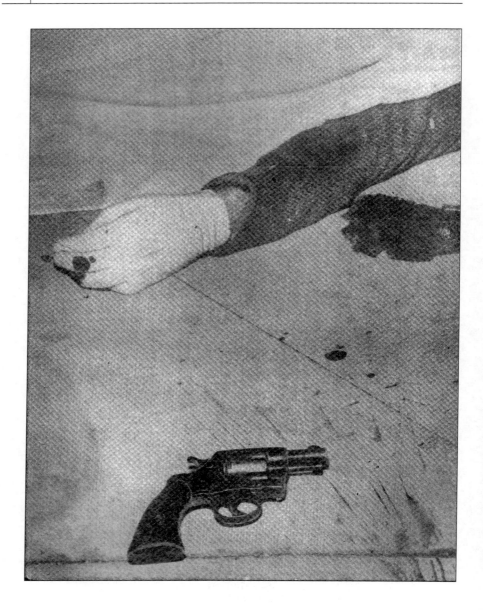

Chapter 16

Trick Mirror Gun Slays AWOL Bandit

"He Wanted the Money Just for the Weekend," Says Hefty Girl Friend.

The Rose-Bud. Dying crabgrass had been my only problem, a random urge for geraniums, maybe, until two weeks ago this afternoon. As I stood on Kat's porch and pondered, Mr. Wispell's brother, neatly dressed in his Southern-Pacific conductor's uniform, trudged up the walk.

"Say, mmm, ah, you'all must be Mr. Typewriter, Ah'm Clarence Wispell?"

His Arkansas accent cain't hardly be reproduced with all its diphthongs intact, so I won't. He had been routed twice around Utah, he said, and went on like a Union Station boarding announcement for the east-bound Super Chief. He had a suitcase with a dufflebag inside, not that he'd need it. I told him the ham equipment was now police property, which was "finer than Ozark air" as far as he was concerned. I let him in to Wispell's bungalow and thought it would be best to let him rummage around alone.

"I'll just leave you to yourself, sir," I said, "Let me know if you need any help, I'll be around," and wondered, what would the Smartee Boys do?

They'd probably discover the lost Zeppelin Tube that powers everything! Who would they give it to? Would they take it home to Pops? Where would they plug it in? Where would they find an electrician?

I rang up Sgt. Cummings. They ought to base a radio cop show on this guy, I thought. It'd open like this:

"Death Squad. Cummings."
(Phone) "I've got somethin' for ya, Sergeant."
"I'll be right there!"

Segue to steady siren under and announcer says, "Cummings of the Death Squad, brought to you by Wrigley's Straw Hat Gum."

"Cummings, Death Squad."

"Tirebiter. I've got some new information for you."

"Like what?"

"I'm not sure. A tin hatbox filled with things stolen from each of the bungalows. I think they're clues."

"I'm gonna move inta one a yer little apartments, Tirebiter, park my coupe in the garage and wait 'til the next crimewave lands on my doorstep. Easier that way. I'll be around."

I'd hardly put the phone down when it rang. It was Shifty on Mr. Pingo's hot-line.

"How'ya doin'? Got a message from Mr. P for Mr. T."

"I'm all ears."

"Ya should be. There's The Armenian Connection ta yer dead Mr. Wispell. It runs from the Middle East ta wouldja believe, Glendale, with a big stop in Vegas. Gang's inta currency, gold, information they can sell or use for blackmail, drugs — hell, petty-theft, whatever pays. Ya with me?"

"The gang wired up Wispell's chair?"

"That's it. Expert job. He was in on somethin' he shoulda not been. Mr. P thought you'd like to know. Nothin' to do with flyin' saucers."

"The police have all this?"

"If they don't, don't give it to 'em. Don't know nothin', right?"

"So right you are, Shifty."

"Howja like a date with Debra Paget?"

"I met her when she played on Lux Radio Theater with Ronald Colman a couple of years back. Beautiful. What's she up to?"

"Should be doin' 'Sheena, Queen of the Jungle,' which part she didn't get. Mr. P is innerested in buyin' her contract. He thinks maybe you should take her out on Saturday, Biltmore Bowl, bill's taken care of, she'll meetcha, see how it goes."

"Isn't she still only about twenty?"

"Don't worry about it. Real reserved, I hear. Mr. P needs yer ears and eyes."

"I'll get back to you after, then."

"Have a good time!"

I hung up again and thought about glamorous Miss Paget and the resplendent rooms at the Biltmore. For a writer, I sure get great dinner dates . . .

I returned to coffee and pondering. It seemed ridiculous that Charlie Vanpool could have been connected to an international gang, but he was pals with Wispell, who was into skimming gold, it seems he dealt drugs, maybe even pharmaceutical ones, and both of them were involved with Mr. Haroot of Armenian restaurant fame. Shifty was right, I was backing out and staying out.

I crossed over to Kat's and turned her lights on and the radio too, in the midst of a passionate Schumann Quartet. There was wind crackling in the palm fronds across the street and a kind of clarity shaping in my mind. At least there would be, once the Church of Science Fiction assembled its believers (and the rest of us) in a couple of hours.

I stared at the open rectangle of stuff arrayed on Kat's table — a jackdaw's nest.

Up from lower left, a photo of me, a photo of Audrey, a CQ card from Armenia, a photo of Tempest Storm. Across the top, an ivory comb on the left, a little pile of "Future" scarf, bootie and babyfood coupon next to it on the right. Down the right side, the circus poster picture, the student's castaways including the "See me" essay. Across from Ol' George, sat a single silver earring.

"Reveal me something!" I said aloud.

"Goes the other way around. What're ya doin' over here?" said Sgt. Cummings from the doorway and came in, pushed his hat back and walked over to look at the collection I'd arranged.

"What're you doin' in with these naked dames?"

"There's a photo or object from each of the bungalows, see? Start with me and work it out."

"Yeah, I get it. You, the radio guy, the model, the sailor, the old lady and the family . . . what's this picture?"

"Circus poster. It came from famous Bungalow Number Seven. The rest belongs to the students and Mrs. Music."

Cummings picked out the photo of the circus poster and stared at it.

"I think I saw this show when I was a kid. Yeah, 1932, Clyde Beatty, Big Top, sideshows, the hippo. Billboards up on walls all over town."

"On walls. What if it's not the circus poster but the date and the wall that's behind it that matters?"

"The wall?"

"Before the garages were built on the alley, the back wall of the Rose-Bud was bare. It's big enough for a billboard or two. That's where the treasure map leads, right?"

Sgt. Cummings turned the photo over and peered at the blank side. "There's a pencil dot here. Right here, see it?"

It was more of a slight depression that showed up in a crosslight, but something might be there.

"Where is it on the picture side?"

He held the photo this way and that under the light.

"Maybe this spot, here in the lion's mane. I can sorta feel it."

"Look, Sergeant, each of these things were chosen to reveal something. This certainly must've been."

"Like where the treasure is buried?"

"Look close. I'd guess the dot is about five-or-so feet above the alley. The wall's about forty-five feet long, though, and there's no end showing, so this could be anywhere."

"We can nail this spot down by magnifyin' the pattern in the bricks, or somethin'. A place to start. Who put all this rubbish together?"

"It could have been the woman I described to you — Kaawi. Or the person with the Sydney Carton alias, who Kaawi says prowled the whole Court and pilfered. One of them left it in Mrs. Music's utility closet, she noticed it this morning and I came over to get it. Too fascinated with it to leave."

"Pack it up, Tirebiter. I'll take it along. More evidence. I may have good news for ya about Wispell in a couple a days. Like I expected, it don't seem he was murdered by little green men."

"Good to know. None of the little green men and/or women coming tonight are murderers. They assured me."

"We'll see ya around six, Tirebiter. You may not see us, OK?" He picked up the tin box and stalked out into the Court. I followed.

Clarence Wispell appeared, suitcase in hand, tipped his cap to Cummings, and said, "Eh-yep, nothin' but a few ol' clothes is all that's lefta Trav'. Salvation Army'll take the rest away for ya, and thankya Mr. Tripewyter."

"Sorry about your brother, sir," I said.

"I know he never owned one, so's I left it on the table there."

"Left one what?" asked Sgt. Cummings.

"Toy. Trav' never liked reg'lar toys. Guns 'n' radio parts. Wind-up space toy warn't his, so's I left it there. Thank ya agin!"

Clarence tipped his cap politely and shambled away. Sgt. Cummings and I exchanged an "I never saw a toy there before" look and went inside to see what it was.

Indeed, there it sat, a spot of bright primary colors shining in the otherwise lifeless room. A wind-up flying saucer, tin, with a small plastic dome on top. An enigmatic "OZ 2K" was printed in red on one side. When wound-up the toy would spin, shoot sparks and crash into furniture legs. We looked at it first, then Sgt. Cummings took out his handkerchief, used it to pick OZ 2K up and turn it over.

"How'd this get here?"

"I haven't been in this bungalow for a week. That wasn't here then and the locks have been changed since. Gremlins. Blue Venusians. Kilroy. Sydney Carton?"

"You told me. If it was him, why'd he leave this here?"

"It's a clue."

"Don't jerk me around, Tirebiter."

"All those things in the box are clues. At least I think so, and one of them might show us where the treasure is. I thought it was Kaawi, leaving things around for me to find, but now I'm sure it's been Sydney, acting by himself. The toy saucer points to the Church of Science Fiction, doesn't it?"

"I'm takin' the damn thing away. We'll dust it, see what shows up." He looked around the room. "Lotsa shelves."

"Wispell put them in, built the transmitter, all before I bought the Court. Either I get another ham to rent it or go into FM radio."

"What's that? Repair shop?"

"It's what they use on flying saucers."

"Sure. The Shadow knows! Don't drink anything I wouldn't." Pleased with himself, the Sergeant strode off, grinning, wishing he could dance like Gene Kelly.

≫◄

Tuesday afternoon. Kat would be on a pizza-run about now. Husky, tanned Santa Monica beach boys competing for a "Hot Date!" with pale inland girls from distant Orange County were on the menu for tonight's show, then the winners would be driven to Vegas. Winners and chaperones laughing and chatting and dozing for hours across the desert, securely housed inside an ample Caddie limo.

I'd turned off the murky chamber music on KFAC and nudged the dial to KFOX's "Harlem Matinee" with Ol' H. H. jivin' his way through "Voodoo Blues" by Jumpin' Joe Williams, some Big Maybelle and Annie Laurie, and the Treniers with "Poontang." What the Rosebud needed was a real change-of-pace.

The screamin' Trenier sax was just fading as three strangers came into the Court and looked at me looking at them.

"Is this the Church of Science Fiction?" asked the older woman. She had very crooked teeth, which made her a little hard to understand.

"Well, yes, ma'm, the Church is having a get-together here *esta noche* as they say in Alien. How did you all hear about it?"

The older man with medium-length patriarch-type whiskers looked around. "Won't rain here will it?"

"Not too likely tonight, sir."

"We got a transmission," said the third person who might have been a young man or woman, covered up by a worn blanket that might have been Navajo.

"Let's get a room, Coral." He looked longingly at Kat's bare front porch.

"Wait, wait, sir. This isn't a motel, it's a bungalow court. These are all rented units. Sorry."

"Thought it was a church the transmission said, didn't it?" This from under the Navajo blanket.

"No, no. I'm the owner here, Mr. Tire . . . Mr. Tee — and I just rented these Church people this little courtyard for the evening. They're going to show some slides. Sounded interesting. Where are you folks from?"

Coral, with the crooked lisp, said "Mert's from Mars. Donno about Nada. I'm from Glendale."

Nada said, "Seedro-Wooly. It's a distant cold planet."

Mert said, "All three of us got the same transmission. Didn't say anything about accommodations. None a these cabins empty?"

"Are you related at all?"

"By transmission," said Nada.

"We could sleep anyplace tonight and then Mert's got a relative in Pomona," said Coral.

"West Covina, I think," said Mert.

"Oh, shit," I thought, but I didn't say it. Instead I said, "Don't worry, I'm sure you'll find others who've received the same transmission. Something has been planned for you all. Planned for later, I mean." Coral raised her eyes upward. "In case you're hungry now, there's a swell hamburger and ice cream shop down on the boulevard." Nada said *nada*. "Good place to wait while things get set up here." Mert nodded. "Going to be busy here soon, so you come on back about 6 p.m., OK?"

All three looked blankly at each other.

"Or," I said, "You could help me bring some furniture out so people — you — have someplace to sit down. How's that?"

Wispell's had two dining table chairs, a rolling office chair and a half-sprung armchair. The co-eds and the Bobs had pretty much the same, so, along with dining and desk chairs from Kat, the Strangers and I brought out a dozen pieces of moveable, sitable furniture and faced them toward the Whitmer and Perry front porches. The Strangers sat in two of the armchairs, with Nada cross-legged on an ottoman. It wasn't even four o'clock yet.

By five, the advance guard of the C of SF had arrived. I introduced myself to Mr. Palmer of the talent agency, another small man, dapper in an elfin sort of way.

"Great booking, neighbor," he said. "Spread the word. Ya need more chairs next time."

Someone I hadn't seen before, a kid wearing a Pep-Boys T-shirt, hauled in the same pretty big movie screen that the Coopers had used at the Saucer Expo. He started to set it up on Mrs. Whitmer's porch and I directed him to the other side. I hadn't seen Mrs. W all day, which was worrisome.

I knocked at her door a couple of times. No response. I knocked a little louder. "Mrs. Whitmer?"

I felt sure she was just sleeping off her long weekend, but her doorway was clear in case she wondered what was going on and drifted outside.

Pep-Boy set up a stand with a slide projector in front of the middle light pole, aimed toward the screen on the right side. I let him plug into an extension from the empty Bobs'. He carried up a table, a phonograph, amplifier, microphone with stand. I brought the end of a second extension out to him.

"No extra chairs?"

"'Fraid not."

"I got a couple." Pep-Boy went out to his truck in the alley and returned with four padded folding chairs marked "MGM Club" on the back. "One for Reverend Cooper, Mrs. Cooper, Marla, one extra for me."

More strangers poked their heads under the Rose-Bud arch, saw that there was activity and came in. The chairs were filled by a party of three deserty-looking men, one with a "Giant Rock" trucker's cap; a tall and heavily bearded man in a hooded robe; a large, sad woman who had been at the Hotel on Saturday, selling the mimeo'd report of her teleportation to Aldebaran; two plain, ordinary couples, both wives clutching Mrs. Cooper's space-travelogue in their gloved hands, both husbands wishing they were watching a Rams game at the Trojan Tavern.

I said good evening to each of them and, after that, I stood back on my porch as about twenty more highly varied, but apparently still human beings arrived, most of them clustering together, a few looking in at the others as if to ask, "Are you from Outer Space?" Finally, right at six p.m., the Coopers arrived and stood in the archway, glowing like newlyweds. Pep-Boy started clapping and the audience turned to see why, then picked the clapping up. The Coopers nodded, chatted and pressed hands on their way through to the table set up by the screen on Will's porch.

Albert Bailey, in his Ol' Prospector overalls, got to the archway, saw me, salaamed me extravagantly and decided he would match my position opposite, by perching on Kat's bungalow steps. Bill Cooper tapped on a live microphone.

"Good evening, Seekers of the Light and the Truth of the Light and the Light of Truth. Welcome to the Church of Science Fiction, founded here tonight on this sacred spot by my adoring and passionate wife and partner, Reverend Alice Cooper. Some of you have already visited with visitors from other planets. This Church believes in your beliefs and can prove it to you in articles and true-life stories in easily readable form in our Church publications. This Church believes that if we believe strongly and sincerely enough, the ruler-beings, the knowledge-beings, the Creators of the New Age will let themselves be known to all of us, and soon.

"The Reverend Cooper will now serve the sacrament to those who will come with us to the Stars."

Little water-cooler cups, a gallon jug, an eyedropper. I kept a distant eye on those who did, and those who didn't take the sacramental drug. I felt like I had the whole situation well in hand. Sgt. Cummings had my back, the Birnbaums could talk to drug-crazed parishioners and nobody was going to get hurt.

Ken Adair, camera bag slung over his shoulder showed up with Gina, the blonde model, and Audrey. I waved and shrugged.

Ken gestured at the celebrants. "Might be a couple a good shots in there. What's goin' on? Think they'd mind, I popped a few flashbulbs?"

"You know what they say about publicity."

"Maybe pix on the Church page Saturday. First Assembly of Christian Saucers, maybe."

"Them or me?" asked Audrey.

"I'm with her," said Gina.

"I'm playin' the cards I got," said Ken and they hurried into Audrey's bungalow.

Bill Cooper shot back a paper cup that I was pretty sure had nothing in it but plain water. He looked upward at the L.A. night sky. "Blessings in the Oneness. I am only a humble servant of the Eternal Source. It is anticipated by the Church that the intensity of the infusion shall soon become greater. Some may use the vibration for their own purposes, but we are here to assist in the battle against these powers."

He went on in this way for a while, then I heard movement in the hedges on the street side of my bungalow. It went toward the rear and I decided to go around the other way to meet it, whatever it might be — Alien, dog or . . . the paper-boy, who stopped in his tracks, thought about ducking under the myrtle, saw it was too thick and stood there.

"What's going on?"

"Oh, heck, Mr. Tirebiter, I just wanted to check out what's going on over here."

"Is this the way you sneak in?"

"Heck. . . . Sometimes, I guess."

"What's your name, paper-boy?"

"Uh . . ."

"Something from Dickens maybe? Sydney Carton?"

"Dickens is my favorite writer. Yeah."

"How about Raffles, The Gentleman Thief?'

"I've read all his stories."

"Inspiring you to burgle through my tenants' homes? Why would you do that?"

Sydney Carton sighed. "This whole neighborhood around here? I pretend it's the wilderness and I have to explore my way around it. There's streams and a swamp and safe places and dangerous ones. I only went inside here once or twice, when Mrs. Kaawi gave me the key and I turned on the light over there. I never stole anything except I took your movie script to look at. The other stealing was her. I've only been ducking behind the houses and through the hedges and alleys and nobody sees me. It's just fun."

"You want to be a writer, Sydney?"

"I think so."

"Start by not stealing some other writer's ideas, especially ones that have been previously heisted from the Immortal Classics, OK?"

"I'm sorry, really. I'll pretend this is a big lake guarded by hippos and tigers and not go near it again."

"Where did you meet Kaawi, Sydney?"

"A month or so ago, maybe, at the Library. I work over at the Public Library putting books away. She sort of got me to think it would be a good joke to just move things around a little, to scare people a little. Then when there were dead bodies, I stopped prowling, for sure."

"I hope that's true. And, look — how about some target practice? Try to hit my porch with the *Mirror* tomorrow otherwise I'm going over to the *Daily News*."

"Yes, sir. Can I stay and watch the show?"

"Just don't drink the water."

"No, sir."

The Reverend Mrs. Alice Cooper was building up to something. "Thousands of people from other planets are living among us," she proclaimed. "They may live next door to you, one of them may be your co-worker! Interplanetary brotherhood depends on a decline in hostility and increase in tolerance and love. Let us join in the Message of the Saucers together!"

Pep-Boy turned on the phonograph. Tonight's smash hit? "From Saucers To You" — Al Bailey and his Venusian All Stars with their interstellar hums, drumming heartbeats and tonal conversations, all summed up with the smallest, clearest of little bells.

At first, I rose above the Court and hovered as high as Wispell's antenna with its new blue neon lights down the side, spelling "S" and "F" with bold serifs. Below, the Court seemed a collage of colored paper bits. All of them seemed to be moving. Maybe the Venusians will stay away tonight. I understand I'm to be your Guide on this Voyage to Io. You can sleep the whole immense journey and arrive a member of the Aquarian Order. I am Regga of Masar. Oara is here. He is the planetary representative from Saturn. You must understand that the Sun is not a hot, flaming body, but a cool body. From above, the Court turns on its axis.

The limo is dark, the desert is dark, and we are sleeping. The light from the blue crystal has power to warn about danger, only somebody took it from me. It would make the mission easier, if I had it now. If I had a cameraman there I'd make the ten o'clock news. Thousands can be healed of their meager lives every day through the Church. Higher Intelligence guides us at a price. A fair price for a trip to Heaven. Hell, maybe. Your choice. I'll be right back.

Now I see the antenna is a guiding light for the saucer. The brilliant blue "SF" turns Rose-Bud red and a white beacon points up and is lost in the cloudless dark sky. The congregation is prepared to board when the ship arrives. Tithing to the Church begins right now tonight. "The Big Green Book of the Church of Science Fiction" has the secrets for your love life and professional success. Seminars at low cost for members. Join now. Everyone is looking up at me and above me the Nomads from Neptune who are descending slowly from Space.

I think the Venusians must be having sex with themselves all the time, like when they're walking down the street and nobody notices, they're having sex. Everything's easier that way and nothing depends on it. We're all asleep.

It's a long scary fall to the ground and I feel myself pitching head-first downward into the Courtyard, into Bugs Bunny's burrow, reaching as I fall for golden bricks, the throbbing Zeppelin Tube, through a vortex of silver dollars for the jangling keys to everything, past a talkative blue Alien speaking through Time, and slam into my own voice, pleading "What's My Name? What's my Name?"

I think it's easier when we're next to each other, in these Space Tubes. Easier to talk, George. I was almost ready for you, almost, and then the Aliens took me over to tell their story. Sorry. Always saying sorry. Aliens won't let me. Wake up all creepy with dawn in my eyes. Sorry.

Albert Bailey was standing over me, asking me if I was alright. I was, just. "Fainted, I guess," I said, busy wondering who the "I" in that statement was.

"OK. Remember your name? What day is it?" asked Bailey in his big carney voice. "I saw ya slump over like a sack o' coal there, Mr. Tirebiter. Not hurt are ya?"

"I'm OK. It was a soft slump, I guess. Where is everyone?"

"Left on the nicest little space-ship you could imagine."

I sat up and looked around. Pep-Boy was coiling up his cables, empty chairs were scattered where they'd been left when the mass abduction took place.

"Coopers told me to thank you for the use of the Rose-Bud. Still, it's a little small for what they got in mind. Not churchy enough, limited parking."

"You think they really wanted the Rose-Bud for a church?"

"I thought they had ya there! Power o' suggestion!"

"Nuts! It was Gideon Selz who wants the place and the police know why. It's not for sale, Mr. Bailey."

"No skin offa mine! Good luck to ya. Coopers are lookin' at a nice soft spot in Pacific Palisades. Cool sea breeze. Saucers everywhere every night. Tell ya this, Tirebiter, between the UFO magazine and the next one I'm puttin' out on all that Fortean phenom b.s., and I figure the Big Green Book of the Science Fiction Church will make us all zillionaires."

He left with his thumbs tucked into his overall straps, happy as only a potential zillionaire could be. The electrical equipment had all been cleared and two extension cords lay neatly coiled on the Perry's porch. As I picked them up, Mrs. Whitmer's door opened a crack.

"Mr. Tirebiter?"

"I hope this all didn't wake you, Mrs. Whitmer."

"Goodness no. I had the nicest dreams. I was Queen for a Day, you see, and I went flying to Hawaii where all the stars and planets are big as oranges and tomatoes. And you were there, too, and Mrs. Music and an orchestra. Is everything all right? I see you've set out some chairs."

"It's over now. I'll get them all put back."

"Goodnight, then."

She closed her door and I carried the cords back to my bungalow. Sgt. Cummings was sitting on the steps, drinking a cup of coffee.

"Took the liberty," he said.

"What happened?"

"You were here weren'tcha?"

"Not really here. Not for awhile, after the music started."

"Yeah, well a lotta people sat and stared at the pictures, some got bored and left. At the end, when there weren't any Martians, the Coopers cleared out, took a little lock-box fulla dough with 'em. Can't run 'em in yet, not 'til I got proof of fraud or maybe manslaughter, what with a poisonous drug."

"I found out about the cat-burglar. My paper-boy."

"Should I bust him for B&E?"

"No point. Kaawi was responsible for the bodies and the stolen clues. She never showed up?"

"Only the usual bunch of nut-bars. Don't worry, LAPD has its eyes open. Got one lookin' at yer friend Bailey."

"I'll evict the Selz's."

"He waited a long time to cash in."

"There must've been more than a single buried treasure here, Sergeant. I think one pot of gold was cached in a chocolate frosting tin and that's lasted Gideon a long time. Maybe there's more, maybe they're all gone. He was obsessed with making sure, though, and that's why he wanted the Rose-Bud. Just to tear it down, starting with that back wall."

Cummings rose, in that unfolding way, and handed me his empty cup. He nodded, pursed his lips and nodded again.

"Thanks for the java. Are we done here?"

"Can't promise. Hope so."

"Gonna have these empty places ready to rent soon?"

"Right away."

"I'll call ya. I could be interested." He didn't look right at me when he said that, so I believed him.

After he drove away, I picked up chairs and returned them to the right bungalows. The last one belonged at Kat's kitchen table. The daisies still drooped, the creaky refrigerator went on, her radio was playing. It was the theme of the Gas Company's show, a big serious piano concerto. I switched it off, turned off the lights, sighed and shut the door.

Across the Court, Audrey's door opened and Ken Adair stepped out.

"What was that party all about, man? Crazy stuff."

"Just a rental. They won't be back."

"Hey! How about a cold beer? Audrey's changin' into a corset thing. Bring yer camera." Ken looked up and down at the almost vacant Rose-Bud. "Nothin' else is happenin' here, that's fer sure." The door closed.

The neighborhood mocking bird was auditioning for the Met from the top of Mr. Wispell's radio antenna. I was listening, liking his stolen ditties better than the big concerto, when a familiar blue glow came alight on my porch.

There it was, the crystal, the "flying saucer alert signal," Kat had called it, sitting upright on a bone white saucer in front of my door.

It sang along with the mocker for a phrase or two. "Thought you were from the prop department," I said. "Guess not." I carried it indoors and set it on my desk where the radiance faded sometime during the night.

Endnotes

THE BUNGALOW COURT

The Bungalow Court got its architectural start in Pasadena around 1910 and, in its many variations (Craftsman, Spanish, Disney), was the basic form of multi-family living in Southern California cities well into the 1930s. It was open, sunny and neighborly. The one pictured above has one-storey bungalows on both sides and a two storey structure at the rear. There's a fountain back there and a Springtime of flowers down the middle. Much, much nicer than apartment living, and perhaps another good reason to move to the Coast.

The Rose-Bud is modeled after a Court only a couple of blocks away from where I lived, from ages 12 to 14, in an older multi-tenented house on University Street. (Mrs. Whitmer and Mr. O'Toole lived there too.)

University Street and that Craftsman-period house with its stocky palm tree in the front yard are no more, erased by the University of Southern California's expanding campus, but some of the surrounding dwellings have survived the conversion to student apartments. Even a few of the ornate Victorians were there, last time I drove through the neighborhood. When I did so, I was excited to see that my own personal "Rose-Bud" was more or less as I remembered it when I delivered afternoon papers there. It was a pleasure to fill it fictionally with George and his tenants.

Here's the "Rose-Bud" around the turn of the 21st Century:

KFAC

The station, KFAC, which George Tirebiter has on his radio most of the time was one of the few all-classical broadcasters in the country. It was located on the dial at 1330 AM and on Wilshire Boulevard in what began as the Fuller auto dealership, which sold Auburn and Cord motor cars — thus KFAC — Fuller Auburn Cord. The studio and transmitter were located on the upper floors of the building and the large-lettered transmission towers were a highly visible presence, towering over the next-door church.

The Southern California Gas Company began sponsoring a two-hour Evening Concert in 1943, hosted by Thomas Cassidy (1917-2012), who also had the job of building the station's record library. The 78rpm albums must have weighed more than all the fancy cars down on the showroom floor. Cassidy and the Evening Concert were cultural institutions in a city with all too little culture in the 40s and 50s.

In 1952 Cassidy began broadcasting concerts from the Hollywood Bowl. He also did intermission features there, live, until the station's horrible descent into jingle-advertising and "youth-appeal" and its dismal demise in 1989.

There were other notable announcers — Tom Dixon in the afternoon, Carl Princi, Dick Joy, Bruce Buell — but Cassidy was the man. I never would have passed my first radio audition without the mellow tones and careful articulation of Tom Cassidy in my ear. Also, he knew how to pronounce the very foreign names that I kept written down in a card file as a record of all the music I liked as I listened.

KLAC was very straightforwardly programmed — 18th and 19th Century orchestral music, mostly. You listened, you got the Classics down. But it wasn't all tone poems. For a while there was a show called "Music Not For Everyone." I dubbed it "Music Not For Nobody" and loved it — Ives, Stravinsky, Antheil, Shoenberg. Musical horizons broadened.

George also listens to "Ol' H. H." — Hunter Hancock playing rhythm and blues on KFVD's "Harlem Matinee," sponsored by Dolphin's of Hollywood, an influential record store on Central Avenue. The owner was an African-American music producer and the store a center for jazz as well as r&b. Hunter Hancock was a white d.j., but his delivery was purely black and the music he played was about to cross-over, big-time.

L.A. and George T. and I were fortunate to be entertained and enlightened in the early 1950s by the radio voices and vivid personalities of Tom Cassidy and Hunter Hancock.

THE HOLLYWOOD BOWL

In the summer of 1953, the year this novel takes place, I was 17 years old and worked at a corner drugstore as a soda-jerk and general factotum. I was hungry for live theatre and music. I'd subscribed to a couple of seasons of musicals at the Civic Light Opera, saw traveling companies perform "Don Juan In Hell" and "John Brown's Body" and was an almost weekly presence at the Bowl.

SYMPHONIES UNDER THE STARS   HOLLYWOOD BOWL - HOLLYWOOD, CAL 385

Bowl tickets were inexpensive, the setting was really beautiful and, for a non-driver, the place was easy to be dropped off at. The season lasted eight weeks in 1953 and I went, most likely with my high school girlfriend, to performances on seven of those weeks. True to date-night preferences, we took in the Kern & Hammerstein and Rogers & Hammerstein evenings the first two Saturdays. The third week I went alone to hear Villa-Lobos conduct his work and an Arthur Fiedler pops concert. The fourth week offered the Cole Porter evening, recalled here as a date for George and Kat. I skipped the fifth week — Liberace, eww.

Gershwin and Jose Greco's Spanish dancers filled in the six and seventh weekends. The final performance was the best one of all. We sat far, far back in the Bowl for Peggy Lee, Victor Young conducting. She was genuinely fabulous and remained that way all her life.

Hollywood High School had its graduations at the Bowl and I was there for both Alizon's and Devin's ceremonies in the late 1970's. Other than in my imagination (the Bowl also serves as a setting in "The Ronald Reagan Murder Case"), my last concert visit was for Ravi Shankar in 1967, the Summer of Love.

U. S. AIR FORCE UFO IDENTIFICATION FORMS

CHANGE 1, AFR 80–17

AIR FORCE REGULATION
NO. 80–17(C1)

DEPARTMENT OF THE AIR FORCE
Washington, *26 October 1967*

Research and Development

UNIDENTIFIED FLYING OBJECTS (UFO)

AFR 80–17, 19 September 1966, is changed as follows:

★**3c.** *Investigation.* Each commander of an Air Force base within the United States will provide a UFO . . . sighting for action.

3e. *EXCEPTIONS:* FTD at Wright-Patterson . . . for separate investigations. The University of Colorado, under a research agreement with the Air Force, will conduct a study of UFOs. This program (to run approximately 15 months) will be conducted independently and without restrictions. The university will enlist the assistance of other conveniently located institutions that can field investigative teams. *All* UFO reports will be submitted to the University of Colorado, which will be given the fullest cooperation of all UFO Investigating Officers. Every effort will be made to keep all UFO reports unclassified. However, if it is necessary to classify a report because of method of detection or other factors not related to the UFO, a separate report including all possible information will be sent to the University of Colorado.

★**6a.** The Deputy Chief of Staff, . . . reported within the United States. All Air Force activities within the United States will conduct UFO . . . investigation with FTD.

8b(6). University of Colorado, Boulder CO 80302, Dr. Condon. (Mail copy of message form.)

★**8c.** *Reports.* If followup action is required on electrically transmitted reports, prepare an investigative report on AF Form 117, "Sighting of Unidentified Phenomena Questionnaire," which will be reproduced locally on 8" x 10½" paper in accordance with attachment 1 (9 pages). Send the completed investigative report to FTD (TDETR), Wright-Patterson AFB OH 45433. FTD will send the reports to interested organizations in the United States and to Secretary of the Air Force (SAFOI), Wash DC 20330, if required.

8e. Negative or Inapplicable Data. Renumber as paragraph 9.

11k. Position title, name, rank, official address, telephone area code, office and home telephone, and comments of the preparing officer, including his preliminary analysis of the possible cause of the sighting. (See paragraph 10.)

By Order of the Secretary of the Air Force

OFFICIAL

R. J. PUGH, *Colonel, USAF*
Director of Administrative Services

J. P. McCONNELL, *General, USAF*
Chief of Staff

1 Attachment
AF Form 117, "Sighting of Unidentified Phenomena Questionnaire"

This regulation supersedes AFR 80–17A, 8 November 1966.
OPR: AFRDDG
DISTRIBUTION: S

AFR 80–17(C1)

SIGHTING OF UNIDENTIFIED PHENOMENA QUESTIONNAIRE

BUDGET BUREAU APPROVAL NUMBER 21-R258

THIS QUESTIONNAIRE HAS BEEN PREPARED SO THAT YOU CAN GIVE THE U.S. AIR FORCE AS MUCH INFORMATION AS POSSIBLE CONCERNING THE UNIDENTIFIED PHENOMENON THAT YOU HAVE OBSERVED. PLEASE TRY TO ANSWER ALL OF THE QUESTIONS. THE INFORMATION YOU GIVE WILL BE USED FOR RESEARCH PURPOSES. YOUR NAME WILL NOT BE USED IN CONNECTION WITH ANY OF YOUR STATEMENTS OR CONCLUSIONS WITHOUT YOUR PERMISSION. RETURN TO AIR FORCE BASE INVESTIGATOR FOR FORWARDING TO FTD (TDETR), WRIGHT-PATTERSON AFB, OHIO 45433, IAW AFR 80-17. *(IF ADDITIONAL SHEETS ARE NEEDED FOR NARRATIVE OR SKETCHES ATTACH SECURELY TO THIS FORM OR ANNOTATE WITH YOUR NAME FOR IDENTIFICATION.)*

1. WHEN DID YOU SEE THE PHENOMENON?
   DAY_____ MONTH _____ YEAR_____
2. WHAT TIME DID YOU FIRST SIGHT THE PHENOMENON?
   HOUR_____ MINUTES_____ ☐ A.M. ☐ P.M.
3. WHAT TIME DID YOU LAST SIGHT THE PHENOMENON?
   HOUR_____ MINUTES_____ ☐ A.M. ☐ P.M.
4. TIME/ZONE   ☐ DAYLIGHT SAVINGS   ☐ STANDARD
   ☐ EASTERN ☐ CENTRAL ☐ MOUNTAIN ☐ PACIFIC ☐ OTHER
5. WHERE WERE YOU WHEN YOU SAW THE PHENOMENON? IF IN CITY, GIVE THE NEAREST STREET ADDRESS AND INDICATE ON A HAND DRAWN MAP WHERE YOU WERE STANDING WITH REFERENCE TO THE ADDRESS. IF IN THE COUNTRY, IDENTIFY THE HIGHWAY YOU WERE ON OR NEAR AND TRY TO FIX A DISTANCE AND DIRECTION FROM SOME RECOGNIZABLE LANDMARK.

6. IMAGINE YOU ARE AT THE POINT SHOWN IN THE SKETCH, PLACE AN "A" ON THE CURVED LINE TO SHOW HOW HIGH THE PHENOMENON WAS ABOVE THE HORIZON, OR SKYLINE, WHEN FIRST SEEN. PLACE A "B" ON THE SAME CURVED LINE TO SHOW HOW HIGH ABOVE THE HORIZON THE PHENOMENON WAS WHEN LAST SEEN.

AF FORM 117

7   (Becomes Attachment 1 to AFR 80-17)

Attachment 1

AFR 80-17(C1)

6A. NOW IMAGINE YOU ARE AT THE CENTER OF THE COMPASS ROSE. PLACE AN "A" ON THE COMPASS TO INDICATE THE DIRECTION TO THE PHENOMENON WHEN FIRST SEEN. PLACE A "B" ON THE COMPASS TO INDICATE THE DIRECTION TO THE PHENOMENON WHEN LAST SEEN.

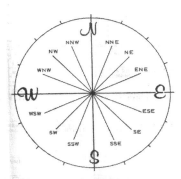

7. IN THE SKETCH BELOW, PLACE AN "A" AT THE POSITION OF THE PHENOMENON WHEN FIRST SEEN, AND A "B" AT THE POSITION OF THE PHENOMENON WHEN LAST SEEN. CONNECT THE "A" AND "B" WITH A LINE TO APPROXIMATE THE MOVEMENT OF THE PHENOMENON BETWEEN "A" AND "B". THAT IS, SCHEMATICALLY SHOW WHETHER THE MOVEMENT APPEARED TO BE STRAIGHT, CURVED OR ZIG-ZAG. REFER TO SMALLER SKETCH AS AN EXAMPLE OF HOW TO COMPLETE THE LARGER SKETCH.

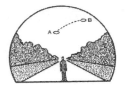

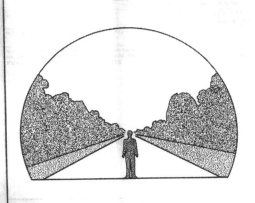

PAGE 2 OF 9 PAGES

Attachment 1
9   (Becomes Attachment 1 to AFR 80–17)

AFR 80–17(C1)

8. WHERE WERE YOU WHEN YOU SAW THE PHENOMENON? *(Check appropriate blocks.)*

OUTDOORS	IN BUSINESS SECTION OF CITY
IN BUILDING	IN RESIDENTIAL SECTION OF CITY
IN CAR ☐ AS DRIVER ☐ AS PASSENGER	IN OPEN COUNTRYSIDE
IN BOAT	NEAR AIRFIELD
IN AIRPLANE ☐ AS PILOT ☐ AS PASSENGER	FLYING OVER CITY
OTHER	FLYING OVER OPEN COUNTRY
	OTHER

A. IF YOU WERE IN A VEHICLE, COMPLETE THE FOLLOWING:

WHAT DIRECTION WERE YOU MOVING?		HOW FAST WERE YOU MOVING?
NORTH	EAST	
SOUTH	WEST	DID YOU STOP ANYTIME WHILE OBSERVING THE PHENOMENON?
NORTHEAST	SOUTHEAST	
NORTHWEST	SOUTHWEST	☐ YES ☐ NO

EXPLAIN WHETHER SUCH MOVEMENT AFFECTS YOUR SKETCHES IN ITEMS 5 AND 6.

DESCRIBE TYPE OF VEHICLE YOU WERE IN AND TYPE OF ROAD, TERRAIN OR BODY OF WATER YOU TRAVERSED DURING THE SIGHTING. STATE WHETHER WINDOWS OR CONVERTIBLE TOP WERE UP OR DOWN.

HOW MUCH OTHER TRAFFIC WAS THERE?

DID YOU NOTICE ANY AIRPLANES? ☐ YES ☐ NO. IF "YES," DESCRIBE WHEN THEY WERE IN SIGHT RELATIVE TO THE TIME OF SIGHTING THE PHENOMENON AND WHERE THEY WERE IN THE SKY RELATIVE TO THE POSITION OF THE PHENOMENON.

9. HOW LONG WAS THE PHENOMENON IN SIGHT?

LENGTH OF TIME	CERTAIN OF TIME	NOT VERY SURE
	FAIRLY CERTAIN	JUST A GUESS

HOW WAS TIME DETERMINED?

WAS THE PHENOMENON IN SIGHT CONTINUOUSLY? ☐ YES ☐ NO. IF "NO," INDICATE WHETHER THIS IS DUE TO YOUR MOVEMENT OR THE BEHAVIOR OF THE PHENOMENON, AND DESCRIBE SUCH MOVEMENT OR BEHAVIOR. INDICATE DISAPPEARANCES ON PREVIOUS SKETCHES.

PAGE 3 OF 9 PAGES

Attachment 1
11   (Becomes Attachment 1 to AFR 80–17)

AFR 80-17(C1)

10. IF THERE WERE MORE THAN ONE PHENOMENON, HOW MANY WERE THERE? DRAW A PICTURE TO SHOW HOW THEY WERE ARRANGED. DID THIS ARRANGEMENT CHANGE DURING THE SIGHTING?

11.	CONDITIONS *(Check appropriate blocks.)*		
A. SKY	B. WEATHER		
DAY	CUMULUS CLOUDS *(Low fluffy)*		FOG OR MIST
TWILIGHT	CIRRUS CLOUDS *(High fleecy or Herringbone)*		HEAVY RAIN
NIGHT			LIGHT RAIN OR DRIZZLE
CLEAR	NIMBUS CLOUDS *(Rain)*		HAIL
PARTLY CLOUDY	CUMULONIMBUS CLOUDS *(Thunderstorms)*		SNOW OR SLEET
COMPLETELY OVERCAST			UNKNOWN
	HAZE OR SMOG		NONE OF THE ABOVE

C. IF THE SIGHTING WAS AT TWILIGHT OR NIGHT, WHAT DID YOU NOTICE ABOUT THE STARS AND MOON?

(1) STARS	(2) MOON	
NONE	BRIGHT MOONLIGHT	NO MOONLIGHT
A FEW	MOON WITH HALO	UNKNOWN
MANY	MOON HIDDEN BY CLOUDS	
UNKNOWN	PARTIAL *(New or quarter)*	

D. IF SIGHTING WAS IN DAYLIGHT, WAS THE SUN VISIBLE? ☐ YES ☐ NO. IF "YES," WHERE WAS THE SUN AS YOU FACED THE PHENOMENON?

IN FRONT OF YOU	TO YOUR RIGHT	OVERHEAD *(Near noon)*
IN BACK OF YOU	TO YOUR LEFT	UNKNOWN

E. SPECIFY THE MAJOR SOURCE OF ILLUMINATION PRESENT DURING THE SIGHTING, SUCH AS THE SUN, HEADLIGHTS OR STREET LAMP, ETC. FOR TERRESTRIAL ILLUMINATION, SPECIFY DISTANCE TO LIGHT SOURCE.

12. GIVE A BRIEF DESCRIPTION OF THE PHENOMENON, INDICATING WHETHER IT APPEARED DARK OR LIGHT, WHETHER IT REFLECTED LIGHT OR WAS SELF-LUMINOUS AND WHAT COLORS YOU NOTICED. DESCRIBE YOUR IMPRESSION OF WHETHER IT WAS SOLID OR TRANSPARENT, WHETHER EDGES WERE SHARP OR FUZZY. DESCRIBE THE SHAPE OR INDICATE IF IT APPEARED AS A POINT OF LIGHT. INDICATE COMPARISONS WITH OTHER OBSERVED OBJECTS, LIKE STARS, A LIGHT OR OTHER OBJECT IN YOUR FIELD OF VIEW.

AFR 80-17(C1)

13. DID THE PHENOMENON	YES	NO	UNKNOWN
MOVE IN A STRAIGHT LINE?			
STAND STILL AT ANYTIME?			
SUDDENLY SPEED UP AND RUN AWAY?			
BREAK UP IN PARTS AND EXPLODE?			
CHANGE COLOR?			
GIVE OFF SMOKE?			
CHANGE BRIGHTNESS?			
CHANGE SHAPE?			
FLASH OR FLICKER?			
DISAPPEAR AND REAPPEAR?			
SPIN LIKE A TOP?			
MAKE A NOISE?			
FLUTTER OR WOBBLE?			

14. WHAT DREW YOUR ATTENTION TO THE PHENOMENON?

A. HOW DID IT FINALLY DISAPPEAR?

B. DID THE PHENOMENON MOVE BEHIND OR IN FRONT OF SOMETHING, LIKE A CLOUD, TREE, OR BUILDING AT ANY TIME?
☐ YES ☐ NO. IF "YES," DESCRIBE.

PAGE 5 OF 9 PAGES

Attachment 1
15 (Becomes Attachment 1 to AFR 80-17)

AFR 80-17(C1)

15. DRAW A PICTURE THAT WILL SHOW THE SHAPE OF THE PHENOMENON. INCLUDE AND LABEL ANY DETAILS THAT MIGHT HAVE APPEARED AS WINGS OR PROTRUSIONS, AND INDICATE EXHAUST OR VAPOR TRAILS. INDICATE BY AN ARROW THE DIRECTION THE PHENOMENON WAS MOVING.

16. WHAT WAS THE ANGULAR SIZE? HOLD A MATCH AT ARM'S LENGTH IN FRONT OF A KNOWN OBJECT, SUCH AS A STREET LAMP OR THE MOON. NOTE HOW MUCH OF THE OBJECT IS COVERED BY THE HEAD OF THE MATCH. NOW IF YOU HAD BEEN ABLE TO PERFORM THIS EXPERIMENT AT THE TIME OF THE SIGHTING, ESTIMATE WHAT FRACTION OF THE PHENOMENON WOULD HAVE BEEN COVERED BY THE MATCH HEAD.

Attachment 1
17   (Becomes Attachment 1 to AFR 80-17)

AFR 80-17(C1)

17. DID YOU OBSERVE THE PHENOMENON THROUGH ANY OF THE FOLLOWING? INCLUDE INFORMATION ON MODEL, TYPE, FILTER, LENS PRESCRIPTION OR OTHER APPLICABLE DATA.

EYEGLASSES	CAMERA VIEWER
SUNGLASSES	BINOCULARS
WINDSHIELD	TELESCOPE
SIDE WINDOW OF VEHICLE	THEODOLITE
WINDOWPANE	OTHER

A. DO YOU ORDINARILY WEAR GLASSES? ☐ YES ☐ NO | B. DO YOU USE READING GLASSES? ☐ YES ☐ NO

18. WHAT WAS YOUR IMPRESSION OF THE SPEED OF THE PHENOMENON? GIVE ESTIMATE OF SPEED_____ . | 19. WHAT WAS YOUR IMPRESSION OF THE DISTANCE OF THE PHENOMENON? GIVE ESTIMATE OF DISTANCE_____ .

20. IN ORDER THAT WE MAY OBTAIN AS CLEAR A PICTURE AS POSSIBLE OF WHAT YOU SAW, DESCRIBE IN YOUR OWN WORDS A COMMON OBJECT OR OBJECTS WHICH, WHEN PLACED IN THE SKY, SIMILAR TO WHERE YOU NOTED THE PHENOMENON, WOULD BEAR SOME RESEMBLANCE TO WHAT YOU SAW. DESCRIBE SIMILARITIES AND DIFFERENCES BETWEEN THE COMMON OBJECT AND WHAT YOU SAW.

21. DID YOU NOTICE ANY ODOR, NOISE, OR HEAT EMANATING FROM THE PHENOMENON OR ANY EFFECT ON YOURSELF, ANIMALS OR MACHINERY IN THE VICINITY? ☐ YES ☐ NO. IF "YES," DESCRIBE.

A. DID THE PHENOMENON DISTURB THE GROUND OR LEAVE ANY PHYSICAL EVIDENCE. ☐ YES ☐ NO. IF "YES," DESCRIBE.

PAGE 7 OF 9 PAGES

Attachment 1
19   (Becomes Attachment 1 to AFR 80-17)

AFR 80–17(C1)

22. HAVE YOU EVER SEEN THIS OR A SIMILAR PHENOMENON BEFORE? ☐ YES ☐ NO. IF "YES," GIVE DATE AND LOCATION.

23. WAS ANYONE WITH YOU AT THE TIME YOU SAW THE PHENOMENON? ☐ YES ☐ NO. IF "YES," DID THEY SEE IT TOO? ☐ YES ☐ NO.

A. LIST THEIR NAMES AND ADDRESSES

24.   GIVE THE FOLLOWING INFORMATION ABOUT YOURSELF

LAST NAME, FIRST NAME, MIDDLE NAME

ADDRESS *(Street, City, State and Zip Code)*

TELEPHONE *(Area code and number)*	AGE		MALE		FEMALE

INDICATE ADDITIONAL INFORMATION INCLUDING OCCUPATION AND ANY EXPERIENCE WHICH MAY BE PERTINENT.

25. WHEN AND TO WHOM DID YOU REPORT THAT YOU HAD SIGHTED THIS PHENOMENON?

NAME_____ DAY_____ MONTH_____ YEAR_____

26. DATE YOU COMPLETED THIS QUESTIONNAIRE.

DAY_____ MONTH_____ YEAR_____

PAGE 8 OF 9 PAGES

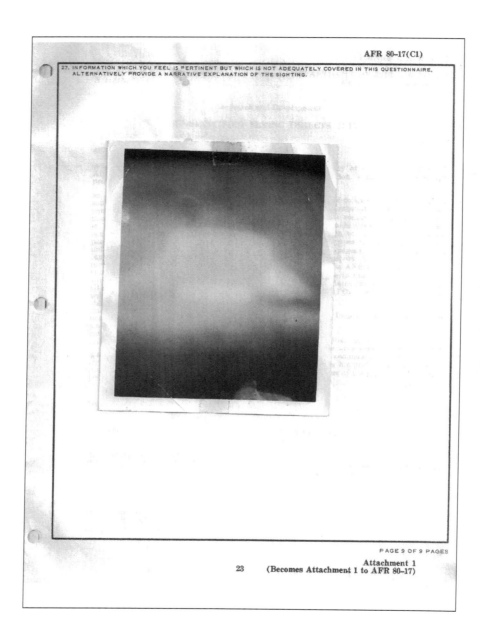

Attachment 1
23   (Becomes Attachment 1 to AFR 80–17)

Made in the USA
San Bernardino, CA
10 June 2018